The GLORY *of the* STARS

ANGIE LOFTHOUSE

Also by Angie Lofthouse

Novels

Defenders of the Covenant
The Ransomed Returning

Short Fiction

Ripped and Other Adventures
Spirits Bright
Joy Ride

The GLORY *of the* STARS

ANGIE LOFTHOUSE

Angella Lofthouse
2016

Dedicated to the prophet Joseph Smith
And the courageous, faithful Saints who followed him

In loving memory of Lynne, David, Dallin, and Kenneth, a
portion of the proceeds of this book will be donated to the
American Foundation to Prevent Suicide.

Chapter 1

L unch break.

Nephi Packard hung back, letting the other telestials working in the aeroponic garden shuffle past on their way out to the cafeteria. No supervisor in sight. He snatched a handful of the blueberries he'd been harvesting and stashed them in a worn plastic bag. Perfect.

He turned around to see Abish Winter staring at him wide-eyed. "You can't take those. You'll get us all in trouble."

"Not if you don't tell anyone." Nephi tossed her a berry. She shook her head and hurried away.

"You're skipping lunch again?" Enoch, his best friend, asked. "I hope she's cute, whoever she is." He socked Nephi in the shoulder.

"Yeah, wouldn't you like to know." Nephi slapped his friend on the back. "Besides," he waggled the bag of blueberries, "these are better than leftover sludge shakes." Leftovers for the leftovers. He shuddered.

"Don't let Brother Sorenson catch you with those." Enoch said.

"How long have we worked here?"

"Since we were twelve."

"Right. Nine years, and have I ever been caught?"

"No, you have not." Enoch took a berry and popped it in his mouth.

"That's right." Nephi slid the bag into the pocket of his faded work pants. His finger found the start of another hole he'd have to sew up. Or maybe Prissa would do it for him. "See ya round, Enoch." Nephi joined the stream of people leaving aeroponics. His long legs carried him past his co-workers and into the hall. He peeled off in the opposite direction from the rest, following the gentle curve of the corridor, whistling a jaunty hymn tune. The words tumbled through his head. *We've found the way the prophets went who lived in days of yore...* He didn't know quite what that meant but he liked the melody.

Thumbing open the access panel, he pushed his too-long hair back from his face. The solid pull of the ship's gravity held him on the landing, but the weightlessness of the core beckoned him forward. The central core of the large globe that was the generation ship the *Kingdom of Heaven*, sported bare metal walls held together by rivets the size of his kitchen table, a narrow landing for each of the hundreds of decks, and, most importantly, no gravity. It was the one place Nephi felt truly free. With a laugh, he launched himself through the opening, caught hold of the narrow railing on the landing, and vaulted over it. Spinning away through the empty space, he whooped in delight. Lights on each deck flared to life as he passed. A thick cylinder ran from top to bottom in the core, housing the engines and other vital systems. Nephi landed with his feet against it, and pushed off into a back flip before letting himself float in the empty, echoing space.

The ship seemed to stretch on forever, and most of it was empty, waiting for the much larger population that would someday reach the planet Canaan, destined to become their new home. The new home of Nephi's distant descendants anyway. It wouldn't happen for four hundred or so more years. The domed ceiling at either end of the core held the ship's reserve water stores. And what lay beyond that, Nephi didn't know.

Technically, only engineers and other specialists were allowed in the core to maintain the engines and such, but no one seemed to mind if a leftover like himself snuck in when nobody was working.

Not that he wanted to be alone.

Where is she?

Elizabeth had come to the core every day for two weeks—except Sundays, of course. She was a little late today. He closed his eyes and relaxed. She'd come.

He imagined he was floating in some vast ocean, the likes of which he had never seen and never would. What did an ocean breeze smell like? The ship's core smelled cold and sterile, especially when compared with the rich odor of the aeroponic gardens and the rest of agri-deck with its gardens, farms, and animal pens.

Another access hatch opened above—or was it below?—him. Above him. She was always above him. His own celestial angel. Elizabeth Black, granddaughter of President Black himself. She emerged from her own deck, taking flight as Nephi had.

He hadn't thought a celestial like Elizabeth would even acknowledge the existence of a telestial leftover like him. But when she had appeared two weeks ago during his lunch-break run to the core, she had not only acknowledged him, she had talked to him, smiled at him, laughed with him, even played games with him as if they were children.

"Hello, Elizabeth." Nephi waved at her. He couldn't stop the grin spreading across his face. Her golden curls were piled on top of her head and bound with a clip that sparkled with multi-colored lights. Nephi's threadbare, dirty work clothes were rags next to her finely woven white blouse. Was it silk? Prissa would know. She worked in sewing. But Nephi didn't know. Didn't much care, either, but it sure looked good on her, tucked into her dark blue pants. Her eyes held a glint of mischief.

Without answering, she caught hold of one of the rungs that ran the length of the engine tower and pulled herself deftly around and out of his sight.

So, hide-and-seek today, was it? Not that there was really any place to hide in the core. She was just teasing him. Being coy. Nephi maneuvered himself closer to the tower. "I have something for you."

Elizabeth didn't answer. Nephi grabbed a rung and started around the tower. He caught a glimpse of Elizabeth's bare foot as she moved back around to the other side. He could picture the playful smile she must have on her face. She enjoyed toying with him. Truth be told, he liked it as much as she did. "I have blueberries," he called. Her favorite.

Nephi reached into his pocket for the berries and tossed them out in front of him. They floated lazily away. Elizabeth came cartwheeling head over heels from around the tower. She was upside down to Nephi's perspective when she plucked the first berry out of the air with her fingers and popped it in her mouth.

"Mmmm." She continued her turn as she grabbed and ate another berry. Each turn, each berry, brought her closer to Nephi.

She could never be his. He knew it. She was a celestial. She was the president's grandchild. Probably she was already promised to some handsome, young elder, and at nineteen she was already old enough to marry.

4

At twenty-one, so was Nephi. But not to Elizabeth Black. Celestial girls didn't marry leftover guys. Period. Yet with her moving closer and closer to him, with the blueberries hanging ripe in between them, anything seemed possible. Nephi could hardly breathe in his longing to reach out and tangle his fingers in those beautiful curls.

She was close enough to touch now, popping another berry into her mouth. Nephi reached out and tapped the little activator button on her hairclip. The lights stopped blinking, and the clip drifted away. Elizabeth's hair floated out in a golden cloud around her head.

"Nephi!" She tried to sound indignant, but she was grinning, trying to hold her hair down. Nephi laughed. Elizabeth let go of her curls to playfully slap his shoulders— the first time she'd ever actually touched him.

Against common sense or any type of decorum, Nephi took her by the shoulder and kissed her, as soft and short as a sigh. He opened his eyes. Elizabeth's were closed, her lips slightly parted. He kissed her again. The taste of blueberries lingered on her mouth. He wanted to hold her, all of her, and make her his forever no matter what the differences between them. He pulled her against him. Her hands came around his neck. Nothing else mattered in that moment.

Until Elizabeth pushed away from him. Her hand clamped over her mouth. There was nothing teasing or playful in her face anymore, only shock and distress.

"Elizabeth." He reached for her.

She shook her head. Her loose hair waved like a strange crown. She latched onto a rung on the engine housing and pulled herself upward. Or was it down? Nephi had lost track of where he was.

Elizabeth didn't look back. If they'd been in a gravity field, she'd have run away, but zero G was ruining her dramatic exit.

"I'm sorry," he called. Elizabeth didn't respond. What had he been thinking, anyway? Celestial girls didn't kiss telestial boys. Not ever. But he still felt warm all over. He could still taste the blueberries.

One of the berries drifted past him. He caught it between his thumb and forefinger and popped it in his mouth. The engineers could worry about the rest of the errant fruit. He wasn't going to.

Elizabeth may be upset now, but she'd be back. He grinned to himself. Give her a day or two. She'd definitely be back.

It was almost time for dinner when Nephi's tab chimed with a message. He turned away from the stinking algae filters he was scrubbing—a punishment for being back late from lunch—with the sudden, wild hope that it was from Elizabeth. That she wanted to meet him again. He took the tab from his pocket.

Nephi Packard, you are summoned to a disciplinary court in the High Council room on celestial deck immediately.

Nephi stared at the message in disbelief. Disciplinary court? Now? "Oh, Elizabeth, you didn't." But it seemed she had. This couldn't be good. He looked down at his work shirt, stained with smudges of purple from harvesting blueberries, smelling of sweat and algae. He couldn't appear before the High Council like this, no matter how soon they expected him.

The High Council. Ugh. Maybe he ought to just run and hide somewhere instead. As if there was anywhere to hide on the ship. Best to just get it over with. How bad could it be, anyway? It was nothing but a five second kiss.

He sprinted from the elevator to his apartment on telestial deck to change into his Sunday clothes. His little sister Priscilla wasn't there, thank heaven. Explaining where he was going would have been tricky. He brushed his hand against one of her scrap metal wind chimes for luck, for all the good that would do.

The elevator climbed with agonizing slowness. Nephi bounced on the balls of his feet and drummed his fingers on his thighs all the way up to celestial deck, level one, a place he'd seen only on the ship newscasts. He stepped off the elevator and into a scene straight from heaven. Pathways of smooth, rounded stone rambled through grass—real grass!—and trees, interspersed with sparkling fountains. Children laughed and ran through the grass or splashed in clear pools while their mothers sat on benches nearby, visiting together or reading from real, paper books, the likes of which Nephi had never seen in person. Their faces held the fullness of the well-fed and a blush of health. The light had a bright, pure quality that Nephi had never seen before. It was a far cry from the plain walls and tiled floors of telestial deck.

Disapproving looks followed him through the park. Even his Sunday best looked faded and shabby next to the celestials in their everyday clothes. Dread sloshed in his stomach. The entrance to the High Council room was a thick wooden door flanked by two enormous trees. There wasn't a buzzer that he could see, so he knocked. Just off to the left, he caught a glimpse of the doors to the celestials' temple.

The door moved upward, proving it wasn't as old fashioned as it looked, and Nephi stepped into the High Council room. Fifteen bearded and somber men in fine black suits sat around a table that looked like dark, stained wood, but couldn't have been real. The High Council. He'd been listening to them give sermons his whole life, but he'd never seen them up close before. He'd never wanted to, either.

Elizabeth was there, too, between her grandfather, President Jeremiah Black, and her father, first counselor Lamoni Black, next in line for the Presidency, and Nephi realized exactly how idiotic he'd been in thinking he could ever mean anything to her. Elizabeth kept her eyes down.

"You've kept us waiting," President Black said. Nephi's mouth went dry. Jeremiah Black was an imposing figure with silver hair and piercing blue eyes. His neatly trimmed salt-and-pepper beard marked him as one of the upper lever celestials. On the *Kingdom of Heaven,* President Black's word was law. It was doctrine. It was the voice of God.

Nephi swallowed. "Forgive me, President. I thought I should change out of my work clothes before I came."

Black's expression didn't waver. He raised his eyebrows slightly. "Sit down, young man."

Nephi took the empty seat across the table from Black, trying not to make the chair clatter in his shaking hands. President Black nodded to his son, who stood.

"You are Nephi Packard of telestial deck, correct?" Counselor Black's mouth twisted as if the words left a sour taste in his mouth.

"Yes, sir."

"Brother Packard, you are accused of the sin of fornication. Will you now confess your fault before this council?"

Fornication? What had Elizabeth told them? She still had her head down, staring at her lap.

"No, sir," Nephi said. "I have not committed fornication."

Elizabeth's father leaned forward. "Are you denying that you kissed my daughter today in the ship's core?"

Nephi cleared his throat. "Yes. That is, no. I don't deny it. I did kiss Elizabeth. Briefly." Her eyes flicked to his for a fraction of a second.

"You lusted after her," Counselor Black continued. "And you led Elizabeth into lust, also."

"No," Nephi said.

Black's face deepened into a scowl.

"When I kissed Elizabeth, she ran away. She didn't lust."

Elizabeth met his eyes, but Nephi couldn't read her expression.

"Young man," President Black interrupted, "I have already heard Elizabeth's confession. I will be the judge of her heart." Elizabeth's face paled.

"With all due respect, President, in the goodness of her heart, Elizabeth may have overstated her involvement. She didn't do anything wrong. It was all me."

"Brother Packard, you forget your place." Lamoni Black pounded his fist on the table. "The President does not require your counsel."

President Black held up his hand to quiet his offended son. "Indeed." His eyes cut through Nephi like spears of ice. "Proceed with the sentencing."

Nephi opened his mouth to protest, but snapped it shut at the look on the President's face.

"Nephi Packard, it is clear to this council that you have no remorse for your sins."

Nephi balled his hands into fists under the table.

"For the sins of fornication and lust you are sentenced by the council to five stripes."

The maximum penalty? For a ten second kiss? Across the table, Elizabeth gasped. Nephi's back prickled with anticipated pain.

9

"And for the sin of leading away another into lust, an additional five stripes."

Ten stripes? Why didn't they just cast him out and get it over with? They must want him to die slowly and in pain. Because telestial boys didn't kiss celestial girls. Ever.

"Thank you, Lamoni." President Black pinned Nephi in his gaze once again. "Because Elizabeth came to me freely confessing her wrongs, I have decided to show her mercy."

That was something, anyway. Of course, the President wouldn't punish his own granddaughter. That relieved him.

"Elizabeth Black," the President said, "for the sins of lust and fornication you are sentenced by the council to three stripes."

"What?" Nephi came to his feet. "You call that mercy? She didn't do anything wrong. Neither of us did."

"Silence," President Black ordered, "or I'll double your sentence again." Elizabeth covered her face with her hands.

"I will take her stripes," Nephi said. "She doesn't deserve them."

President Black stood. "Isn't that noble? Especially for a leftover." He spat out the word. "Elizabeth has her own lessons to learn."

Elizabeth let out a muffled sob.

"Enough," Black said. "Take Brother Packard to the penance room before I lose my patience."

Nephi glared at him. Elizabeth's father stood and bound Nephi's hands with electronic cuffs, a larger version of Elizabeth's hairclip, minus the lights and easy release capabilities.

Elizabeth continued to cry. Neither her father nor grandfather made any move to comfort her. Nephi wondered why she'd confessed in the first place. Surely she'd known what it would mean. Maybe she truly believed she'd committed a sin. "I'm sorry, Elizabeth." This time he really meant it. She didn't look up.

Counselor Black grabbed Nephi's arm and led him out the back door, not into the park, but into a quiet hallway lined with doors. Nephi stayed silent during the long walk down the hall.

Black opened a door at the end of the hall and shoved Nephi inside. The room was bare of furniture, the walls white, and the floor covered in dull tiles. "Brother Packard, your penance will serve the purpose of bringing your will back in line with the will of God." His voice was nearly monotone. Nephi guessed it was a rote and meaningless speech, much like his sermons. "Let these stripes remind you of your nothingness before God and your need for His correction."

Nephi clenched his teeth. Counselor Black released the band from around his wrists. "Remove your shirt."

Nephi pulled his best shirt over his head and let it drop to the floor.

"Stand there." Lamoni Black pointed. "And place your hands against the wall."

Nephi did so. The wall tingled with heat for a moment when his hands came into contact, and he could not pull them away. Panic washed over him.

"May God show forth His mercy unto you." Counselor Black left the room.

Nephi tried unsuccessfully to control his breathing. Trying to yank his hands free did him no good at all. If Elizabeth's father was not going to deliver the stripes, who was? And how long were they going to leave him stuck to the wall? Maybe the High Council expected him to think about the severity of his sins first. But all he could think about was the way his lungs refused to take in air and his heart wanted to escape from his chest.

The door opened. Nephi looked over his shoulder expecting one of the High Councilmen, but it was a much younger man who came in. Ammon Nielsen, heir apparent to Lamoni Black, who had no sons of his own. Of course. Who else would Elizabeth be promised to? He hoped she would be okay. Ammon held the rod—a slender strip of metal humming and crackling with blue bolts of energy. Nephi instinctively tried to pull away from the wall again.

Ammon stepped up close behind him. "Did you really think you could violate my bride-to-be and get away with it, leftover?"

Nephi lowered his head. He didn't want to give Ammon the satisfaction of rising to the bait. He wondered if Ammon realized all the time he and Elizabeth had spent together in the core.

"I can't deny that I'll enjoy punishing you," Ammon said. His face twisted into an ugly smile.

"Will you enjoy punishing Elizabeth, too?"

Ammon brought the rod down across Nephi's back with savage force.

Nephi cried out. His back spasmed as the flesh tore away. A burning stench rose around him. He jerked as an electric shock coursed through his body, but the wall held him firmly in place. His throat clenched. Tears came to his eyes. He squeezed them shut. He would not let Ammon Nielsen see his agony. His breath came out in hollow gasps.

"One," Ammon said with cruel satisfaction.

Chapter 2

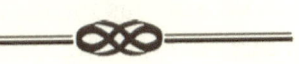

Cold tile beneath his cheek.

Nephi blinked.

Blobs that might have been people swam in his vision, hazy and distorted.

He hurt. Oh, how he hurt. Breathing hurt. Blinking hurt. Living hurt. How was he still alive? He tried to remember how he came to be—wherever he was—but he couldn't.

Voices. Feet moving around him. The brush of air across his back was a fresh torture, as if Ammon Nielsen stood behind him still, inflicting stripes with the rod. He closed his eyes and silently pleaded for release from this agony.

"Nephi? Can you hear me?"

He knew that voice. "Prissa?" he whispered. She shouldn't be here, shouldn't see him like this. She rested her hand on his cheek.

"Nephi?"

He forced his eyes open. His sister Prissa crouched beside him. Words stuttered on his tongue, trying to tell her he was fine. Not to worry. But it wasn't true. Judging from the look on her face, Prissa knew it, too.

"We're going to get you home, okay? I'll fix you up."

"Prissa." He tried to touch her, but couldn't move. His eyes fluttered closed. Hands slid under his shoulders and lifted him. He groaned.

"Hang on, buddy." That was his best friend Enoch. Nephi tried to get his feet under him. His head swam. *Guess I got caught,* he thought blearily.

"Hold still," another voice commanded. "I've got you." He ought to know that voice. Someone lifted his feet. Another cry tore loose from his throat. His head bobbed and dangled as they carried him. Every step they took, every sway, every jostle added to the suffering. His stomach heaved, and sour vomit splashed on the floor. His rescuers kept moving.

Time turned fuzzy in his brain. Voices swirled around him. Someone may have been talking to him, but he could no longer find the words to answer. Minutes later there was a pillow against his face, a bed. His bed. He knew the coarse feel of the sheets, the lumps in the mattress. He sank at last into numbing blackness.

It didn't last long. He jerked awake when a cold sting touched the wounds on his back. "Nephi, be still."

He recognized the voice now. Phoebe Sharpe—long-time friend of his deceased mother—sat at the head of his bed. "Let your sister care for you."

"I'm sorry, Nephi," Prissa said from behind. "I know it stings, but it'll help."

Nephi grimaced. At least he felt more coherent now.

"It hurts," Phoebe said. "But the ointment will dull the pain and prevent infection."

Phoebe had taken Prissa and Nephi under her wing when their mother had passed four years earlier, and was teaching Prissa all the healing techniques she knew.

"After she applies the salve, we'll bandage you up. You need to be awake for that, but when we're through, I have something that will help you sleep," Phoebe said.

Nephi nodded and tried not to flinch under Prissa's ministrations. The look on Phoebe's face reminded him of the hours she had spent at his mother's bedside before she passed, trying to find some way to heal her friend of the illness that ravaged her. It was Phoebe who'd come to tell him and Prissa that their mother had gone to join their father in the telestial realm. Nephi shuddered. What would Prissa have done if she'd lost him, too? He winced as her hands moved further down his back. Phoebe was right, though. Already the pain had lessened.

"What happened?" Prissa asked.

"Ten stripes."

"Ten? What did you do? Try to assassinate President Black?"

"I kissed Elizabeth."

"Elizabeth Black?" Prissa's voice rose. "You have some kind of death wish?"

"No." He closed his eyes. "I didn't think she'd go tattle to grandpa first thing."

Prissa snorted. "What else can you expect from a celestial?"

Nephi sighed. What had he expected? "I just hope they gave her some medical care after her stripes."

"They did this to her too?" Prissa fell silent for a moment. "I hate celestials."

"No sense complaining about what isn't going to change," Phoebe said, her face hard. She was right. Celestials kept their own counsel. Nothing a leftover could do about that.

"I need you to sit up so we can bandage you," Phoebe said. "Can you manage?"

Though Prissa's salve had helped, it was still torture pushing himself up and over into a sitting position. He was shaking when he finished, trying hard not to puke again. Or pass out. His eyes met Prissa's. Her short unruly curls stuck out every which way.

"Nephi—" she started and shook her head.

"I know. Stupid, huh?"

Her brown eyes turned watery. She blinked the tears away. She was only sixteen, and all they had was each other.

"Lift your arms up," Prissa ordered, shaking off the tears. She and Phoebe wound a soft, linen bandage around his torso and shoulders like a tight-fitting shirt. He wondered what had become of his good Sunday shirt. Maybe he should have worn his work clothes after all.

Work. He sagged. If he didn't log enough work hours, he wouldn't get enough credits to eat. Prissa couldn't work enough hours to feed both of them. No matter the pain, he'd have to be back on agri-deck tomorrow.

"Here." Phoebe handed him a cup. Nephi sniffed and pulled a face. "It will ease the pain and let you sleep," Phoebe said. "Bottoms up."

Nephi swallowed the foul-tasting concoction as quickly as he could.

"Healing will take time," Phoebe said. "You can't rush it."

Nephi lay back down on his stomach, too tired to protest. Arguing with Phoebe Sharpe was useless anyway. He'd just get up and go to work in the morning when she wasn't here.

The sleeping potion took rapid effect. As he drifted off into a comfortable, hazy dream, he heard Phoebe say, "Take care of him, Prissa."

He awoke alone, unsure how much time had passed. "Prissa?"

No answer came. A deep breath caught in his throat. His stripes ached and stung and itched something awful. He tried to push himself up to sitting again, but the pain was too intense. His skin felt like it might split open at the slightest movement.

He rested his head on the pillow again, defeated. So much for working. The tattered curtain that separated his bed from Prissa's stirred fretfully in the breeze from the air circulators. Prissa's scrap metal creations clinked together almost musically. He wondered what time it was and how long he'd been asleep. Craning his neck around to look at the clock proved impossible, and he had no idea where his tab was.

His stomach rumbled. This helplessness was unbearable. He tried again to get up, and again fell back to his bed with a groan. Hopefully Elizabeth was in better shape than he was. The memory of their brief kiss rose in his mind, along with their days of harmless flirting and children's games. As if they were children. As if it had been harmless.

What had prompted Elizabeth to confess to her grandfather, anyway? She could have simply stopped meeting him in the core, and it would have been over. Forgotten. He sighed. It would have broken his heart, but that would have been a whole lot less painful than recovering from stripes. Funny how he didn't feel any closer to God's will now than he had before. He snorted.

Someone buzzed at the door and came in. "Nephi?" He recognized Enoch's voice.

"I'm in bed," he called. "Come on back."

Enoch pushed aside the larger curtain that separated the front room from the sleeping area. He sat on the edge of Nephi's bed. "How you feeling?"

"In pain. And hungry."

"Prissa is getting you lunch right now," Enoch said. "Did you really kiss Elizabeth Black?"

"Yep."

"Man, you sure got some guts."

Nephi lifted his mouth in a half-smile. "Yeah, turned out great, didn't it?"

"How did you even get near her?"

"She's been coming to the core during lunch, like me."

"And you never told me?" Enoch threw up his hands and rolled his eyes.

"I didn't think anything would come of it." But maybe he had. And the secrecy had been fun. Exciting. "I just got carried away yesterday."

"Yeah, I get it," Enoch said.

Both of them were quiet for a minute. "Thanks for bringing me home," Nephi said.

"Whoever brought you down from celestial deck just threw you out of the elevator." Enoch sounded disgusted. "Like they didn't want their holy feet to touch telestial ground."

"I don't remember that," Nephi said. "I think I blacked out after about the seventh stripe." He winced at the memory.

"Must have been some kiss," Enoch said, a bitter edge in his voice.

"It lasted about ten seconds, but I guess that qualifies as fornication."

Enoch scoffed. "For celestials, maybe. You could 'fornicate' with half the telestial girls out in the hall, and the celestials wouldn't even care."

"What did you say?" Prissa pushed through the curtain with a sludge shake in her hands.

"Nothing." Enoch came to his feet, his face turning red. "I'll see you later, Nephi. Bishop Behling wants to come down and see you tonight. Is that all right?"

"Like I really have a choice." Nephi wrinkled his face, wondering what his terrestrial bishop would have to say.

"Bye, Prissa," Enoch said. He slipped through the curtain and out the door.

Prissa set the shake on the bedside table. "Do you feel up to eating?"

"I'm starving," Nephi said. "But sitting up his hard."

"You have to. I need to change your bandages." She looked back over her shoulder. "Maybe I should get Enoch back in here to help. Phoebe's delivering a baby."

"Don't worry, Prissa. I'll cooperate." He gritted his teeth and pulled himself up through the pain. He flipped himself over to sitting with a cry he couldn't hold back.

"Nephi!"

"I'm all right." But his stomach was unsteady again. "Let's get this over with."

"Hold still." Prissa unwound the bandages and applied more salve. It hurt, if possible, worse than it had the night before. Nephi bit his tongue, determined not to cry.

Prissa wasn't fooled. By the time she got the fresh bandages around him, her own eyes brimmed with tears. She swiped them away fiercely. Prissa wasn't one to cry. Nephi took her hand.

"I promise you I won't be that stupid ever again."

"You'd better not." She turned away, dumping the dirty bandages into the wash bin next to his bed, and handed him his lunch. He'd lost his appetite, but he forced himself to drink it anyway, for Prissa's sake.

"Did you get lunch?" he asked her.

"Yes." She sounded irritated. "You still had some work credits left over from yesterday, and Phoebe gave me extra for helping patch you up, so we're fine."

For today, maybe. "I'll go back to work tomorrow."

"No, you won't. You can't." Prissa put her hands on her hips.

"I have to. We'll starve."

Prissa shook her head. "You'll make your stripes worse. You haven't seen how bad it is."

No, but he could feel it. She was right.

"We'll get by." She sat down on the bed and took his hand. "Just like we always have."

"Just like always."

They fell silent. Nephi guessed Prissa, like him, was thinking about their parents. "It's not right what they did to you," Prissa said quietly. "Enoch has a point."

"I hope you're not planning on fornicating in the halls, young lady," he said in his pompous imitation of the High Council. He winked.

"Nephi!" She swung a playful punch toward his shoulder, but stopped just short. "I have to go help Phoebe with the birth, and I'm expected back in sewing after that. I'll come check on you again later. Get some rest, okay?" She stood up. "You need another sleeping draught?"

"Nope. I'm fine."

She cocked her head and gave him a look that said she knew he was lying. He waved her off. "Go. I'll survive."

"Okay." She kissed his cheek and gathered up the wash bin. Nephi stretched out on his stomach, exhausted, and drifted off again.

———⚬⚬⚬———

Bishop Behling, of terrestrial deck, came by that evening after Prissa had changed Nephi's bandages again. Enoch followed the bishop in with a wink at Nephi.

"Hello, Bishop." Nephi started to sit up, but the bishop held up a hand.

"Please don't get up. I'm told you are in a lot of pain."

"Yes, but my sister is taking good care of me." Nephi relaxed into his pillow.

"Good, good. I'm glad to hear it." The bishop seemed distracted. He stood beside the bed, his hands clasped. His dark hair showed gray around the edges. He sported a short beard, his right as a bishop though he was only a terrestrial, better than a leftover, but not quite up to celestial standards. "Brother Packard, it is unusual for the High Council to convene a disciplinary court so quickly and not invite the bishop of the offender." He cleared his throat. "Not that my presence would have changed the outcome."

"I know, Bishop." Nothing could have changed that outcome. It had been decided before he walked into the room.

"Perhaps you feel your sentence was harsh and unwarranted."

"Maybe." Nephi bit back any further response.

"Yes." Bishop Behling sniffed. "But you have done your penance now. It is over. I hope you will remember this lesson."

"It will be impossible to forget."

Behind the bishop, Enoch rolled his eyes. Prissa came in and stood by Enoch. She looked angry. Bishop Behling didn't seem too happy, either.

"Nephi," he said, "the most important thing to learn here is that God has given each of a us a station in life. You must accept yours, just as I must accept mine. It is the only path to peace."

"So, it wasn't kissing that was wrong. It was kissing Elizabeth Black?"

The bishop hesitated. "Lust is a serious sin. You must guard yourself against it."

"Yeah, I will." Could this conversation just end please?

"All right, then." The bishop dusted off his pants. "Your penance is sufficient. God bless you, Brother Packard."

"Thanks." But he doubted God had any blessings in store.

Chapter 3

By Sunday, four days after his stripes, Nephi could get out of bed well enough to move to the sofa in the front room. Bishop Behling had granted him special permission to have church services broadcast to his home. He thought he might be the only person on the *Kingdom of Heaven* not going to the chapel, except maybe Sister Morrison and her newborn baby. And Elizabeth. Where would she be? Celestial deck had an actual hospital, and Nephi hoped three stripes wouldn't be nearly as bad as ten. Really, that was his biggest regret. That Elizabeth had suffered because of his poor choice.

The wall screen flared to life, showing the 11,000 or so residents of the *Kingdom of Heaven* filing into the chapel for church. The camera tightened onto the stand where President Black and his counselors sat front and center behind the podium. The High Councilmen were spread out to either side of the Presidency, all with their neatly trimmed beards to mark their lofty station. Behind them were the elders, with less impressive beards. Nephi always thought it odd that such young men were called elders. But lots of things on the *Kingdom of Heaven* didn't make sense. Behind the elders sat the terrestrial bishops.

Nephi caught sight of Ammon Nielsen whispering something to his buddy, who nodded and laughed. Seeing it made Nephi's back hurt worse, remembering the glee with which Ammon had delivered the stripes. He bent forward with his elbows on his knees so his bandaged wounds didn't touch the couch.

The celestials sat in the front of the chapel, with the terrestrials in the back. The telestials got the upper balcony, as far away from the stand as the president could get them. But regardless of how far away the celestials might want them, the leftovers still had to come to church same as everyone.

This was the first time in his twenty-one years that Nephi wasn't in the chapel on Sunday morning. He couldn't turn off the wall screen or even mute the sound, but he supposed no one would know if he went back to bed and slept through it. It was a testimony to his level of boredom that he preferred watching church to going back to bed.

The services proceeded as usual, with singing and prayers. The camera shifted to a small army of the terrestrial men and boys administering the sacrament of bread and water to the lower chapel. No one took it up to the balcony. Nephi found the scene intriguing. He'd never actually witnessed the passing of the sacrament before. He usually spent this part of the service daydreaming or teasing any children sitting nearby.

He cocked his head to the side, contemplating the trays of bread and water moving up and down the quiet pews. Some people had their heads bent as if in prayer. What did it mean to them? He shifted his gaze to the painting of Jesus that hung behind the choir seats, larger than life. Nephi pulled his eyebrows together. He had never thought about it before. Certainly, he'd never wished to take the sacrament. That's just the way it was.

But was it the way it should be? The stripes stung and itched. Where were these thoughts coming from, anyway?

The sacrament ended, and President Black stood. That caused a stir in the congregation. President Black only addressed them in person maybe once or twice a year. Nephi shifted into a more comfortable position. The thought of being subjected to one of Black's sermons left a sick feeling in his stomach.

"My brothers and sisters," Black said. "It is a privilege for me to address you today." He gripped the edge of the podium and stared straight at the camera. Nephi flinched. No wonder they'd let him stay home. Black would not have been able to stare him down like that if he was up in the telestial balcony.

"I feel impressed this morning to speak on a topic familiar to us all, but one it would do us good to remember."

Nephi rolled his eyes. No doubt a lecture on morality was coming.

Black hefted his thick leather-bound scriptures onto the pulpit and made a show of rifling through them until he had the right spot. Only the president had the right to read scriptures directly.

"The book of Doctrine and Covenants teaches us that the kingdom of heaven is divided into three separate degrees of glory."

Okay. That wasn't what Nephi expected.

"The lowest of these, the telestial kingdom, is likened in glory to the stars; the terrestrial kingdom to the glory of the moon; and the celestial, the highest kingdom, to the glory of the sun."

So, Bishop Behling was right. It wasn't the kiss so much as it was who he'd kissed. Maybe Enoch was right, too. They wouldn't even care what he did with leftover girls. He shifted again, but it didn't help the pain.

25

President Black closed the scriptures with a thump. "Before we were born, our Father in Heaven knew us. He looked into our hearts and saw what we had been, what we were, and what we would become. He saw our true nature and the quality of our hearts. Then he placed us here on our little *Kingdom of Heaven* journeying to our own promised land in the place where we belong. It was a mercy, brothers and sisters, for a telestial spirit would not be happy in the celestial kingdom, and neither could the reverse be true."

Nephi recalled the grass and trees and clear water of celestial deck. He didn't think he'd be too unhappy there. Then Prissa's voice echoed in his head. *I hate celestials.* Maybe Black had a point. The only way the park would be nice was if Prissa was there, and Enoch and Phoebe and his other neighbors.

"It is not for us to question the judgment of God," Black said. "We must not covet that which we cannot attain."

Is that what Black thought? That Nephi had been trying to kiss his way onto celestial deck? "No," he told the screen. "You're absolutely right, President. I wouldn't be happy there. Not at all."

"Of course, we must always be vigilant," Black said. "We must take care to strictly keep God's commandments, lest we should lose our assigned kingdom and fall into outer darkness after this life."

Nephi tuned out as President Black went on about the need for complete obedience, but Black's words continued to tumble around in his brain. God had looked on his heart and found him—less. He'd been taught that all his life. And since God had no use for Nephi, Nephi had never had any use for Him. Outside of sitting through church on Sunday morning, Nephi rarely spared God a moment's thought. When it came right down to it, he wasn't certain he believed in God at all. But it was certain that his penance had not brought him any closer to believing.

He must have dozed off, because when he focused on the wall screen again, the congregation was standing for the closing hymn. The broadcast shut itself off after the closing prayer, and Nephi's stomach rumbled right on cue.

While the celestials and terrestrials had various Sunday school classes to attend, the leftovers were free to do as they pleased with the rest of their Sabbath. Sunday afternoon was Nephi's favorite time of the week, with no work to worry about and plenty of friends to visit with. And it always started with lunch. The one day of the week the leftovers got actual food and not just sludge shakes and scraps. Not this week, though. Not for him. He stood up slowly, still shaky on his feet. The pain left him lightheaded. The room swayed under him. It was only three steps over to the little table, but he didn't know if he could make it.

The table held small gifts from his neighbors. A few apples, a loaf of bread, even some cookies. Nobody wanted him and Prissa to go hungry, but no one had much to spare, either. It would do, though. Nephi took one step toward it and stopped. His legs trembled. The wounds across his back burned. This wasn't going to work.

Someone buzzed at the door. Nephi lowered himself back onto the couch. "Come in." No way could he make that far. It raised open to reveal his friend, Salome Hunsaker, with a pie in her hands. There were perks to having friends who worked in the kitchens. Nephi grinned, frustration forgotten. "Hi, Sal. Come on in."

Sal stepped inside and stood like she didn't know what to do with herself. She still wore her Sunday dress, and as short as she was, it made her look like a little girl, though she definitely wasn't. Her straight, dark hair was cut even shorter than Prissa's. Nephi pushed his own hair out of his eyes.

"I made a pie." Sal held it out to him. "Actually, I made it yesterday, but I couldn't sneak it out before. Blueberry."

Of all the treats Sal had baked and pilfered for him over the years, pie was his favorite. But blueberry? He wondered if he'd ever enjoy the taste of blueberries again. She handed it to him. It did smell wonderful. "Thanks, Sal. That's really sweet of you." He looked at it for a second, wondering what to do with it without getting up. "You want to get us both a piece?"

"Oh, yeah," Sal said, turning pink under her olive complexion. She took the pie, found a couple of plates and forks, and cut them each a slice. She handed one to Nephi and sat down on the couch beside him. "How do you feel? Does it hurt?"

"Yeah, but I'm getting better." Nephi shrugged, which made his stripes hurt worse. He winced. "Slowly."

"I think it's wrong—what they did to you." Sal shook her head. "Prissa said all you did was kiss Elizabeth once."

"Uh—yeah." His cheeks warmed. "Stupid of me. I didn't even enjoy it." Sheesh. Why had he said that? He took a bite of pie to cover his embarrassment.

Sal didn't seem to notice. She looked at his wall screen. "Did you have to watch church today?"

"Yep."

"What did you think of President Black's sermon?"

He almost shrugged again, but stopped himself just in time. "I don't know." He took another bite. "Most of the time I don't think about the sermons at all. But this one seemed—personal. Like he thought I was getting above myself or something."

"I think it's all a bunch of crap," Sal said, stabbing at her pie. "Why doesn't God love us all equally?"

Nephi took another bite of pie, unsure how to answer. "Do you really believe God exists?" he asked after a minute. He'd never discussed the subject with anyone before.

"You think He doesn't?" Surprise laced her voice.

"I don't know. If He does, like you said, why doesn't He love us all equally?"

She drew her legs up under her. "I've been reading my second great-grandmother's journals, and you know what?"

"What?"

"I don't think things were always this way on the ship. Divided up by decks and all." Sal stabbed at her pie again.

"Really?"

"Yeah, but if I try to read any farther back, my access is blocked."

"That's weird."

Sal glanced at him sharply.

"Weird that it's blocked," he said. Maybe it was weird that she was reading her ancestor's journals, but he didn't need to point that out. He shoveled in another bite. "This is delicious."

"Thanks." Sal stared down at her empty plate. Her cheeks had turned pink again. He'd always found that cute. Nephi scooped up his last bite.

"It is weird," Sal said. "I should be able to read the journals of my own family, but they're blocked just like the scriptures."

"You tried to read the scriptures? In the computer system?"

"Yes." Her blush deepened. "They're in there, but not accessible. It makes me wonder—if the president with his precious leather book is the only one who can read and interpret scripture, why is it in the public database at all?"

"Who knows? Why were you trying to read the scriptures, anyway?"

Sal stood up. "I shouldn't be talking about it, should I?" She stacked Nephi's plate on her own and put them both in the sink.

"Don't worry about it. What's a little heresy between friends, right?" Nephi quipped.

Sal stiffened.

"I'm kidding," Nephi said. "Just between us, right?" Heck, saying he didn't believe in God was far worse heresy than trying to read the scriptures. Sal was right. They shouldn't be talking about this at all.

Sal relaxed a little. "It's just that, I read a quote in my great-great-grandmother's journal. It said that everyone is the same to God. That He doesn't turn anyone away. That we can all receive eternal life. I don't know where it came from. She didn't name her source. But it makes you think, you know?"

"Yeah, it does." In fact, he'd never thought about any such thing, but listening to Sal, feeling the sting of his stripes, and seeing church services from a different perspective had left him uncomfortably contemplative.

"I should go," Sal said, glancing over her shoulder like she expected the High Council to swoop in and carry her away for penance. "My dad's expecting me in the cafeteria for lunch."

"Oh, okay. Thanks for the pie."

"Yeah." Sal opened the door and nearly ran smack into Prissa and Enoch.

"Hi, Sal." Prissa gave her a hug. "Are you leaving?"

"I have to go. Sorry." She glanced back at Nephi.

"Sal brought us a pie." Nephi pointed to the table.

"Blueberry. Mmm." Prissa clapped her hands. "Thanks, Sal. I see you've already had your share, Nephi."

"Best pie I ever tasted," Nephi said, just to see Sal blush again. "Thanks for coming to see me, Sal. Come back later if you want."

Sal turned cherry red and hurried out the door.

Prissa faced Nephi with her hands on her hips. "Were you flirting with Sal?"

"Was I?" He gave her his innocent look.

Enoch laughed.

Prissa rolled her eyes. "You'll never learn, will you?"

"What am I supposed to be learning? To stop talking to women?"

"Something like that."

"I was just teasing her. It's so easy to make her blush."

Prissa sighed and stepped past him and Enoch to fuss with the food on the table. Tension stretched her shoulders beneath the thin fabric of her dress. She carried more burdens than a girl her age should. Burdens Nephi had added to.

"Prissa?"

"Hmm?"

"Do you believe in God?"

Prissa stared at him. "What kind of question is that?"

"The kind that will get you cast into outer darkness," Enoch said. He sat down next to Nephi. "Don't go there, my friend."

"Yeah, but just between us. Do you?"

Neither answered for a minute. "What difference does it make?" Prissa said. "It doesn't change anything, does it?"

"I guess not." Nephi rested his arms on his knees. Prissa turned back to the table to cobble a meal from the gifts. They had no more credits for food this week. She was right. It made no difference at all.

Chapter 4

"Nephi, you have to see this."

Prissa's cry roused him from his early morning stupor. He slid out of bed and pushed back the curtain leading to the front room. He wore only his threadbare pajama pants. Six weeks since his penance, and his stripes were healing. But that didn't mean the pain was gone.

"What is it?" he asked, and stopped, staring at the wall screen. "Oh." The morning news spotlighted the marriage of Ammon Nielsen and Elizabeth Black. They were both dressed in white, smiling and waving at the camera. They stood in front of the ornate doors leading to the celestials' temple. Nephi didn't know or even care what went on in there. A place where the celestials could go congratulate themselves on their holiness, probably.

Elizabeth looked happy enough. She had her golden hair piled up in an elaborate coif and her wedding dress glittered with a thousand tiny diamonds. So. They still let her in the temple, still let her marry Ammon in spite of her stripes. Why did that surprise him? It ought to make him happy, right? She hadn't done anything wrong, after all. But a penetrating sense of loss settled in his chest. The real question was why would Elizabeth marry someone like Ammon Nielsen?

The answer was obvious. He'd be the president someday.

It still disappointed him.

"I'm sorry, Nephi."

He bristled. "What for? It's not like I thought she'd marry me."

"I know, but—" She shrugged.

"Sorry, Prissa." He put his arm around her shoulders, thin as bird bones. The generosity of their friends would not feed them indefinitely. "I'm going back to work today."

"Don't push yourself." Prissa looked over at his exposed back.

"All the stripes have scabbed over. I'll be fine." He stretched his back, trying not to show how much it still hurt.

"You're not working until Phoebe says it's okay."

"Phoebe's babying me, and so are you. I can work just fine. I don't want you going hungry."

"I'm not." Prissa lifted her chin. "Enoch shares his dinner with me every day, so you can have mine."

"That's nice of him. But nobody's going to do with less on my account. Not anymore."

"What's all this?" Phoebe asked, coming in the door.

"Nephi thinks he can go back to work today," Prissa said. "He thinks I'm going to starve or something."

Phoebe clucked her tongue. "That's not a good idea. You're still weak. You have to give it time."

"I've given it enough time. It's healing fine. I'm tired of being cooped up in here, alone."

"All right," Phoebe said. "You can take a walk around telestial deck today, as long as you have someone with you. That's enough activity. It'll start building up your strength again, okay?"

34

"No." Nephi folded his arms. "I'm getting dressed and reporting to agri-deck. I've had enough coddling."

"Come on, Nephi." Prissa shook her head.

"No more arguments." He slapped the curtain aside to get his work clothes, refusing to cave in to their wishes. Let Elizabeth and Ammon have their perfect celestial life. What did he care?

Prissa and Phoebe whispered to each other on the other side of the curtain. He ignored it. His work clothes were waiting for him, neatly folded in his single drawer. *Thanks, Prissa.*

By the time he finished showering in the tiny bathroom, which stung his stripes horribly, the women were gone. He sat on the edge of the bed for several minutes, working up the strength to stand again. Maybe Phoebe was right, but so what? He had to do this. He couldn't sit around any longer.

Gritting his teeth, he forced himself to his feet. The walk to the elevator and then across agri-deck had never seemed so long. He had to lean on the wall and catch his breath before he entered the aeroponic garden.

Brother Sorenson, his terrestrial supervisor, put a hand on his pudgy hip. "So, you're back, huh? I won't tolerate slacking, you know."

"I know." Nephi stood up straighter, hoping he didn't look as lousy as he felt. He brushed his too-long hair out of his eyes. Brother Sorenson gave him a squinty-eyed look.

"Go harvest peppers until lunch." He held out his tab so Nephi could log in and start earning work credits. Nephi entered his passcode. For some reason, it reminded him of Salome digging through old journals. What might he find if he had a terrestrial tab like Brother Sorenson?

"Packard! Stop daydreaming," Sorenson barked, snatching back his tab. "You're already late. Get going."

Nephi shook off the odd thought and headed for his assigned area. Sorenson must have been in a good mood. Enoch was there harvesting peppers too. "Hey, welcome back," he said. "You sure you're up to this?"

"Sure. Anyway, I don't want Prissa going hungry."

"I've been taking care of Prissa," Enoch said. "You don't have to worry about her."

"I know, and I appreciate it, but she's my sister. It's my job to take care of her." He dropped a pepper in the large metal collection bin between them. Even that small movement sent ripples of pain across his back.

Enoch frowned. "I was just trying to help out."

Nephi gave him a long look. "She's only sixteen," he said softly.

"I know how old she is." Enoch slammed a pepper into the bin. "If you don't want my help, just say so."

"I appreciate your help, Enoch." Nephi sighed. "I'm sorry. I can't sit around being useless anymore."

Enoch nodded, but didn't answer. They worked in silence. After a while Nephi found he could hardly lift his arms, and he stopped to rest for a moment with his hands on his thighs, breathing hard.

"Are you all right?" Enoch asked.

"I'll be fine," Nephi panted. "Just give me a minute."

"You're bleeding," Enoch said. "It's coming through your shirt." He rested his hand on Nephi's shoulder.

"Packard, what's going on over there?" Sorenson bellowed, coming up the row.

"He's hurt," Enoch said. "I should take him home."

"He can get his own sorry butt home," Sorenson said. "I don't want to see him back here until he can actually work."

"I can work," Nephi said, but he knew it wasn't true. His arms were still trembling from the effort he'd already exerted. "I just need to rest a minute."

"No slacking, Packard. Now get out of my garden."

Nephi's jaw tightened. Sorenson was a real jerk, but for Prissa's sake Nephi had to try. "Sir, I'm sorry. Please give me a chance. I need the work credits."

Brother Sorenson shook his head and his fat cheeks quivered. "I have no use for someone who can't give a full effort. You brought this on yourself. You'll have to deal with the consequences." He tapped on his tab a few times. "You're off the clock. No credit for this paltry amount." He gestured to the half-full bin.

"But I'm trying," Nephi protested.

"Not hard enough. Don't make me ask you to leave again." Sorenson stomped away.

Nephi balled his hands at his sides. That wasn't right. It wasn't fair. He just needed a chance.

Blood seeped through the back of his shirt.

"You'd better get Phoebe," Enoch said. "Can you make it back to your place?"

"Yes," he said through his teeth.

"Don't worry about Prissa, or anything. We'll take care of you guys."

Nephi nodded. He wanted to be grateful. He knew he should. But his anger at the whole stupid situation wouldn't let him. "I'll see you later." He stalked toward the door, ignoring the smell of fresh blueberries and Brother Sorenson's disgusted glare. Out in the hallway, he pounded his fist against the bare metal wall. Another half-healed scar ripped open. Nephi leaned his forehead against the wall and choked on the bitter tears forcing their way up his throat.

The thought of going back to his room was more than he could take. He didn't want to have to admit to Phoebe or Prissa that they were right.

The core. That's what he needed. To just float, just be. As long as he didn't think about Elizabeth. His fists clenched tighter. That shouldn't be too hard.

Nephi pushed himself away from the wall, wincing, and shuffled toward the access panel. He had to lean on the walls for support as he made his way along. It was foolish. He ought to take Enoch's advice to go home and message Phoebe. What would he do if he didn't have the strength to get back out of the core again?

Would he be any worse off than he was now?

Dark thoughts crowded his mind. The walls of the *Kingdom of Heaven* constricted around him. There was nowhere to get away, no way off the ship. Except…

Only one.

Nephi stopped where he stood. No. Death was not what he wanted, was it? Not like his father. Hopelessness seeped into his bones, black as the endless night of space that surrounded them.

He continued forward until he reached the access panel and pounded it open with his fist. The core stretched away in darkness, waiting for him. He closed his eyes and let himself fall. If only, he thought. If only he could fall, fall, fall until he hit the bottom. Or would it be the top? And what then? An eternity in servitude to celestials like Black taught. Or just…nothing?

But he wasn't falling. Only drifting like a leaf on a pond. He almost laughed. As if he'd ever seen an actual leaf on a pond. He imagined the clear, blue pools and trees on celestial deck. Did they ever allow stray leaves to drop onto their ponds? No. That would disturb the perfection of the water, wouldn't it? Couldn't have that on celestial deck. No blemishes there. At least not visible ones.

He wondered if Elizabeth had scars on her back or if they'd gone easy enough on her and fixed her up quick enough that she didn't. A lump filled his throat. He wasn't supposed to be thinking about her.

But he could still see her standing beside Ammon Nielsen with a smile as bright as the aeroponic grow-lights. Did she really mean it? Was she really happy to be marrying him?

Of course she was. He was to be the president someday, after all. What did it matter, anyway? What did any of it matter?

His parents were dead, his sister going hungry. He was permanently scarred. Did any of that matter? Not to President Black and his celestials. Not to Ammon. Not to Elizabeth.

Nephi opened his eyes. Bright red drops of his own blood hung in the air around him. He stared up—or was it down—to the faraway dome of the ship's edge. What did any of it matter? They were locked in here. Had been for generations. Was there anything outside of it? Planets, stars, dirt, sunshine, ponds? God? Was all of it nothing but a daydream? Why was he made to suffer while Elizabeth and her pals lived in ease? Why did his parents have to die? Why did Prissa have to suffer and fear? Why? A single tear wet his cheek for a moment before slipping into the weightlessness to join his blood. He squeezed his eyes shut.

Something had changed, or broken inside of him. And from that broken place, an indescribable longing something more flooded out, something beyond telestial deck, beyond the confines of the *Kingdom of Heaven*. And a longing to know if anyone really watched from above, or if he was truly unworthy of anything more than this.

Behind his eyelids, he sensed the core growing brighter. He cracked open his eyes and quickly squeezed them shut again. Even that couldn't keep the intensity of the brightness from blinding him. He threw his arm over his face. The engine must be exploding. It was the only explanation. He would die anyway, like it or not. So would everyone else.

A heartbeat passed. And another. How long did it take an engine to explode, anyway?

Cautiously, he lowered his arm. The light had receded enough that Nephi could open his eyes. A man was there in the core with him, surrounded by the light. A scream died in his throat. The man didn't appear to be floating in zero G. His brilliant white hair and clothing were unaffected. He simply stood in mid-air, calm and serene. He had a kind face and a benevolent smile.

Nephi tried to speak, to ask the man who he was and where he came from, but all that came out was a breathless squeak.

"Nephi." The man held out a hand toward him. "Do not be afraid. I am Uriel, the archangel, sent from the presence of God to deliver a message."

"I—uh—" Nephi bowed his head, unable to look the archangel in the face. He felt keenly the sting of every stripe on his back. He was nothing but a lowly leftover. "F-forgive me."

"Nephi."

Blinking, Nephi raised his head again. The angel, Uriel, smiled mildly. He didn't look angry or ready to exact justice. "Your sins are forgiven, Nephi. The Lord has looked upon your heart."

Nephi brought his hand to his chest. "Before I was born, the Lord looked upon my heart and saw what I would become."

"Yes." Uriel smiled again. "But not in the way you've been taught. The Lord saw what you could be, and it is more than you are now. More than you can comprehend."

"Me?" Nephi's head swam trying to understand what he was seeing. What he was hearing. Maybe he was worse off than he thought. Maybe he was hallucinating. Or— "Am I dead?"

"No." The light around the archangel shimmered, and Nephi had the distinct feeling the heavenly being was laughing. "I've come to deliver a message, as I said." Uriel's countenance grew serious again. "The people of this vessel called the *Kingdom of Heaven* have gone far astray. They no longer worship God in spirit or in truth."

"They don't?" Nephi absently brushed at the hair that wasn't hanging in his face because of the lack of gravity. He could hardly think. In reality, he had never worshipped God at all.

"They have lost the truth their fathers once held dear. Nephi, God has chosen you to restore them to the true worship of their Lord and Savior."

"What? Me? How? I mean—" Nephi looked down at his bloodstained work clothes. "I'm just a telestial leftover."

"You are much more than that," Uriel said. "This division among you into kingdoms is not pleasing to our Father in Heaven. All men and women stand equal before him. All are judged according to their works and the intent of their hearts. Not on the station of their birth. All can receive eternal life through the Atonement of Christ."

"All of us?" Isn't that what Sal had read in her grandmother's journal? A spark ignited in his heart, warm and bright as the light around the angel. It grew to fill Nephi's being until he thought he might be glowing, too. He had never before experienced such peace and well-being. Such love and acceptance. And he knew, without any doubt, that the angel Uriel spoke the truth.

"Your Father in Heaven and His Beloved Son love you," Uriel said. "Just as they love all His children. Even those now cut off from the face of the Earth."

Everyone. Not just a chosen few born on celestial deck. His mind caught a sudden vision of the universe beyond the walls of the *Kingdom of Heaven*. Of worlds without number, peopled with beloved sons and daughters of God. He gasped aloud.

"Nephi, the Lord has chosen you to bring His children on this ship back to Him and to His truth."

"Why me?" What would he have to do? The thought of preaching made him cringe. "I'm the least important person here. No one will listen to me."

"I once felt the same," Uriel said. "But you'll be surprised at what you can do with your hand in the hand of God."

"What do you mean? You're an archangel. Not a telestial deck farm worker who doesn't know anything."

Uriel laughed aloud this time, and the light rolled out in waves around him. The sound filled the core, and the walls rang with echoes of delight. "You have a lot to learn, young man," the angel said. "Starting with the fact that God calls the weak and the simple to accomplish His marvelous purposes."

"Weak and simple, huh? I do fit that description."

"Here." From somewhere in his glowing robes, Uriel produced a small book. "We'll start with this."

Nephi took the book. It had a soft, brown leather cover, warm under his fingers.

"What is it?"

"The Book of Mormon. The beginning of your studies."

Nephi let go as if it had burned him. "That is forbidden. I'll be cast out for having it." The stripes were bad enough.

Uriel pressed the book into Nephi's hands. "No one should be forbidden to read the word of God." The laughter was gone from his voice. "Take it. Read it."

Nephi resisted the urge to toss it away again. "If the celestials catch me with this, I'm dead."

Uriel grinned. "In all your twenty-one years, have you ever been caught?"

"Just once." Nephi looked the angel in the eyes. His breath stalled. "Am I dreaming?"

"The Lord has called you to do His work," Uriel said. He spoke softly, but the words seemed to reverberate through Nephi's bones. "Will you do it?"

A chill passed through him. He'd come into the core unsure if God existed and now he was talking to an angel. Either he'd cracked under the strain or God had quite a sense of irony. The book rested heavily in his hand. He didn't know really what he was supposed to do, but he couldn't deny what he had seen. What he'd felt. Maybe things could change for him. For those he loved.

"I don't know if I can," he said. "But I will try."

Uriel nodded. "That is enough. Remember, with God, nothing shall be impossible."

"Nothing?"

"Nothing." Uriel took a step forward on thin air. "Bow your head."

Nephi did so, his eyes on the forbidden book he held in his hands. Uriel placed his hands on Nephi's head.

"Nephi Joseph Packard, in the name of Jesus Christ, I consecrate and set you apart for the work you are called to perform. I bless you with the strength you will need to accomplish it."

Nephi could feel the wounds on his back knitting themselves together. The pain receded. Healing warmth washed over him. His breath hiccupped in his chest. What was happening?

43

"If you will give your heart, might, mind, and strength to God, He will always be with you. Amen."

"Amen," Nephi whispered. He raised his head. "My stripes."

"The scars remain, I'm afraid."

Yes. Nephi could feel the skin stretching in odd directions, but there was no pain. None at all. "Thank you." The words didn't seem adequate.

"Go now," Uriel said. "Begin your reading. Do not forget what I have told you."

"I won't."

"I will meet you here again in one week."

"O-okay." He shuddered.

A soft smile graced Uriel's face. "You can do this, Nephi. I promise you."

"How?"

But Uriel was already leaving, rising upward on a pillar of light. Or was he falling into it? In a moment he was gone, and Nephi was alone. The core seemed small and dark without the presence of the angel. His limbs trembled. It took a long time before he dared tuck the Book of Mormon into the pocket of his work pants and pull himself up the rungs of the engine housing toward the exit.

Chapter 5

Nephi checked the time once he was out in the hall again, surprised at the amount of time that had passed. It was just past the lunch hour, and he was starving. The book in his pocket thumped against his thigh. It was still there, so maybe he hadn't hallucinated the whole thing after all. A combination of elation and terror tumbled through him.

He used the worker's entrance to the kitchens, which opened onto the long rows of fridges and freezers. A stainless steel counter ran the length of the opposite wall. The clatter of dishes and conversation came from the area beyond, but the fridge room was empty.

He thought about taking something from one of the fridges but that didn't seem quite right after talking to an angel. Besides, there was someone he wanted to see. He just wasn't sure where to find her.

A girl came into the room.

"Hey, Leah," Nephi said.

Leah jumped. "What are you doing back here?" Her eyes narrowed. "Is that blood on your shirt? Are you okay?"

"I'm fine. I was looking for Sal. Do you know where she is?"

"Yes." She rolled her eyes. "But she's working. Why aren't you?"

"Long story. Can you get Sal for me? I promise I won't keep her long."

"Fine." Leah shook her head. "Just don't get caught by our supervisor."

Don't get caught. He felt a little light headed. "Thanks, Leah."

Leah took some lettuce from one of the fridges and left. A minute later Sal came in. "Nephi, where have you been? Are you bleeding? Prissa is searching for you."

"She is?" She must have talked to Enoch. "I'm not bleeding anymore. I was in the core, that's all."

Sal arched an eyebrow. "Alone this time, I hope."

What was she, his mother? "Not exactly." He winked and was rewarded with a red flush in her cheeks. She scowled her disapproval.

"Sal, I—" He stopped, unsettled. What would she think if he told her what happened? Probably that he was nuts. But she was the one who had started him thinking, so—

"What?" She put her hands her hips. Maybe now wasn't the time.

"That old jack—I mean Brother Sorenson—wouldn't let me work. Do you have any leftover shake or something I could have?"

She studied him for a minute, perhaps gauging his sincerity, before she nodded. "Wait right here."

Something fell out of her back pocket as she turned. Nephi went over to see what it was. A book with a red fabric cover. It reminded him of the book he had stashed in his pocket. He reached his hand in to see if the Book of Mormon was really there. It was. He wasn't crazy.

Sal's book didn't have anything on the cover. It looked handmade. He wondered what was in it. He glanced toward the main kitchen, but, no. She wouldn't like that. He'd better respect her privacy. Instead, he picked it up and set it on the

46

counter and leaned back on his elbows to wait for her. It felt good not to worry about hurting his back anymore. *Thank you, God.*

She came in with a sandwich wrapped in a napkin. Thin slices of roast beef with grilled peppers—maybe the same peppers he'd harvested that morning. His mouth watered. "That's no leftover."

She handed him the sandwich. "You look like you need it."

"Thanks." He took an enormous bite. "It's delicious. This won't get you into trouble will it?"

"It won't be missed." Sal spotted her red book off the counter and froze.

"That fell out of your pocket," Nephi said around a bite of sandwich. "What is it?"

"Nothing," Sal said, too quickly. "It's just my journal." She slid it into a pocket on her apron.

"Don't you keep your journal on your tab? Saved in the database for future generations and all that?"

"Yes." She shrugged. "This one is more personal, that's all." She looked at the floor. "It's where I keep my poetry," she mumbled.

"You write poetry?"

"Sometimes." She went pink again.

"That's fantastic. Can I read some?"

"No way. Nobody reads them but me."

"Oh, come on. Please?" He took another bite of sandwich. It really was delicious. Sal shook her head. "Some other day, then." He winked again.

Sal sighed. "I have to go back to work. Enjoy your sandwich."

"I am. Thank you." He watched her walk away, suddenly wishing she didn't have to go.

"Hey, Sal."

"Hmm?"

"You're right, you know."

"About what?"

"The ship and how things are supposed to be. You're absolutely right."

"Oh." She looked surprised. "I'm glad you think so."

"I'll talk to you later, okay?"

"Sure. See you." She left with a wave of her fingers.

Nephi finished his sandwich as quickly as he could to avoid getting Sal in trouble, and folded the napkin neatly on the counter. So, Sal was secretly a poet? She was just full of surprises.

Both Prissa and Phoebe were waiting for him at home. Phoebe had a jar of ointment in her hand.

"Where have you been?" Prissa cried. "I've been worried sick."

"I went to the core. No big deal." Except it had been a pretty big deal.

"You should have come straight home," Prissa chided. "Enoch said you were bleeding." She put her hands on her hips.

"I'm fine." Better than fine, actually.

"I'll be the judge of that," Phoebe said. "I told you not to work today."

Nephi hesitated. If they saw his scars, he'd have to tell them what had happened in the core. He didn't know if he was ready for that yet.

"I'm fine, Phoebe. Really. It was just a little blood. It's stopped now. It doesn't hurt."

"Quit being so stubborn." Prissa stamped her foot. "You don't have to act all manly around us. Let Phoebe look at you."

Phoebe gestured with her hands. "Off with the shirt, young man."

"Okay." Nephi closed his eyes and pulled the shirt over his head. For the first time, he saw the bloodstains. No wonder they didn't believe he was fine.

He took a deep breath and turned around so Phoebe and Prissa could see his back.

Neither said a word for many long seconds. Nephi turned around again. "See? I told you."

Prissa's mouth hung open. Phoebe had her hand pressed against her heart. Not knowing what else to say, Nephi stepped around them and through the curtain to his bedroom. He tossed his work shirt on the floor and grabbed the only clean one left in his drawer. It didn't fit anymore, but he wrestled it on anyway.

Phoebe came in behind him. "Nephi, those scars. That's months, if not years, of healing. That's not what I saw this morning."

Nephi faced her. Prissa stood just behind Phoebe, her eyes wide. "I know," Nephi said. "When I had to leave work, I was upset. Hopeless. I went to the core. Just to cool off, or something."

He sat down on his bed, rested his arms on his thighs, and folded his hands. Nothing else to do but just come right out with it. "An angel appeared to me there."

"What?" Prissa's voice rose.

Nephi looked over at her, his hair falling down into his face. "He said he was an archangel—Uriel. He healed my stripes. But that was after..."

"After what?" Phoebe asked. She spoke softly, carefully. Like she thought he'd gone crazy.

"After he told me that things are wrong on the ship. That we aren't following the true gospel anymore. He said that it doesn't matter what deck we are born to, that all of us are equal before God." He couldn't keep the wonder from his voice. "He said the Lord wants me to set it right again. To restore the truth."

"Nephi." Prissa sat beside him and rested her hand on his arm. Her forehead creased with worry. She should be worried. Nephi was.

He stood, pulling Prissa up with him. "The angel gave me this." He took the book from his pocket.

"What is it?" Phoebe asked. Nephi handed it to her. Phoebe opened it. Her face went pale. "You can't have this."

"I know."

"What?" Prissa looked between Nephi and Phoebe with fear on her face.

"It's the Book of Mormon," Nephi said. He took it back from Phoebe. "Uriel told me to read it. He said no one should be forbidden to read the word of God. No one."

"Where did you get this, Nephi? Tell me the truth." Phoebe pushed the book back toward him.

"I told you the truth."

"They'll cast you out," Prissa cried, her eyes filling with tears. "That's much worse than stripes."

True, being thrown out of the airlock to suffocate in space was worse than a few stripes. Nephi put his arms around Prissa. "I won't get cast out." He remembered Uriel's words. "I won't get caught."

Prissa stepped away, wiping her eyes. "Just toss it in the incinerator. It's better that way."

"I agree with your sister," Phoebe said. "I don't know where you got it, but it's dangerous. Just leave well enough alone."

"You saw yourself my stripes are healed." Nephi held up the book. "I didn't find this floating around in the core. I saw an angel. I talked to him. He put these scriptures in my hands. I can't pretend that didn't happen."

Phoebe and Prissa exchanged a worried look. Nephi slumped back down on the bed and lowered his head.

"Nephi—" Phoebe paced in the small space. "Are you sure it was an angel and not a…devil appearing as an angel or a trick of some kind? Maybe you're being tested."

Nephi remembered the light, the peace and love, the touch of Uriel's hands on his head. He didn't understand what it all meant or why the Lord would send an angel to him of all people. He shook his head. "It wasn't a devil or a trick. I know it. How else can you explain my scars?"

"I can't," Phoebe said.

"And besides that, I felt something when I was in his presence. I felt—light and peaceful. Happy. I can't really explain it." He ran his fingers through his hair. "When I went to the core, I was in despair." He shivered, remembering the wish to die. "I came out with…hope."

"Hope for what?" Prissa asked.

Nephi thought for a second before replying. "I'm not sure. Maybe for whatever's in here." He held up the book. "Or for the way things should be."

Prissa's eyes grew teary again.

Phoebe folded her arms. "Things are what they are. What they've always been."

"Maybe they haven't always been this way," Nephi said. "Maybe they shouldn't be this way at all."

"It's dangerous," Phoebe said. "Think of your sister. She needs you."

"I know that. And I'm going to be here for her no matter what. I promise."

Prissa grabbed his hand and squeezed it. "I can always count on you."

"Then trust me, okay?"

Prissa nodded, smiling through her tears. Nephi looked at Phoebe. "I've trusted you like a mother since we lost our own. Can I count on you not to say anything about this? Not to anyone?"

"Your mother was my dearest friend. I would never do anything to put you or Prissa in danger. That's why I want you to think very carefully about what you intend to do next."

"I will."

"You'll do the right thing," Prissa said. "I believe in you."

"Thanks, little sister."

Phoebe put her hand on Prissa's shoulder. "I think I've kept you away from the sewing room as long as I can get away with. You'd better get back to work."

"Okay. I'll see you tonight, Nephi." She kissed his cheek and left. Phoebe gave him a long, searching look. She set her jar of salve on the nightstand. "I'll leave this here just in case. Prissa knows what to do with it."

"Thanks, Phoebe. I don't know what we'd do without you."

"Just promise me you'll think about what I said. This could have serious consequences."

"I realize that."

"Good." She looked like she wanted to say more, but disappeared through the curtain. The door opened and shut again. He was alone. Prissa's scrap metal chimes tinkled faintly, but otherwise all was silent.

Nephi studied the plain, unassuming volume in his hands. *Just throw it in the incinerator.* Good advice, maybe. No one had been cast out in Nephi's lifetime, but he'd heard the stories of those who had. Sent to their deaths in the cold silence of space because they dared to defy the authority of the president.

If he understood what the archangel had told him, he was about to defy President Black in more ways than merely reading a book.

I can't do this.

Just toss it in the incinerator.

He stood up, ready to do it, when the angel's injunction shivered through his bones again. *The Lord has called you to do His work. Will you do it?*

His hands trembled, and he felt caught between Prissa's tears, Phoebe's disapproval, and Uriel's soul-piercing gaze. He had promised the angel he would read it, hadn't he? What was he getting himself into here?

Nothing good will come of this.

And yet, he hadn't been lying when he'd talked about the peace. The hope. The real joy he'd experienced there, bathed in Uriel's heavenly light.

I have to do this.

He sat back down on the bed and opened the book to the first page. Interesting. *Translated by Joseph Smith, Jr.* Huh. Who was that? He flipped the page over and began.

Chapter 6

In the quiet hours of the early morning, Nephi closed the Book of Mormon and lay on his bed with the book clutched tight against him. The stories he'd been told at church all his life were the same, yet completely different from what he'd been taught.

His thoughts spun in dizzy circles trying to take in all the passages, the new ideas. Possibilities he had never imagined. If President Black and his predecessors had indeed read this book, they had not taught it. He could only imagine what the Bible and the rest of the scriptures must contain.

Prissa was sound asleep on the other side of the curtain. She'd brought him dinner, but otherwise hadn't said a word to him all evening. He'd have worried about it more if he hadn't been so engrossed in what he was reading. Now, he wanted to shake her awake and tell her what he knew. That they'd been lied to. All of them. And that God knew her and loved her and wanted to give her everything He had. What a concept.

Nephi closed his eyes and drew in a deep breath. Ask, the book had said. Ask and get an answer from God. He'd never done anything of the sort before. Prayers were something someone else said to begin and end church. He didn't know how, but he could try. He cleared his throat. "Dear Lord," he whispered. "Can this all be true?"

It didn't seem like much of a prayer, but there in the semi-darkness, the same feeling he'd experienced in the core rushed into him.

Yes. Oh, yes. It's all true.

If only he could stay right here and bask in the warmth forever.

Nephi rolled onto his side. How wonderful to do that without pain. A smile spread across his face, as sleep stole over him with a gentle caress. This had been the most intense, crazy day of his life. The only thing he knew for sure was that he would never be the same.

Nephi woke hours later with a start. Prissa was already up and gone. Why hadn't she roused him? The time glared red from the clock on the wall. 9am. She'd left the lights down too. Great. Now he'd missed breakfast and was late for work.

He brought the lights up to full and climbed out of bed, in the process knocking the Book of Mormon onto the floor. He bent to pick it up. The warm, tingly feeling filled his heart again. Everyone needed to know about this. But first things first. He hid the book under his mattress, and went to shower and dress as quickly as he could.

His work shirt still had bloodstains on the back. Nephi winced. He'd forgotten to throw it in the wash. It didn't smell great, either. It would have to do. Wrinkling his nose, he put the shirt on and ran to agri-deck. It felt good to run.

Brother Sorenson was unimpressed with his newfound stamina. "You expect me to let you in here an hour late? After yesterday?"

"I overslept. It won't happen again. I'll stay an extra two hours."

Sorenson shook his head. "You can't have healed that fast, and I don't need you giving me a half effort. Besides, you brought it on yourself. You don't deserve to be working until you've paid the price for your sins. You are the worst kind of leftover there is. Now, get out of my sight."

The door snicked shut. Nephi's cheeks grew warm. "You're wrong Sorenson," he whispered to the implacable door. But he wasn't about to go in there and try to change Sorenson's mind. Instead, he took an elevator down three more decks to the algae filtering room. It smelled like a rotting corpse down there, but Brother Ryan was not nearly as bad as Sorenson.

"Can you use me today? I know I'm late, but Brother Sorenson doesn't want me in aeroponics."

"I heard what happened yesterday. Are you sure you're up to this?" Ryan sounded more concerned than disapproving.

"I'm much better than yesterday. It won't be a problem. I'll even work extra hours."

"How could you be that much better after one day?" He raised his eyebrows.

Nephi hesitated. He doubted Ryan would buy "healed by an angel," and saying so might land him back in front of the High Council. "Phoebe Sharpe. She has some powerful concoctions," Nephi said. "And—God is merciful."

Ryan's eyebrows nearly reached his receding hairline.

"Even to leftovers," Nephi muttered.

"Yes." Ryan tapped his tab. "Indeed He is. Come on in. Don't worry about being late. If you work hard, I'll give you a full day's credits."

"Thank you, sir." Nephi clocked in on the tab, and Brother Ryan waved him inside.

The algae filtering system was much smaller than the aeroponic garden. Only brothers Hyrum and Zeniff Bradshaw shared the workspace with him.

"Howdy, Nephi," Hyrum said. "Back on your feet, huh?"

"Yep." Nephi pulled out the nearest filter and began to scrub with a bristled brush. Had to keep the fountains on celestial deck pure and pristine.

"Heard you fainted in aeroponics yesterday," Zeniff said. Hyrum choked back a snicker.

"I didn't faint. I maybe overdid it a little, not used to being up and all. And I could have stayed, but Sorenson is a jerk."

"That he is," Zeniff agreed.

"So, hey," Hyrum nudged Nephi with his elbow. "You and Elizabeth Black in the core, huh? That takes some guts, man."

"Not really." Nephi attacked the filter with the brush. "Since nothing happened."

"Nothing? You got ten stripes for nothing?" Zeniff whistled.

"Pretty much," Nephi said, wishing they'd change the subject.

"Harsh," Hyrum said. "Anyway, I heard her grandpa married her off yesterday. Guess he didn't want to risk any more fornication." He and Zeniff laughed.

Nephi pressed his lips together and kept silent.

"Hey, no offense, big guy," Zeniff said. "We're just joking around, that's all."

"I know." Nephi continued scrubbing, jaw tight.

Hyrum and Zeniff settled down and went back to work, though they continued to regale each other with stories of the adventures and pranks they'd supposedly gotten away with. Nephi didn't believe any of it, but he found himself smiling at the outrageous banter and laughing along with them. It was so normal, like there had never been stripes or an angel or reading the word of God. Like maybe nothing had changed at all.

He imagined telling these two about what he'd seen, what he'd read, what he knew. Or thought he knew. They wouldn't believe him. Prissa and Phoebe barely believed him, and they'd seen actual proof. And if Prissa couldn't believe him, who would? No one, that's who.

Do not doubt the power of God.

Nephi jumped at the sound of Uriel's voice in his mind, clear as day.

"Hey, tell us what really happened," Hyrum said.

"What?" Nephi had the sudden, absurd thought that Hyrum had heard the angel's voice.

"What happened in the core?"

Nephi gaped at him.

"You and Elizabeth?" Zeniff prompted, stepping up beside Hyrum.

"Oh." His heart stopped jackhammering inside him. "Like I said, nothing happened. Barely even a kiss. That didn't stop her from running to tattle to grandpa, though."

Brother Ryan came out of his office then, his face stern. "I hope you young men aren't perpetuating the rumor that Elizabeth Nielsen-Black was in the core with Nephi." Nielsen-Black? Nephi stifled a smirk. Of course Ammon had taken Elizabeth's name. There had always been a President Black on the *Kingdom of Heaven.*

Brother Ryan scowled. "Because slandering her like that is a rotten thing to do." He looked Nephi in the eye. "I hope you're setting the record straight."

Well. That was the official story? So Elizabeth could marry Ammon without casting any shame on his family? The

59

lie was more of a betrayal than her wedding. She would deny even knowing him. That hurt.

"Yes, sir. I was just telling them that Elizabeth—er, Sister Nielsen-Black, I mean—is perfectly innocent."

Brother Ryan nodded. "Good. I don't want to hear anymore talk about it. Got it?"

"Yes, sir." Nephi glared at Hyrum and Zeniff as Ryan walked away.

"Who were you with, then?" Zeniff asked.

"Apparently no one." Nephi sighed.

"Too bad." Hyrum snorted.

Yeah. Too bad. Nephi went back to his scrubbing. Too bad it wasn't the truth.

"You should read it," Nephi told Prissa when they sat on their small couch after dinner. He'd never truly appreciated the satisfaction of eating a meal he'd earned himself, even if was just scraps and a sludge shake. He held the Book of Mormon out to his sister. "It's all there. The stories you know. Lehi and Nephi. Alma and Ammon. Mormon and Moroni. But not like we've been told. There's so much more. It's hard to explain it all. It's a real eye-opener. Do it for me. Please?"

Prissa folded her arms and shook her head. "I can't. I'm scared, Nephi. Don't you get that?"

"My Prissa? Scared? I never heard of such a thing."

Prissa sniffed. "Phoebe thinks you've lost your mind."

Nephi frowned. Phoebe had always loved him like a son, even before his own mother died. Now she thought he was crazy? "How does she think I got this?"

"That you found it. Or stole it. I don't know."

"And what about my back? I wasn't in any pain today."

"She says maybe…maybe you got something stronger than her salve."

"Yeah. The power of God."

"She says maybe you're trying to trick us."

"Trick you? Like, what—I'm in cahoots with the celestials to try and get you cast out? That's ridiculous. You don't believe that, do you?"

"No." Prissa flopped down on the couch and leaned forward into her hands. "I don't know what to think. You say you saw an angel. That's just…just…"

"Crazy?"

"Yeah." She lowered her head. "I'm sorry, Nephi."

"Okay." Nephi set the book down and put his arm around her. "I didn't mean to make you uncomfortable. I've learned so much. I want to share it with you."

"But I'm frightened. You could be cast into outer darkness. I don't know what I'd do without you. You're my only family."

"Oh, Prissa. That's not true. You've got Phoebe and Enoch. And lots of people. You'd get along just fine and you know it."

"Maybe." She gave him a sad smile. "But I wouldn't want to."

"Neither would I." Nephi patted her knee. "I'm not going anywhere, okay? Look at me."

Prissa faced him.

"I did see the archangel. He gave me the book. I'm not crazy and I'm not making it up. Trust me. Have I ever lied to you?"

"No." Prissa shrugged. She looked away. "I trust you, but—"

"No buts. This is real, Prissa."

"You really want to change everything?"

"I don't. God does. Don't you think it's time for it? Time we were treated as equals? Time we were all taught the truth?"

"Time we stopped losing our loved ones because the celestials think we aren't worth saving?" Their mother's illness and death was always fresh on her mind.

"Exactly. This is exciting, don't you think?" Nephi stood. "It's high time we started rocking this boat."

"Phoebe says things are what they are. We can't change them."

"Phoebe is a wonderful woman, but in this case, she's wrong. We can change it and we will. God is on our side."

"You really think so?"

"I really do." He took her hands and pulled her up. "I don't know how many people will believe me, but at least I need to know I have you on my side."

"I'm on your side. Forever." Prissa tightened her grip on his hands. "I guess you'd better tell me what's in that book."

Chapter 7

O n Sunday, Nephi sat with Prissa and Enoch in the far corner of the large, curved balcony of the chapel and listened with new ears to Elizabeth's father, Lamoni Black, deliver the sermon. He'd never listened so intently in his life.

"Obedience," Counselor Black said, "is the key to our salvation."

Nephi scrunched his forehead.

"Our level of obedience before this life determined where we were born and where we can go after this life. Our obedience here insures that we are not removed from our promised kingdom."

Nephi leaned forward and rested his arms against the railing.

"Who is it we are to obey?" Counselor Black asked.

"God," Nephi muttered.

"What was that?" Enoch asked.

"Nothing." Nephi looked at Prissa. She had her brows knit together.

"Jeremiah Black is the voice of God on this ship," The younger Black said. President Black sat behind his son with a smug little half-smile on his face.

"You're wrong," Nephi whispered.

"What are you doing?" Enoch elbowed Nephi in the ribs.

Nephi sat up straight again. "Just listening."

"Listening? Why?"

"Shh."

"Are you serious? Since when do you want to listen to him?"

"I don't. Sorry. Don't know what got into me."

Lamoni was still talking about his father and word of God, and Nephi wanted to find the truths among the lies.

Enoch rolled his eyes. "What do you want to do when they let us out of here?"

Nephi mentally sized up Enoch and made a decision. "You can come over to our place."

Prissa, perhaps sensing his intention, nudged him with her elbow. He gave her his it'll-be-fine smile, but she wasn't impressed.

"Okay," Enoch said. "We could play cards or something. And you should see if your girlfriend will bring another pie." He winked.

"She's not my girlfriend," Nephi said, looking around for her. He spotted Sal a few rows over with her father and younger brother. She was scribbling away in her little red notebook, intent on that and nothing else. She of all people had a right to know the truth.

"I'll invite her," Nephi said, "but there's no guarantee of pie." He grinned.

Prissa let out a strangled cough in his direction. Nephi put his arm around her as they stood up for the middle hymn. "Don't worry," he whispered in her ear. "They're our friends. They should know."

Prissa looked none too happy, but she nodded her acceptance. Nephi squeezed her shoulders and belted out the hymn with unusual vigor. *Come, rejoice, the King of glory/Speaks to earth again./Gladsome words ring out from heaven,/Joyous, wondrous strain.*

The four of them played three hands of Saints and Angels, and had just started on Sal's apple pie when Nephi decided he'd better speak up before he lost his nerve. He pushed back his chair. Prissa's fork clattered to the table. Enoch and Sal looked at her and then at Nephi as if their heads were attached to the same puppeteer's hands, which struck Nephi as hilarious, and he had to spend a few seconds getting his composure back before he could start. He took a deep breath and cleared his throat.

"Okay, there's something I want to tell you two, since you're my closest friends."

There went Sal, blushing again. Man, he didn't even have to try.

"What's up?" Enoch asked.

"Prissa already knows about this." She looked rather pale. "I don't think she wants me to tell you."

"Oh, go on," Prissa said. "I guess you know what you're doing." She took a bite of pie.

"Okay." He let out his breath. "I can't keep this secret any longer, and I think you deserve to hear it straight from me."

"You got her pregnant, didn't you?" Enoch said.

"What?" Nephi's eyes popped.

"Elizabeth. You got her pregnant. That's why she turned around and got married so fast."

"Are you kidding me? No!"

Prissa punched Enoch in the shoulder. "This is serious, you twit."

"Sorry." Enoch rubbed his shoulder.

Nephi sat down again. "I already told you nothing happened with Elizabeth."

"Yeah, well supposedly she was never there at all so—" He shrugged.

"Don't you trust me? Because if not…"

Enoch held up his hand in appeasement. "I trust you. You just seemed so dramatic and all. Sorry."

Nephi turned to Sal. "Do you trust me?"

Sal gave him a long look. "I believe what you said about Elizabeth."

"Good." He hoped it was trust enough. He glanced at Prissa, who gave him a tiny shrug.

Here goes nothing.

"The other day, when I had to leave work, I went to the core."

"Alone?" Enoch asked. Prissa shot him a dirty look.

"Yes, alone." Nephi said. Sal pressed her lips together. "At least I was alone at first. I was discouraged and depressed. Hopeless, really. I thought about what had happened, and about the things you'd said, Sal."

She raised her eyebrows.

"Anyway, I started thinking about things. Wondering if there really was a God at all."

Enoch had a half-scowl on his face, like he didn't know what to think. Sal's eyes were wide. Prissa just looked terrified.

"So, the core started to get bright, really bright. I thought the engine was overloading or something. But it wasn't that at all. It was an angel."

For a moment, no one even breathed.

"What did you say?" Enoch asked. Prissa had gone white. Sal leaned forward eagerly.

66

"I saw an angel." Nephi explained about Uriel and what the archangel had said. Then he brought out the worn Book of Mormon and set it on the table. For a moment, no one breathed.

"That's it?" Sal reached for it, but stopped just short of touching the soft leather. "The Book of Mormon?"

"Yep. The real deal. I read it all."

"That could get you in a world of trouble, my friend," Enoch said.

"That's exactly what I tried to tell him," Prissa said. Nephi shot her a wounded look. "But…then I read it, too."

"You read it?" The envy was apparent in Sal's voice, and in the hungry look on her face.

"Well, not all of it. I'm not as fast as Nephi. I've read enough to know he's right, though. We haven't been taught the truth."

"I knew it," Sal said. "I knew things weren't right on this ship."

"Do you want to read it?" Nephi slid the book toward her.

"Oh." Sal picked it up and opened the front cover. She ran her hand down the title page. "Could I?"

"Of course." Nephi grinned. "I would be glad if you did."

"Wait." Sal looked over at Prissa. "Did you want to finish it first?"

"Go ahead and take it," Prissa said. "I'm much too slow. I've already read the highlights, anyway."

Sal closed the book and held it to her chest. "I have wanted this for as long as I can remember." A rare smile lit up her face. For a second, Nephi couldn't breathe.

He shook himself out of his stupor. "Be careful with it. Don't let anyone else see it. These guys are right about the danger."

"It's worth the danger," Sal said.

"Yes it is." Nephi leaned back in his chair. This was going better than he'd thought.

Enoch stood up. "Are you nuts? You're risking death in outer darkness here. Death! Don't you get that?"

"Would you rather be kept in the dark all your life?" Sal snapped.

"I'd rather be alive." Enoch's face flushed.

Nephi held up his hands. "Settle down, you two. No need to argue. You can each make your own decision about whether or not to read it."

Enoch sat again, scowling. Sal turned away. Prissa looked on the verge of tears.

"Believe me, I understand," Nephi said. "I know the risks. And you're right, Enoch. It's frightening. But Sal's right too. What we stand to gain is far more than what we might lose."

"More than our lives?" Enoch asked in all sincerity.

"Yes," Sal said. "We'll gain the truth." Nephi wondered how she could sound so sure. Like she had no doubts at all. He couldn't say the same. He believed the angel, of course, and the scriptures. But the implications sat like a terrifying lump in his stomach. With Enoch's, Phoebe's, and Prissa's doubts tumbling through his brain like loose blueberries in the core, he was glad to have Sal's belief to cling to.

"I don't want to put anyone's life in danger," Nephi said. "Especially you guys." A chill passed through him as the inevitability of it all blossomed in his brain. "Things are going to change. They must. It won't be easy, but I know it will be a change for the better."

"I hope you know what you're doing," Enoch said.

"No, not really." Nephi slapped his friend on the back. "But God knows."

Sal nodded in agreement. Nephi grinned. "So, who's ready for more pie?"

Nephi went back to the core on Wednesday during his lunch hour, standing at the access panel, filled with misgivings. Maybe he shouldn't have told anyone. Maybe he shouldn't have shared the Book of Mormon. Sal still had it, though he was pretty sure she'd finished reading it—maybe more than once. He should have asked for it, in case Uriel wanted it back, but it was too late now. Anyway, he couldn't ask for it with the way her eyes lit up like stars whenever they whispered about it over lunch in the fridge room.

How was he going to explain that to the archangel? And besides, Sal understood the Book of Mormon a lot better than he did, seeing connections he hadn't known were there. Really, it ought to be her here meeting with Uriel. For a second, he considered going to get her. But maybe this was supposed to be a private meeting.

He stretched his arms above his head and bounced on his toes. He could do this. Really, he could. The access panel slid open at his touch. The core was empty, dark, just like any other time he'd come. He stood at the threshold, his head bowed. Maybe he'd been judged unworthy after all.

Footsteps sounded behind him, and he whirled around to see a terrestrial woman walking past. She stopped.

"Do you have authorization to be in the core, leftover?"

"Uh—" Nephi cleared his throat. "No."

She put her hand on her hip. "Then you'd better leave, hadn't you?"

He stuffed down a surge of irritation. The access panel slid shut of its own accord. The woman continued to stare at him.

"I was just going to lunch," Nephi said, and stalked off in the direction opposite the one the woman was headed. He took a few deep breaths to calm himself down. When he was reasonably sure she was gone, he jogged back to the access panel. The hall was deserted, so he opened the panel and leaped into the core before anyone else could stop him.

The lights flared to life around him, calming him. His fears dissolved. He closed his eyes and began to pray.

"Oh, Lord, forgive me. I know I am weak and foolish. Please send thy angel to me again. I have so much to learn."

"Nephi."

He opened his eyes. The archangel in all his glory stood before him again. Relief came first, followed by a sharp spike of anxiety.

"I read the Book of Mormon," he said quickly. "Then I gave it to my sister and to a friend of mine. I hope I wasn't wrong to do so. I wanted so badly to share it."

Uriel laughed, sending ripples of pure joy in Nephi's direction. At least he was capable of amusing an archangel, he thought wryly.

"No. You are not wrong," Uriel said. "You are exactly right. Forgive my merriment. I know that was not easy to do."

"Yeah. Phoebe Sharpe is frightened of it. So is my friend Enoch. They think we'll get cast out. I suppose they have a point." He shrugged. "But I thought—"

He looked up at Uriel, who was patiently waiting for him to finish. "Well—to me it seems worth the risk. I never imagined what I was missing until I read that book. Now I think everyone should know the truth."

"Good." Uriel put his hand on Nephi's shoulder. Nephi gasped at the warmth that flowed into him. "You must believe in this work with all your heart, with all your mind, with all your soul. If you don't, you will surely fail."

"I do," Nephi said. "At least, I want to. I have so many questions."

"That's why I'm here." Uriel dropped his hand from Nephi's shoulder. "What do you want to know?"

Nephi thought about all the questions filling his head. Which one did he want to ask first? "Where is my mother?" he blurted out. It surprised him, but now that he'd asked, the longing to know grew stronger. "I was taught she'd passed on to her telestial reward, whatever that means. It doesn't sound like much. More slavery to celestials. I don't know that I ever believed that. I guess I thought she...and my father...just didn't exist anymore. Now—I don't know what to think. Where are they?" He stopped for a breath, far more emotional than he'd anticipated. He had tried so hard not to think about his parents at all.

"Your parents are in the bosom of God, awaiting the day when you can be joined eternally as a family in the celestial kingdom," Uriel said.

"Really? Even my father? After how he died?" The thought struck a painful spot in his heart. He'd been angry over the suicide for so long.

"Even him." The angel smiled. "That was an excellent question. That is part of what you are to do, Nephi. Make it possible for all who are or have been on the *Kingdom of Heaven* to be saved in the celestial kingdom."

"How?" He brushed his hair back against his head, but it floated up again instantly.

"With the truth. Nothing can stop it. Nothing can change it. The truth will always prevail. God remembers all of His children, and you are part of His covenant people. Do you know what that means?"

"I have some idea." The theme of God's covenant people had imbued every story in the Book of Mormon. He really needed to read it again.

"God's promises will be fulfilled. They must be. You will be an instrument in His hands."

Chills shivered down Nephi's arms. He stood on a precipice, caught between running back to his old life and plunging headfirst into something wild and dangerous. And beautiful and life-changing too. What could he do but throw himself into it?

"What do I need to do?"

"For now, you need to learn. Check your tab. You'll find you now have access to everything in the database."

"Everything?" Nephi took the tab from his pocket and tapped open the database. Sure enough, he could see it all. He blinked, dizzy. "Won't the information specialists know about this?"

"What's a little computer system to God?" Uriel folded his hands in front of him and grew serious. "You have a good foundation with the Book of Mormon. Now you must study the Bible and other holy scriptures. Also, read the ship's logs. You must understand your people's history if you are to be an effective teacher and leader."

"That sounds like a lot of studying," he said before thinking about how it would sound. "Oh, er, I mean, I'm not the best student around." He cringed. Reading the Book of Mormon in one night was definitely an aberration.

"I understand," Uriel said. "But I believe God has given you someone who can help."

"Salome." Of course she could help. She loved reading and studying. She'd always been the smartest in their class, and she was curious and thoughtful and…

"Her wisdom and insight will serve you well." The light began to gather around Uriel, and he rose toward the distant, rounded top of the core.

Nephi had another moment of panic. "Will I see you again?"

"When you need me."

In moments, the angel was gone. The core lights were dim and cold in comparison. "I'm sure I'll need you," Nephi whispered.

Chapter 8

Sal actually teared up when she saw Nephi's access to the database. "This is top level access," she whispered. They stood together, bent over a counter in the refrigerator room after dinner.

"I know." Nephi could hardly believe it himself. So many books, articles, ship's logs, passenger logs. He didn't even know where to start.

"I would guess only Jeremiah Black himself has this much information." Sal shook her head. "You sure nobody's going to notice you're accessing all this?"

"What's a little computer system to God?" Nephi grinned. "Will you help me study all this? I don't even know how to begin, but you're good at that kind of thing. We could learn together. What do you think?"

Sal pursed her lips and scrunched her forehead. She touched a button on the tab. "I want to," she said, looking up at Nephi. "But you're the one who saw the angel. You're the one with all the access." She handed his tab to him. "Maybe I shouldn't."

"Don't be silly." Nephi handed the tab back to her. "The archangel told me to ask you for help.

Sal's eyes popped. "He did?"

"Yes."

"Me specifically?"

"Yes, you. It's not that surprising."

Sal turned red. "It is to me."

"It shouldn't be. You're the smartest person I know. You should be getting a celestial education and working with the engineers or something. Not stuck here in the kitchens." He paused. "Although you are a great cook." Too bad he didn't get to eat it more often. His stomach growled. Sludge shakes weren't very filling.

"I like to cook," Sal said. "I don't mind working in the kitchen. I don't need some big, important job. I just want to know the truth. I want to be treated fairly. Equally, you know? I want to worship God."

"I know." His scars pulled tight as he straightened his back. "Things have to change. That's what Uriel said." He shrugged. "But I don't know if I'm the right person to change them."

"You are." She set down the tab and moved over to pick up some dirty dishes. "You're a natural leader. People look up to you."

"What people?" He thought of Brother Sorenson in aeroponics. He sure didn't look up to Nephi. Who looked up to a telestial, anyway?

"Lots of people." Sal stacked the plates on the counter. "I look up to you."

"Thanks." Nephi grinned. She'd gone pink again. "I look up to you too, Salome. That's why I want you to help me."

Sal ducked her head. "I'm happy to help you," she muttered, then looked up again and almost smiled.

"Great. When can we start?"

Late that night, Nephi knelt by his bed. He folded his hands, then his arms, then his hands again. No words would come. He couldn't understand it. If anyone needed to talk to God, it was him. "Father in Heaven," he began, quietly so as not to wake Prissa. He could hear her breathing on the other side of the curtain. She'd been asleep when he came back from studying with Sal. Though it hadn't been studying really. More like just trying to figure out what to learn first. Which was why he now found himself on his knees. The only prayers he'd ever heard, offered by priesthood holders in church, always began with "Father in Heaven."

"I—uh—I thank thee for sending an angel to me." That seemed like a good start. Now what else? "Oh, and I thank thee for letting me read the Book of Mormon. And for access to the rest of the scriptures and…everything else. It's a little overwhelming." He stopped. This was God he was talking to, after all. No sense trying to lie. "Okay. It's a lot overwhelming. I don't know why you would choose a guy like me—a nobody even among the leftovers." He paused again. "I've been rebellious, too. I never paid much attention in church. Maybe that's okay since we haven't been taught right anyway. But I am sorry for what happened with Elizabeth in the core." The scars on his back tingled and itched. "I never meant to do wrong or get Elizabeth in trouble."

He sighed. "I'm not up to the task you've given me, and that's the truth. But I'll try. And I have Sal to help, so that's good."

"Nephi?" Prissa's voice startled him out of his prayer.

"Prissa? Sorry, I didn't mean to wake you." He stood up and sat down on the edge of the bed.

Prissa turned on a soft night lamp and pushed the curtain aside. "Who were you talking to?"

"I was praying. I didn't mean to be so loud."

"Praying? Alone? I thought prayers were just for public."

"Nope. You can talk to God anytime. You should try it."

Prissa pulled her knees up to her chest. "I don't know. What would I say to God?"

"Whatever you want."

"I'd rather talk to you," Prissa said "Where have you been?"

"In the lounge with Sal. We were reading some things."

"The Book of Mormon again?"

"Yeah. And—other things."

"What other things?"

Nephi leaned forward with his hands on his knees. "I saw the archangel again today. He gave me access on my tab."

"Access to—?"

"Everything."

"Everything?" Prissa's voice rose incredulously.

"Pretty much everything."

"Wow."

"I know. I asked Sal to help me sort it all out."

Prissa was quiet for a minute. "You like her, don't you?"

"Who? Sal? You know I like her. She's a good friend."

"I think you like her more than that," Prissa said.

"Sal is very…smart. And I need smart friends since I'm so dumb." Nephi yawned.

"Okay." Prissa giggled. "Whatever you say."

Nephi grew serious. "I asked Uriel where our mother is."

"What did he say?" Prissa whispered.

"That she is in paradise. Waiting for us to be together as an eternal family. That we'd all be together in the celestial kingdom someday."

Prissa sniffed and Nephi looked over to see tears trailing down her cheeks. "I miss her so much. And Dad too."

Nephi went to sit beside her on her bed and put his arm around her. "I do too." Though his heart still grew uneasy thinking of his father.

"I never thought I wanted to go to the celestial kingdom at all," Prissa said, "but if that's true—well—I want to see them again."

"You will. And it won't be like the celestials have taught us. Or maybe it will, but it's not just for them. All of us have an equal chance of getting there. All you have to do is follow Jesus Christ."

"I don't think I know how to do that," Prissa said.

"I think you're already doing it." Nephi squeezed her shoulders. "But we can learn more together."

Prissa wiped her eyes. "Can we? I mean, President Black would say we leftovers aren't capable of following Christ. That's why we were born to telestial deck." Prissa rested her head on Nephi's shoulder. "If that's not true, then why were we born to telestial deck? Why were our parents and our friends? Why don't we have what the celestials get? We could, you know. It's not like there isn't enough to go around." She lifted her head. "I don't know. Sometimes it sure seems like God doesn't care about us. At least, I never thought He did."

"I never thought so either. When I got the stripes, I didn't think He even existed."

Prissa nodded.

"But Sal said something that first Sunday after the stripes. That everyone was equal before God. That got me thinking. And I had lots of time to think, you know. Then at my darkest moment, God sent an angel." The memory gave him goose bumps. "I don't think God would do that if He didn't care, right?"

"I guess so." She smiled through her tears. "But you'd better be right about this."

Nephi ruffled her hair. "Don't worry. I'm right."

Studying the scriptures with Sal was unlike anything Nephi had done before. Certainly not like school when he was a kid. He'd barely paid attention and been bored most of the time.

His and Sal's studies were anything but boring. He felt like someone had opened up his brain and was pouring information into it. As if having been in the dark all his life, he was finally stepping into the light, and, oh, there was so much to see!

"It's like we're on our own journey through the wilderness." Sal's eyes danced. "But our desert is the stars."

"And we've been wandering a lot more than forty years."

"More like four hundred," Sal agreed. "With at least that many more to go." She opened up her red journal and began to write.

"Working on a poem?" Nephi asked.

"Just taking some notes." She shut the book quickly, turning pink.

"Are you ever going to let me read any of it?"

Sal shook her head. She tucked the journal into her pocket.

Nephi knew it wouldn't do any good to pester her about it. "You think God is leading us to our own promised land?"

"Our ancestors thought so," Sal said. "They named it Canaan, after all, like the children of Israel." She tapped something on Nephi's tab. "But I'm not sure they were acting under God's direction. The early ship's logs are hard to decipher."

"Even if they were acting under God's direction back then, they aren't now."

"But you are." Sal's cheeks turned a deeper red.

Nephi stood up and pushed his hair out of his eyes. He paced around the sitting area.

"I think that proves he's leading us to a promised land," Sal said. Her eyes followed him as he wandered. "We're another branch broken from the olive tree."

Nephi stopped pacing and sat across from Sal. "Even though we've never seen Earth and never will?"

"Yes. And we won't see Canaan ourselves, either, but our descendants will, and God will give us everything we need right here on the *Kingdom of Heaven*." Sal drew her legs up underneath her. "It's wonderful, isn't it?"

"Yeah, it is." Chills prickled up his arms. Again, he felt himself teetering on the precipice of something huge. Something that would change everything forever.

"Nephi," Sal gave him a pointed look, "don't you think it's time we shared this with more people?"

Nephi stood up to pace again. "Other people know. Prissa and Enoch and Phoebe Sharpe." All of whom still thought he was crazy.

"But everyone deserves the truth. I want to tell my father. He grieves so much for my mother and sister. I want to give him comfort. I want him to know what I've learned. It might do him good. He's just wasting away in sorrow. I worry about him so much." She stopped. "I'm out of line, aren't I? I'm sorry."

Nephi sat beside her. "Don't be sorry. You can tell your father. You could have from the start."

"I didn't want to violate your trust."

"I know you wouldn't." Nephi picked his tab up off the couch. "I trust you."

"I think we should hold a meeting. With people we trust. We could do it on a Sunday afternoon, while the higher decks are still at church."

He looked at her in surprise. "You've given this a lot of thought."

Sal shrugged. "That is what the angel told you to do, isn't it?"

"Yes, but...I don't know if I'm ready for that. What would I even say? What if no one believes me?"

Sal stood up abruptly, folding her arms. "Do you believe it?" She frowned, the serious expression almost as cute as her smile.

"Of course I do." He couldn't stop the laughter bubbling up inside him. What would he do without Sal to keep him on his toes?

Her frown deepened. "You don't need to be scared. You just need to open your mouth." She walked out.

Nephi stifled another laugh, hoping he hadn't offended her. She really was terrific. And she was right. He flopped back on the couch and covered his eyes with his arm. "How are we supposed to avoid getting caught?" he asked the empty room. And what was he supposed to say, anyway?

Speak the truth.

Nephi felt a twinge of pain in the scars on his back. The truth could get him put to death. And anyone who believed him.

Sal's words echoed with unusual power in his mind. *You don't need to be scared. You just need to open your mouth.*

All right, then. He would do it.

Chapter 9

Nephi pushed his hair out of his eyes and cleared his throat. A dozen people had gathered in Sal's living room, the Hunsaker's apartment being much larger than his own, if just as sparse. Sal and her father and brother were there, of course; Enoch with his parents and sister and younger brother; Phoebe Sharpe and her husband Thomas; and Prissa. He'd known all of them forever and had no reason to be afraid, but nerves still made his hands shake and his stomach dance.

"I guess you all have some idea what I'm about to say," Nephi began.

"You really claim to have seen an angel?" Enoch's father, Alma Johnson, asked.

"Yes." Nephi stood up a little straighter. "The archangel Uriel appeared to me in the core. Twice, actually." Alma looked skeptical. "He healed my stripes, as Phoebe can attest."

"That's true." Phoebe didn't look pleased. "I've never seen anything like it."

"What did you do to deserve stripes?" Enoch's mother, Naomi, asked. "I've heard a lot of different stories."

Nephi pushed his hair back again. This wasn't how he pictured the meeting going. His eyes slid to Sal, but she wasn't looking at him.

"I know the Black family has denied it, but the truth is, I was in the core with Elizabeth Black. In a moment of sheer stupidity, I kissed her." He glanced at Sal again. "It was nothing, really. But I was accused of fornication and sentenced to ten stripes."

"How could anyone survive ten stripes?" That from Sal's brother, Reuben. "Are you making it up?" Sal slapped her brother's arm.

"He isn't making it up," Prissa said, her curls bouncing as she tossed her head. "You should have seen him. It was awful."

"Okay, okay." Reuben threw his hands up. "It seems like too harsh a punishment is all."

"You're right. It was too harsh. I believe it was more about Elizabeth's station than the actual kiss." His cheeks must have been as red as Sal's right then. "I only survived thanks to Phoebe and Prissa. And like I said, the angel healed me. Look." He turned around and pulled off his shirt so they could all see the scars criss-crossing his back. No one spoke, but someone drew in a sharp breath. He thought it might be Sal. He put the shirt back on and faced them again.

"I believe you," Reuben whispered.

"It's like a symbol," Sal said, coming to her feet. "A symbol of everything we're fighting for."

"Fighting?" her father asked.

Nephi started to answer, but Sal spoke first. "Yes, fighting. We're fighting for truth and freedom. To overturn lies and false doctrines." With each declaration, she grew more passionate. "We're fighting against the poverty and illness unfairly imposed on us by celestials, who have no right to rule us as they do, and—." She stopped and touched her rapidly flushing cheek. "I'm sorry."

Nephi squeezed her shoulder in what he hoped was a reassuring gesture. "Don't be. You're right, Sal. The angel told me that we have gone far astray from the true gospel. We don't understand true doctrine. Sal and I have been reading the scriptures and other materials, including the history of the ship. This division into kingdoms is false. It began back with the plague, when the sick and their families and friends were quarantined. Fear of the sickness kept them divided and deprived. Some justified the action by preaching that those who suffered and died in the plague were afflicted because of unworthiness. That falsehood spread until we arrived where we are today." He glanced at Sal, hoping he'd got all that history part correct. She nodded. "But that is not what God wants for us. All of us have an equal chance to return to our Heavenly Father through the grace of Jesus Christ. This scripture is one example." He turned on his tab. "'And he denieth none that come unto him, black and white, bond and free, male and female; and he remembereth the heathen; and all are alike unto God, both Jew and Gentile.'"

"That's what was quoted in my second great-grandmother's journal," Sal said. "She had the scriptures. Or someone taught them to her."

Thomas Sharpe came to his feet. "This is blasphemy. Only President Black can read and interpret the scriptures."

"If he's been reading them, then he's deliberately deceiving us," Sal said.

"You cannot speak about the president like that." Thomas took Phoebe by the hand. "We're leaving." Phoebe looked over her shoulder at Nephi as they left, but he couldn't tell if she was upset with her husband or with him.

Sal sat down again next to her father with her mouth pinched tight and her hands trembling. Her father whispered something in her ear and she shook her head. Nephi wanted to disappear.

"All right. I admit, Thomas has a point," Nephi said. "I for one don't want any more stripes. But—" He paused, gathering his thoughts. "I must speak the truth."

He looked over the small gathering. Sal looked miserable, but Prissa grinned at him. That, at least was encouraging. Everyone else looked worried, or at best confused. Maybe Brother Sharpe was right to walk out. Nephi swallowed.

"I have told you the truth. I know it would be easier to ignore me and go on with life as normal. This is a dangerous journey I'm asking you to take with me." It was as if someone else was speaking through his mouth. The words left him heavy with fear, and floating in the core at the same time. "I can promise you this journey will take us somewhere we've never imagined."

"Back to God," Sal whispered.

"Yeah." Nephi grinned. "To God."

"I'm going with you," Prissa said. Nephi nodded his thanks.

"Me too." Sal didn't smile, but she looked him straight in the eyes.

"I want to know more," Sal's father said.

"I do too," Enoch's mother said. His father nodded.

Enoch stood up. "Nephi, you've done a lot of crazy things over the years, and I've done most of them with you. This is probably the craziest you've come up with, but you know I've got your back like I always have."

"Thanks, man," Nephi said. "I'm going to need it. We're all going to need it."

A couple of days later, a group of celestial children came to tour the aeroponic garden where Nephi was working again. Ordinarily, he would have ignored them, but one of their chaperones caught his attention. Elizabeth.

He turned hastily back to his planting, determined not to meet her eye. The group passed behind him. Brother Sorenson droned on about the aeroponic system and the goodness of God in providing a way to feed themselves on their long voyage through the stars, etc. He didn't mention the people like Nephi who were actually doing the work.

Nephi watched them sidelong as they passed. A little girl with big, brown eyes looked back at the same moment and caught his gaze. She gasped when she saw he was looking at her, but cocked her head, studying him for a moment, and smiled before turning away.

Nephi shook his head. It was a shame, really, that the innocent children were being raised to believe lies. They were as much a victim of Black's control as any of the telestials.

Enoch nudged him, clearing his throat.

"Huh?" Nephi turned his head and nearly choked. Elizabeth had stopped beside him.

"We need to talk," she said in a whisper.

Nephi glanced at the celestial children moving out of sight. "Here?" He didn't want to be accused of sneaking off with her.

Elizabeth nodded tersely. Enoch coughed. "So, I'll just—" He pointed over his shoulder. "Yeah." He walked away.

"I want to apologize," Elizabeth said. "I didn't mean for you to get punished."

He wanted to ask why she'd said anything to her grandfather in the first place, but he didn't. "I'm the one who should apologize. You didn't deserve punishment, either."

Tears gathered in Elizabeth's bright blue eyes.

"I'd go back and change it if I could," he said. But when he thought of all that had happened since, maybe he wouldn't.

Elizabeth shook her head. "It wasn't your fault. I should have known better."

Better than to hang out with leftovers? Nephi didn't ask. "I hope you're feeling all right now. All healed?"

Elizabeth stood up straighter. "Yes. Thank you. I'm fine."

They fell silent. "Congratulations on your marriage," Nephi said after a few awkward seconds.

"Thank you." She lifted her chin. "Ammon is a good man."

He wondered why she felt the need to tell him that. "Good. You deserve every happiness." He had a sudden urge to tell her everything—about the archangel, the scriptures, all of it, but he didn't get the chance.

"Goodbye, Nephi." She raised her hand for a moment as if she would touch him, then hurried away after her group.

"Goodbye," Nephi said to her retreating figure. Odd how looking at her now did not bring back the feelings he'd had for her before. If anything, it just made him sad for her.

Enoch was back a moment later. "What was that all about?"

Nephi shrugged.

"Huh. I bet she regrets marrying Ammon Nielsen." Enoch elbowed him in the ribs.

"Maybe so." Nephi frowned and resumed his planting. It wasn't any of his business anyway.

"Maybe you should have told her," Sal said at their late night study session in the lounge. She pulled her legs up under her on the sofa. "I mean, everyone deserves to know, right?"

Nephi thought about the little brown-eyed girl. "Yes." He leaned forward and rested his elbows on his knees. "But Elizabeth doesn't have a great track record for keeping confidences."

"That's not fair," Sal said. "She apologized, didn't she? You ought to forgive her."

"I have forgiven her," Nephi said. "But that doesn't mean I have to trust her. Besides, it doesn't matter. She walked away before I could say anything anyway. I'm certainly not going to seek her out. One five second kiss caused enough trouble. I don't need to go creating more."

"I know." Sal shifted her position. "I guess I feel sorry for Elizabeth."

"You do? She's got the best of everything. Probably never had to work a day in her life, and never will. Why would you feel sorry for her?"

"Look at it from her perspective. On celestial deck, a woman's position in society is dependent entirely upon her husband's place in the hierarchy."

"No problem for her there," Nephi said.

"Yes, but no celestial man wants a wife with scars from stripes—evidence of her unrighteousness."

"So why'd Ammon marry her?"

"He has to marry her if he wants to inherit the presidency."

"So he married her in spite of her stripes." He wrinkled his nose. "You know, he may have been the one to give her the stripes."

"Eww." Sal shuddered. "That makes it even worse. Elizabeth knows he only married her for his own gain, and he has these secret scars on her back to hold over her. Keep her in her place."

"In her place? Why would she need keeping? She's clearly not going to give her place up."

"Maybe not. But it seems obvious she wants something more. Or at least something different. She must have thought she was doing right in confessing her sins, but it ruined her life. Now she's stuck living up to the expectations of people who hold her in contempt. Her husband, her grandfather, her parents. She must be miserable. At least, that's how I'd feel in her place."

"Yeah, but you're not very much like Elizabeth." He meant it as a compliment, but Sal didn't take it as such, judging by the look on her face.

"I suppose I'm not. Maybe she is glad to have her position and power, but in a lot of ways the celestial women have it much worse than I do."

"What do you mean?"

"I've never been made to feel that my worth depended on what kind of husband I got, or that I had to act a certain way in order to please a man." She looked away. "There's a lot of pressure on the celestial women to be, well, perfect. I don't know how they deal with it."

Nephi cocked his head. "How do you know all this, anyway?"

"I'm observant," Sal said. "And I read." She held up his tab for emphasis.

"And you're brilliant. You ought to lead tomorrow's meeting."

Sal shook her head. "I don't speak in front of groups. You do it."

Nephi raised his eyebrows. "You spoke at the last meeting. It was perfect."

Sal's cheeks colored. "That was only our families. There will be twice as many tomorrow. Besides, it wasn't perfect. I made a fool of myself. I'm not doing that again."

"You didn't make a fool of yourself. You showed everyone how passionate you are about this. How passionate we should all be."

Her eyes got big. "I'm not doing that again. No way." She stood up and handed him the tab. "Goodnight, Nephi."

"Goodnight." He watched her walk out and wondered what he was going to say to twice as many people the next day.

It turned out to be more like three or four times as many people. Nephi watched in astonishment as forty or more of his friends and neighbors tried to cram into the Hunsaker's apartment. It wasn't going to work.

Sal tapped Nephi's shoulder and leaned over to shout in his ear over the noise and confusion. "Somebody's already using the lounge, but the cafeteria has emptied out. Let's go there."

Nephi nodded. He cupped his hands around his mouth. "We'll meet in the cafeteria. Head that direction."

A general grumble moved through the crowd as they started out the door.

"Just a few at a time," Nephi called. They didn't need everyone heading en masse to the empty cafeteria. That would surely arouse unwanted curiosity.

"Where'd they all come from?" he muttered to Sal.

"Word spread. They want what you have to offer. We all do."

Nephi raised his eyebrows. "What exactly does everyone expect?"

Sal didn't hesitate. "Truth. Freedom. Eternal life."

Nephi didn't answer. Is that really what he had to give them? "I don't know what I'm doing."

91

"Yes, you do," Sal said. She nudged him forward. "Be brave."

"Right. This from the girl who won't speak in front of a crowd."

"But you're great in front of a crowd." Sal pushed him again. How would she know? She'd never seen him in front of a crowd. He'd never been in front of a crowd. He wasn't sure he wanted to be.

Speak the truth, he reminded himself.

It took ten minutes for everyone to trickle down to the cafeteria. Nephi waited in the hall until everyone was inside. He stood there for a minute alone in the quiet hallway. The lights were dimmed to evening levels. Nephi closed his eyes and silently prayed. He was growing more used to the sacred communication every day.

Dear God, help me to speak thy words.

Nephi, I am with thee.

"All right, then." Nephi squared his shoulders and went inside.

The crowd seemed less formidable in the large cafeteria than it had at the Hunsaker's. He moved to the front of the room. Everyone watched him intently, looking curious, eager, a little fearful. Leah, from the kitchens, was there, along with Abish and other friends from aeroponics. He was surprised to see that Thomas and Phoebe Sharpe had come again. He waved his fingers to Phoebe, who returned the gesture. Her husband remained still.

Prissa and Sal sat together up front with Enoch beside them. Prissa gave him her brightest, most encouraging smile.

Nephi folded his hands behind him. "My friends, I'm glad you've come tonight. I guess you all heard about the angel already." He swallowed the lump in his throat, and tried to recapture the spirit he'd felt out in the hall. "I have something very important to share with you."

Chapter 10

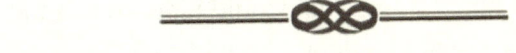

"That was quite a speech you gave last night," Enoch said.

Nephi smirked as he pinched back a bud on a strawberry plant. "Is that supposed to be a compliment?"

"Sure." Enoch shrugged. "You were like a whole different person up there."

Nephi snipped a couple more buds off before answering. "I'm still the same person."

Enoch shook his head. "You've changed. I'm not saying it's a bad thing."

Nephi considered that. He really didn't feel any different. "I haven't changed. I've just learned more."

"What have you learned, Brother Packard?"

Nephi tried not to look as startled as he felt as he turned around to face Brother Sorenson. How long had he been standing there? Sorenson glared, his beefy arms folded, looking for an excuse to send Nephi down to scrub the algae filters again.

"I've learned how important proper pruning is, sir." Not a total lie. For a second he felt like he had when he'd talked to Elizabeth—like he ought to tell Sorenson everything.

"Is that so?" Sorenson leaned in, nose to nose with Nephi. "Let me tell you something, Packard. Guys like you don't know squat about gardening or anything else. You barely have enough brains in there to do what you're told without screwing it up. I don't want to hear you talk about learning. You're not capable of it. You're a leftover. Don't forget it." He poked a finger into Nephi's chest and stepped back with his hands on his hips, his glare daring Nephi to respond.

Nephi didn't flinch. "You're wrong. I know a lot more than you think. I know things that would blow your mind."

Sorenson's face turned redder. "I ought to—"

But his threat was cut short when the ship's all-hands-assemble whistle echoed through the space. Nephi looked over at Enoch. They didn't sound that call for no reason.

Sorenson narrowed his eyes as if he thought Nephi was responsible. Nephi swallowed hard, hoping he wasn't. He glanced nervously at Enoch again.

With a final glare, Sorenson turned away from them to shout above the whistle. "Everyone to the chapel. Now!"

Enoch grabbed Nephi's arm and pulled him away before Sorenson could turn on them again.

"See what I mean?" Enoch said as they made their way toward the door. "You've changed."

Nephi chuckled. "Back talking Brother Sorenson? That's not much of a change. Trust me, friend. I have a lot more changing to do." He slapped Enoch on the shoulder. "I'll see you in the chapel."

A meeting in the chapel meant putting on Sunday clothes, and he'd have to do it in a hurry. President Black did not tolerate tardiness. Nephi arrived home to find Prissa already there, smoothing out the wrinkles on her dress. It was getting too small, but they didn't have the extra credits to replace it. They still hadn't caught up from what they'd lost during his recovery.

"What's going on?" Prissa asked. "Do you know?"

"No." A tremor went through him. It couldn't be about him, could it? His scars itched something awful, a reminder of the danger of defying the president.

"You'd better get changed," Prissa said.

Right. Get changed. Go to the chapel. Pretend nothing was wrong, nothing had happened. He ducked behind the curtain and got into his Sunday shirt.

He took Prissa's arm as they made their way to the chapel. She was trembling, her lips pressed together like she was holding back tears. "Don't worry," he whispered. "This has nothing to do with us."

"How do you know?" She clung tighter to his arm.

"They'd have already arrested me if it did."

She looked up at him, her eyes huge.

Nephi squeezed her hand. "It's okay. I promise."

The telestial balcony was nearly full when they arrived. Nephi spotted Enoch. He motioned Nephi and Prissa over to where he sat, down in front near the railing. Sal was with her father in the next row back. Nephi waved to her. Her hands fidgeted restlessly on her lap. Her forehead was creased. Her father looked just as nervous. Actually, when he looked around, he saw almost all of the people who'd come to the meeting last night had congregated together, and all of them were staring at him with fear in their faces.

Nephi pushed the hair out of his face and tried to give them all a reassuring smile. He sat down next to Prissa and Enoch, trying not to panic. Down below, the High Council, elders, and the terrestrial bishops filled the seats on the stand, every one of them looking unusually somber behind their beards. Or maybe that was just his imagination.

That's when he noticed the empty seat among the High Councilmen. Leaning forward, he saw the casket. A man-sized boat made to resemble polished wood, covered and curved upward on each end. A casket of a celestial. Relief washed over him. The death of a High Councilor would warrant a meeting like this. Nothing to do with him at all, just like he'd said. He nudged Prissa and pointed out the casket. She scowled. "Who died?"

Nephi shrugged. President Black stood up, and the chapel fell silent. "My brothers and sisters, today we must bid farewell to one of the *Kingdom of Heaven's* finest men. Helam Lawrence."

Of course. Brother Lawrence was almost a hundred years old and couldn't even remember his own name half the time.

Nephi relaxed into his seat and tuned out President Black's eulogy. Brother Lawrence had gone on to celestial glory to be waited on hand and foot by telestials, and so forth. His thoughts turned to his own mother. He remembered standing hand in hand with Prissa, watching their mother's body be ejected into space. Just the two of them, alone. No one had spoken any words about her life, about what kind of person she had been. The workday had not stopped for his mother's death. she had not had the chance to live to be a hundred and forget her own name. And of course his father had taken the casting out into his own hands. All he remembered of his father's death was his mother's misery—and his own. Would it ever stop hurting?

Uriel had said they were waiting for him in heaven. He wondered idly what had actually become of Brother Lawrence. He closed his eyes and for a moment he caught a glimpse of something. Light brighter than the growing lamps, people clothed in white, and were those...? Yes—his mother...and his father, together, laughing and joyous. His father looked straight at him and held out his hand. "Nephi, hurry. We need you."

"Dad?" Nephi's eyes popped open, his breath stolen away by the vision. What did it mean?

President Black's speech rang suddenly loud in his ears. "Before we send our beloved brother Helam on his final journey through the stars, we must fill the spot he has left in our High Council."

Nephi leaned forward.

"To that end, I have called Brother Ammon Nielsen-Black to be our newest High Councilor. May it be according to God's will.

"All in favor of this action so indicate," Black said.

Hands went up all through the chapel. Nephi froze. His scars stung beneath the coarse fabric of his shirt, a hand-me-down from Enoch to replace the shirt he'd lost when he'd gotten his stripes. He knew he should raise his hand as expected, but he couldn't. Not for Ammon. Not for any of them. Not anymore.

It was over in a blink. President Black hadn't so much as glanced at the telestial balcony. His small rebellion had passed unnoticed. And yet, Nephi could feel the significance of it.

Prissa reached for him, and he squeezed her hand. That's when he noticed Enoch held her other hand. He raised an eyebrow at that, but kept quiet.

Ammon came forward, smug and self-satisfied, and made a big show of kneeling before President Black while Black and the rest of the High Council gathered in a circle around him and laid their hands on his head to ordain him a High Priest on the Council.

Nephi pictured Ammon with the glowing rod raised to strike and he shivered. He wondered what Elizabeth thought about it. Was she pleased? Remembering what Sal had said about Elizabeth's position, he wished her happiness.

His eyes flicked back to Sal. She sat forward in her seat watching the circle with her forehead creased in concentration. He wished he knew what she was thinking. She caught his eye, then, and he winked at her. The hint of a smile wisped across her face before she turned her attention back to the front. Nephi did the same. Ammon stepped up to the pulpit, but Nephi didn't listen. He reflected on the vision he'd seen just before President Black had called Ammon to the High Council. *Hurry.* They were waiting for him, but what was he supposed to do for them? The answer must surely be in the endless data on his tab. He'd have to ask Sal to help him figure it out.

Ammon went on about how he'd humbly fill Brother Lawrence's shoes.

Humbly, my left big toe.

Then he paused for a moment and looked in Nephi's direction. "And I promise you that wherever heresy exists on this ship, I will root it out and destroy it."

Heresy, huh? "I'm not afraid of you," Nephi whispered.

Prissa bumped his shoulder with hers. "Maybe you should be."

After watching old Brother Lawrence take his final journey out the airlock in his fancy casket, Nephi and the rest went back to work. Brother Sorenson, apparently perturbed by the interruption and still irritated with Nephi, sent him to scrub algae filters with Hyrum and Zeniff for the rest of the day.

It seemed that the service had replaced lunch hour, because he never got one. By the end of the day, he was starving and exhausted and covered in slime. He went up to his room to shower and change for a third time, and finally made it to the cafeteria for dinner.

He'd hoped to talk to Sal, but she wasn't there. Nephi figured she was on the upper deck helping with the funeral banquet. The celestials loved to throw gigantic parties for their dearly departed. Instead he took his sludge shake, and sat with Prissa and the Sharpes. He nudged Prissa. "Where's Enoch?"

She shrugged, turning pink. "How would I know? Weren't you working with him?"

"Nope. I got sent down to the filters again."

"Again?" Prissa giggled.

"Yeah. Be glad you don't have to do it." Nephi poked her playfully in the shoulder.

"Nephi." Thomas Sharpe cleared his throat. "I wanted to tell you that I…well, I was impressed with the things you had to say last night."

"Oh." Nephi pushed back his hair. "Thank you, Brother Sharpe. I was glad you both came back."

"So are we," Phoebe patted her husband's arm. "But, Nephi, you really must exercise a little more caution. Not raising your hand today—"

"I didn't know anyone noticed."

"Some did." Phoebe leaned forward. "It would be unwise to draw the attention of the High Council again."

"I know." Nephi sighed. "But how can I pretend to support something I know is wrong?" He shook his head. "I can't do that anymore."

"I admire your integrity, but I think you should be more careful," Phoebe said.

"I will. I promise."

"Good." Phoebe and Thomas excused themselves.

"So," Nephi said when they were gone, "I saw you holding hands with Enoch at the meeting."

"So what?" She fiddled with one of her curls. "I was holding your hand, too."

"Enoch's just another big brother to you, huh?"

"That's right." She pointed her fork at him. "Just like Sal's your very smart friend."

"I see." He tousled her hair, which always drove her crazy. She swatted at his hand. "But, seriously, you're only sixteen," Nephi said.

"You think I'm still a baby." She stuck out her lip in a mock pout. "But I'm not. I can make my own decisions."

"Fine. I only want you to... exercise a little more caution." He winked.

"Why? Don't you trust Enoch?"

"I trust him." He put his arm around her. "But if he hurts you, I will smash his face in no matter how close of friends we are."

"You're very gallant." Prissa stood up, her leftover shake finished. "But that won't be necessary. We're just friends." She poked out her tongue. "Are you studying with Sal tonight?"

"Yep. Want to come?"

Prissa shook her head. "Phoebe thinks Sarai Jenson will have her baby tonight. She wants me to help." She smiled. "I like doing that."

"Good. I'll see you later, then."

Prissa waved goodbye and left. Nephi finished his tasteless dinner shake, wishing he could have some of the funeral banquet Sal had prepared for the celestials. He had so much he wanted to talk to her about. He hummed to himself half an hour later as he walked to the lounge.

Sal wasn't there, but Hyrum and Zeniff were. They sat at one of the tables looking at a small, handmade, red notebook. A familiar-looking notebook. Hyrum pointed at something and they both laughed.

Nephi crossed the room in two strides and snatched Sal's journal from Hyrum's hand. "What do you think you're doing?"

Hyrum smirked. "Enjoying a little—poetry." His lip curled. Zeniff snickered behind his hand. "You'd probably enjoy it too," Hyrum said. Nephi resisted the urge to remove Hyrum's grin with his fist. With Zeniff here, that wouldn't end well.

His teeth clenched. "Where's Sal?"

"Oh, gee." Hyrum pretended to look around the lounge. "She was here a few minutes ago." His smile turned malicious. "What are you two doing in here this late at night, anyway?"

"Yeah." Zeniff stood up. "We want all the juicy details."

Nephi tightened his grip around Sal's journal. "You two oozing algae-balls wouldn't understand even if I told you."

Hyrum came halfway out of his seat, but Nephi stomped out without waiting for his response. He had to find Sal.

Her father answered the door at their place.

"Is Sal here?"

"No." He wrinkled up his forehead. "I thought she was with you."

"She's supposed to be. Don't worry. I'll find her."

She was in the back of the kitchens, sitting on the floor against the tall refrigerator doors with her arms wrapped around her knees. Her shoulders shook with crying. Nephi seriously considered going back and breaking Hyrum's nose.

101

"Hey."

Sal lifted her head. Tears streaked her cheeks. Nephi sat beside her and handed her the journal. "I think this is yours."

"Thanks." She ran her hand over the cover, blinking away a fresh batch of tears.

"I didn't look at it," Nephi said.

"I know." She pressed the journal against her chest and sniffed. "But Hyrum did. I'm so humiliated." Her voice broke.

Nephi put his arm around her. "I could go break every bone in his body. Would that help?"

She shook her head and laughed, though it sounded more like a sob. He tightened his arm around her. It was nothing more than what he'd do to comfort Prissa. Except Sal was not his sister and he was quite distinctly aware of how nice it felt to hold her close to him. "You shouldn't be humiliated, anyway. I'm sure everything in that journal is just as beautiful as you are."

Sal looked away from him. She was nothing like Elizabeth; small and dark where Elizabeth was tall and golden. Looking at Sal, Nephi couldn't imagine why he'd ever felt anything for Elizabeth. He tucked his finger under Sal's chin and turned her face to his. His lips touched hers softly, and she pulled away, shock written on her face. It was just like Elizabeth, only a thousand times worse because this was Sal, and at that moment he knew he couldn't live without her and her wisdom and amazing strength.

"Sal, I'm…" He trailed off as she reached up and brushed the hair out of his face. Her delicate fingers trailed across his forehead. He closed his eyes. Sal pressed her lips awkwardly against his. Nephi pulled her closer and showed her how to kiss properly. She was a fast learner.

When they parted, her eyes were wide. Nephi grinned and was rewarded with her rare and lovely smile. But then she buried her face in his shoulder and started to cry again. He tightened his arms around her, a bit perplexed. "I didn't mean to upset you."

"Y-you didn't." She scooted away from him and stood, scooping the journal off the floor. Nephi stood too.

"Listen, Sal…"

"I'm sorry." She swiped at the messy tears on her cheeks. "It's been such a strange day, you know."

"I know."

"And that jerk stole my journal. I know he read it." She bit her lip. "I could just die."

"Don't do that." Nephi took her hand. "What would I do without you?"

Sal waved her hand to brush away his comment.

"I mean it." He wanted to kiss her again so badly it hurt.

Sal looked down at the journal in her hand and her eyes went wide. "Nephi, I wrote about you in here."

"Something steamy?"

She didn't smile like he'd hoped. "No. About the angel. About everything. She dropped his hand and raked her fingers through her hair. "This is a disaster."

Nephi reached for her, eased her closer to him. "Don't worry. Hyrum and Zeniff can't even read."

Sal chuckled, though it wasn't a happy sound. "You know they can. They did." Her voice quavered.

Nephi squeezed her shoulders. "They didn't have it all that long." He thought about Hyrum taunting him. *You'd like it too.* Oh, how he wanted to punch the guy.

"Long enough." Sal shuddered. "And those two don't seem like the type to be sympathetic to our cause."

No, they didn't, especially not after Nephi had yelled at and insulted them. Not that they didn't deserve it. "Whatever they read, we can't change it now. No sense worrying about it."

Sal stepped away from him, clutching her journal against her chest. "There'll be plenty to worry about if President Black gets wind of what we're doing. I should never have written it down."

"It's not your fault." He almost reached for her again, but she was already backing away.

"I just want this day to end." Her eyes grew glassy again. She turned and hurried toward the door.

"Salome." Nephi's throat felt tight.

Sal turned halfway back, her cheeks red, but not in the usual cute way. She looked sickly.

"I love you," Nephi said.

Sal looked at him for a moment. "You probably say that to all the girls you kiss."

She was out the door before he could say anything back.

Chapter 11

Nephi flopped onto the worn couch in his apartment. The broken crossbeam pressed against his backside. He grumbled. The cushions were shot too, and it would take ages to save enough credits to put in for a new one. One the celestials had thrown out anyway. Leftovers didn't get new stuff.

Prissa looked up from the project she was working on at the table, wrapping thin scraps of fabric around two short lengths of plastic tubing. Where she came up with her bits and pieces, Nephi didn't know.

"Not studying tonight?" Prissa asked.

"Nope." Nephi stretched out on the couch and covered his eyes with his arm. "Why do women have to be so complicated?"

"Why do men?" Prissa snapped.

Nephi sat up. "Did something happen between you and Enoch?" His fists still itched to punch someone's lights out. Enoch might do just as well as Hyrum.

"No." Prissa rolled her eyes. "Absolutely nothing happened between me and Enoch." She gave the fabric strip an extra hard twist. "What happened with you and Sal?"

Nephi relaxed his hands. "I'm not sure what happened. Hyrum and Zeniff stole her journal. She was pretty upset."

"What? Those oozers. Did you get it back?"

"Yeah, I did." He lay back on the couch again. "What's that you're making?"

"It's called a God's Eye. I found the instructions in the database. It should be made with yarn, but I didn't have any." She held it up to show him the interesting pattern created by her twisting and wrapping.

"God's Eye, huh?" The mention of deity sent shame seeping through his skin. He'd lost a night of important studying because once again he couldn't control his impulses. Maybe God should choose someone else.

His chest constricted. What would become of him then? *I'm sorry, Lord.*

"What do you think?" Prissa asked, still holding her God's Eye.

Nephi forced himself to breathe. "It's pretty. When are you leaving?"

The door chimed.

"Right now." Prissa bounced up, dropping the God's Eye on the table, and opened the door.

"Ready to go?" Phoebe asked.

"Yes." Prissa grinned, her ire forgotten. "Bye, Nephi. I'll be back later."

"Don't wait up." Phoebe waved, and Nephi lifted his hand in response as the door slid shut again.

He let his arm fall back across his eyes. He ought to get up and study on his own. Or maybe he ought to get on his knees and ask forgiveness for his weakness. But all he could think about was Sal's kiss and the look on her face when she had left him. The sadness in her eyes. The regret. He groaned. Sal was right. It was time for this miserable day to end. He rolled off the couch and dragged himself to bed.

———— ∞ ————

He awoke some time later to the sound of muffled sobbing.

"Prissa?" He turned up the nightlight and pushed back the curtain. Prissa had her face buried in her pillow. Her body quivered with crying.

Nephi came to sit on her bed. "What's wrong?" He rested his hand on her back.

Seconds ticked away while she tried to catch her breath. Finally, she rolled over and sat up. "Sarai Jenson," she choked out. "She's dead. And her baby." Her face crumbled.

"Oh, no. I'm sorry. So sorry."

"It was awful. There was so much blood. And the baby...the baby never had a chance."

"I'm sorry you had to go through that, Prissa."

"I couldn't do anything. Neither could Phoebe." She turned her face against Nephi's shoulder, and he held her until her tears were spent.

His heart felt like someone had increased the gravity in his chest. Prissa lifted her head, sniffing. "Poor Jarom is beside himself. You should talk to him, Nephi. He needs you."

Sarai's husband. He was a couple of years older than Nephi, and a friend. Prissa was right. He needed to go see him, but what in the galaxy would he say to him? *I'm sorry* was so inadequate. Hard experience had taught him that.

"I can't leave you like this," he told Prissa, his voice gruff.

Prissa sat up straight and brushed her sleeve across her nose. "I'll be okay. If I'm going to follow in Phoebe's footsteps, I have to learn how to accept it." She pulled her face into an expression she probably thought was stoic, but only looked young and sad.

Nephi kissed forehead. "Get some sleep."

Prissa nodded and slid back under the blanket. Her eyes misted up again. "You'll go see Jarom?"

It was almost one in the morning, but he knew he had to go. Maybe it would make up for everything he'd messed up tonight. "Yes, I will."

"Good." She rolled onto her side, and a moment later was asleep.

Nephi quietly changed out of pajamas and headed for Jarom Jenson's apartment, two levels up from his own on one of the nearly empty levels of telestial deck, with apartments waiting for newly married families. Maybe someday Nephi would move up here with his own bride. He pictured Sal, but that thought made his heart even heavier.

He pressed the chime at Jarom's door. It was Jarom's bishop who answered, frowning beneath his beard, looking Nephi up and down with a dour expression. "Come in," the bishop said. "I was just leaving."

Nephi and the bishop swapped places in the doorway, and the door slid shut between them. The tension and grief in the room pressed against his skin. Jarom sat on a straight-backed chair, his head hanging, his hands dangling between his knees. He looked up at Nephi with empty eyes, and lowered his head without speaking.

Nephi sat in the empty chair across from him—a seat no doubt vacated by the bishop. "Prissa told me what happened. I'm so sorry. I know that doesn't help." He pushed his hair back, waiting for words of wisdom to come to mind, but nothing did.

"Sarai's already gone," Jarom said, his voice flat. "The baby too. Out the airlock ten minutes ago. That's what my bishop came to tell me. No goodbyes. No memorial. Just out into space like a piece of garbage."

"They didn't deserve that." Nephi said. "And neither do you. What did your bishop say?"

"What do bishops ever say? That our own sinful nature caused this to happen. If she were more worthy, she would have lived." Jarom's voice broke bitterly.

"It isn't true," Nephi said, and the words he'd been waiting for flooded in. "Sarai and your child have gone to the bosom of God. They are happy there, and they are waiting for you. You can be with them eternally in the celestial kingdom."

Jarom's head snapped up. "How can that be?"

"The angel told me." Nephi said. "And I've seen it. In a vision. I saw my parents and others too."

Hurry, Nephi. We need you. He shivered at the memory of his father.

Jarom's forehead wrinkled. "We went to your meeting last night. Sarai was excited about it." He lowered his head into his hands.

"I know it doesn't take away the pain now, but you will see Sarai and your baby again. You will be with them forever. She is in God's hands, and so are you."

"I don't know if I can believe that," Jarom said. "But I want to. Sarai was a good person. She was kind and generous. She worked hard."

"I know." Nephi thought for a second. "We'll hold a service for her and for your baby."

"A funeral service?"

"Yes. We should honor their lives, like they deserve." He stood up. "And not just Sarai and the baby. All our loved ones. They are precious to the Savior—every one." He stopped.

Jarom nodded slowly. "I like that idea. For my brother and my grandparents, too."

"Anyone we want to remember." He would have to talk to Sal about the best way to go about it. If Sal was even speaking to him anymore.

Jarom nodded, his eyes growing redder. "You really think I'll see her again?"

"I know you will." Nephi stood and rested his hand on Jarom's shoulder. "Be strong."

"I will." Jarom stood too and shook Nephi's hand. "Thank you for coming." His hand trembled in Nephi's.

"I pray the Lord will comfort you tonight." Words could be so inadequate sometimes. Nephi took his leave, scowling at his feet as he walked. A memorial service would be nice, but it wasn't enough. Something was still missing. Something more to do.

Another pair of feet appeared in his line of sight—petite, olive-toned feet. He stopped short just before running into her. "Sal?" She looked awful with her dark hair standing straight up as if she'd been raking her fingers through it, and her eyes almost as red as Jarom's. "Are you okay?"

"I couldn't sleep. Prissa told me where to find you. It's so awful about Sarai Jenson and her baby." She wilted a little. Nephi remembered her own mother and baby sister had died in childbirth.

"It is awful." He wanted to take her in his arms and comfort her, but he kept his hands at his side.

A shudder ran through Sal's body. She pulled herself up straighter. "I wanted to apologize."

"I'm the one who should apologize." He pushed his hair out of his eyes. "I didn't mean to upset you. I just—I don't always think before I act. You may have noticed." He felt a grin tugging at his lips in spite of everything.

"Yes, I've noticed." Sal almost smiled, too. "And I think too much. I shouldn't have run out like that. It was rude. I'm sorry. I didn't want you to think—" She flushed.

"Think what?" He couldn't hide the grin now.

"To think I was angry with you. I'm not." She looked down at her hands. "I was flustered because no one's ever…kissed me before."

"Probably because you haven't let anyone know the real you before." He reached for her and she took his hand. The weight of the day settled on him. There was only one place he wanted to be now. "Will you come to the core with me?"

"What?" Sal's eyebrows leaped toward her wild hair.

Nephi stuffed down a laugh. "That's where I go to think. Unwind. I need that right now. And—" he shrugged— "everything's better when you're with me."

"Oh." She squeezed his hand. "Sure. It sounds nice."

"Good. Let's go."

Nephi led her to the access panel on Jarom's deck. The tension in his jaw eased as soon as the panel slid open, but Sal hung back. "It's so dark in there."

"Don't worry. The lights will come on. And you can't fall. There isn't any gravity."

"I don't know." Sal bit her lip.

Nephi took both her hands in his. "Trust me. We'll step off together. I won't let go of you, okay?"

"Okay." Her hands tightened around his.

Nephi bent over and kissed her softly. She didn't seem to mind. Then he stepped backwards off the ledge, pulling Sal with him. She gasped.

The lights came on along the length of the engine housing. Sal let out a terrified squeak and wrapped her arms around Nephi's neck, burying her face in his shoulder. His arms closed around her. "Don't worry," he whispered in her ear. "We aren't falling. Just floating. You're safe, I promise."

Sal only clung to him tighter. If that's what she wanted, he wasn't going to complain. He should have brought her to the core a long time ago—like before he'd ever met Elizabeth.

Nephi patted Sal's back in a way he hoped was reassuring. "We can go if you want." Though he hoped she didn't.

"How?"

"I can get us back to the access panel. No problem. Do you want to leave?"

Sal drew in a deep breath and lifted her head. "No. I can do this."

"Of course you can." With some reluctance, he eased his arms away from her. She let go of his neck and caught hold of his hands before she floated too far away.

"Are you all right?" Nephi asked.

Sal nodded, letting out her breath. She tipped back her head to look at the dome high above—or was it below?—them. "It's so big."

"Sure is." They spun in a slow, lazy dance, and Sal relaxed.

"So, this is where it happened, huh?"

"Uh—" Nephi felt his cheeks flush as hot as Sal's ever did.

"Where the angel appeared?"

Oh, that. "Yes. Twice, actually."

"I can tell. It feels different in here. Holy."

Not nearly as holy as when Uriel was present. He didn't tell her that. "I started coming here after my mother died. I always feel peaceful here."

"I can see why. But it makes me dizzy." She closed her eyes.

"You have to get used to it," Nephi said. He intertwined his fingers with hers. "Is your stomach okay? Are you going to be sick?"

"I don't think so—oh!"

The light in the core brightened. Goose bumps prickled over Nephi's skin.

"What's happening?"

"The angel is coming." He pulled her close to him. "Don't be afraid."

"I shouldn't be here," she whispered.

"Sure you should." He squeezed her hands.

The light coalesced around the figure of the archangel, obscuring the engine housing and layers of decks, leaving them bathed in light. Sal sucked in her breath and tightened her grip on Nephi's hands.

"Salome Hunsaker." Uriel inclined his head toward her. "I am honored to meet you."

"Y-you're honored?" Sal's voice rose a full octave.

"I am." The light around Uriel rippled. "You are a beloved daughter of God with an important work to accomplish."

Sal blinked. "I—uh—I—" She looked at Nephi, lost for words.

"That's what I keep trying to tell you, Sal. You're amazing. Even an archangel knows it."

Sal cleared her throat. She faced Uriel. "I am awed to be in your presence."

The light rippled again with silent, angelic laughter, sending joy and well-being washing through Nephi, taking away the worries and pains of the day.

"I let Hyrum get a hold of my journal. He stole it from me." Sal's words came tumbling out in a rush. "I wrote about your coming to Nephi, about reading the scriptures. All of it. I'm afraid I've ruined everything. I'm so sorry. I should never have written those poems."

Nephi put his arm around her. "It's okay, Sal."

The archangel studied her for a moment. "Tell me, Salome. Why did you write them?" His voice was gentle, not accusing or angry. Nephi held his breath, waiting for her answer.

"I wrote them because…" She paused. "Because it means so much to me. Knowing the truth, reading the word of God. I had to put my gratitude into words." She lowered her head. "I shouldn't have."

"You did well, dear sister. Your expression of faith and gratitude is pleasing to the Lord. Never apologize for or be ashamed of the beauty that comes from your heart."

"But if Hyrum and Zeniff—"

The archangel held up his hand to stop her. "Know this. Both of you. Nothing can thwart the work of God. No matter what opposition you face, no matter how many dangers and trials you must endure, even unto death, the purposes of God will continue to unfold. You may help the work or hinder it, but no one can stop it. Remember that."

The light around them intensified until the core had entirely vanished, leaving them in a fiery, golden glow. Sal's hand slipped from his. He glanced toward her. She was glowing almost as bright as the angel. The startled look on her face made him wonder if he looked the same.

"Nephi, Salome, kneel," Uriel commanded.

How? But when he tried, he found he could, in fact, kneel. Either they weren't in the core anymore or the light itself had gained substance.

Uriel stepped toward him and Sal. Nephi could sense more people around them—heavenly beings he couldn't quite see in the burning light. Uriel's hands came down on his head. His skin tingled. Warmth filled him as if the light had entered his body and was flowing through his veins. When Nephi thought he couldn't hold any more light without bursting apart, Uriel began to speak.

Chapter 12

Nephi didn't become aware of his surroundings again until he and Sal were back in the hall on telestial deck. He didn't recall how they got there. The ship had turned dark and cold, empty. The same could be said of himself—his own capabilities reduced to nothing without Heaven's touch upon him. He blinked, trying to clear his head.

"Nephi." Sal touched his arm. She still glowed. Not exactly like in the core, but her eyes were alight and a smile brighter than he'd ever seen before graced her cheeks. "Will you baptize me?"

"Baptize you?" His thoughts crept sluggishly through his brain.

The smile left her face. "Weren't you even listening in there?"

"I was listening." He tossed the hair out of his eyes. Of course he'd listened. The words were burned into his heart. But he hadn't wrapped his head around what all of it meant yet.

"Then you should realize that we were never baptized under proper authority. What President Black calls the priesthood isn't really anything. But now—"

"Now I can do it." He couldn't breathe. He had more power—more real power—than even President Black. It left him dizzy.

"Yes." Sal's smile returned. "So, will you?"

"Sure." He shrugged.

"Great." She tugged him toward an elevator.

"Whoa. Wait. You mean right now? It's the middle of the night." Maybe that was why his brain didn't seem to be functioning.

Sal's hands went to her hips. "Would you rather do it when everyone's awake?" She closed her eyes and took a deep breath. "I need this, Nephi. You're the only one who can give it to me. Please."

The look in her eyes made shame squirm uncomfortably in his chest. She was so much better than he could ever hope to be. That was clear from all the archangel had said to her—and about her. It was a wonder God had any use for a screwup like him at all.

"I'm sorry, Sal." He rested his hand on her shoulder. "My brain's all muddled and overwhelmed. I'm not thinking straight. I'd be happy to baptize you. Actually, I wonder how I'm even worthy of that honor."

Sal regarded him like maybe she thought he was teasing her.

"I mean it," he whispered.

Sal relaxed. "All right. Let's go."

The baptismal font, where Bishop Behling had baptized them as children, was on the lowest level of terrestrial deck, where the hallways sported soft carpet and cream-colored walls adorned with artwork, some of which dated back to Earth before their long journey had begun. It was a huge step up from the bare walls the leftovers lived with, but it didn't rise to the level of the grass and trees on celestial deck. Nephi had heard the terrestrials had a park of their own, but he had never seen it. At this time of night, the hallways were deserted, and Nephi saw the wisdom of an early morning baptism.

Hand in hand, they made their way to the font. The door was unlocked, and the room dark. The lights came on when they entered. Sal knelt beside the empty font and found the button that turned on the many nozzles that streamed warm water into it. Nephi stuck his hands in his pockets. "I don't actually know how to baptize somebody."

"It's right here." Sal pulled out Nephi's tab and brought up the appropriate passage of scripture. "See? Easy." She stepped over to a closet full of towels and white baptismal clothing. "This could be a problem," she said. "These are all made for grown men and eight-year-old children."

She rifled through the closet. Nephi watched, amused. Finally, she settled on the largest girls' dress she could find and went into the little dressing room to change. Nephi picked out a jumpsuit and did the same.

He looked at himself in the mirror. It felt so odd to be standing there all in white, waiting to perform a baptism like he was a bishop or something. But then the same feeling that had consumed him in the core came rushing back. He was a servant of God. He didn't know why God would choose him, but He had. Nephi nodded at his reflection. He could do this.

The font was nearly full when Nephi stepped out of the dressing room onto the stairs leading down into the water. Sal stood on the opposite side of the font in the too-small dress. The sleeves barely reached her elbows and the fabric stretched tight across her chest. She tugged at the bottom of the skirt, trying to get it to cover her knees. Nephi laughed. Sal was no little girl anymore.

She looked up at him and shrugged. "It will have to do." Her face settled into a beatific smile that made his heart skip. This was a side of Salome that no one got to see but him.

The nozzles automatically shut off and the water sat clear and still between them. Their quiet breathing echoed off the tiles. A feeling of sacredness permeated the space unlike Nephi had ever felt. It was quieter and more personal than what he felt in the presence of the archangel. "Ready?" he asked Sal.

She nodded, and they both descended into the font.

"What if I don't do it right?" Nephi rested his hand on her back.

"You will." Sal put her hand on his arm. It seemed to him a gesture of complete trust. In that moment he realized exactly how much he loved her. She had her eyes closed, waiting for him to begin. He almost couldn't speak.

Slowly, he raised his arm. "Salome Hunsaker—" Even saying her name sent shivers through him. He cleared his throat. "Having authority, I baptize you in the name of the Father, and of the Son, and of the Holy Ghost. Amen."

He lowered her into the water and brought her back up, clean and new. Words popped into his mind and out of his mouth. "You're a new person now, Salome. Reborn in Christ."

"I know." She threw her arms around him. "I think I've been waiting for this my whole life."

He squeezed her tight, resting his cheek on the top of her head. After a minute she pulled away, looking embarrassed. "I guess we should get changed." She turned pink. "It is pretty late."

"Yes it is." He grinned. Too bad the baptismal font wasn't an appropriate place to try and kiss her again.

It was close to 4am when they finally arrived at the Hunsaker's rooms.

"This has been the oddest, worst, best day of my life," Sal said.

"We've sort of drifted into tomorrow, so maybe it's the oddest two days of your life."

"Maybe." She yawned. "I guess we'll see what happens in the morning."

"Anything's possible, right?" Nephi took her hand.

Sal looked up at him, a half-smile on her face. "Right. And, Nephi—thank you."

"I'm glad you were with me." There was so much more he wanted say, but the depth of his feelings he couldn't put into words. He settled for kissing her cheek, though he wanted so much more. "Goodnight."

"Goodnight."

He started down the hall, whistling to himself. A very strange day indeed.

"Nephi!"

Prissa's shriek roused him from a dreamless sleep. His clock read 6:10. He groaned and buried his face in his pillow. Two hours of sleep was better than nothing, right?

"There's no water," Prissa shouted from the tiny bathroom.

Nephi sat up and rubbed his face. "What are you talking about?"

"The shower won't turn on. The toilet doesn't flush. Where's the water?" Panic had crept into her voice.

"Hang on a sec." Nephi stumbled out of bed and into the front room. He punched the button on their little kitchen

119

sink. Nothing. "Maybe something's gone wrong with the pumping system." He frowned.

"How is that even possible?" Prissa pushed through the curtain dressed in her work clothes with her curls in a frizzy sleep-induced knot. "Ship systems don't malfunction."

She was right about that. Their ancestors had built the *Kingdom of Heaven* to last for generations. Their careful designs and the constant automated maintenance of the repair bots kept the systems in perfect order. Always. Nephi had never seen a malfunction or even heard of one. He shrugged. "Guess we hope it comes back soon. What else can we do?"

Prissa groaned. "What am I supposed to do with this—" she pointed at her hair. "Without any water?" Her eyes widened. "Why am I worrying over such petty things after what happened to Sarai?" She collapsed on the couch and pulled her knees up to her chest. "I must be the most selfish girl on the whole ship."

"Don't be silly. I'm sure there are some celestial girls more selfish than you." He sat down and bumped her with his shoulder. "Just joking. You're allowed to worry about your hair. Your life doesn't have to stop, you know."

"I know," she whispered into her knees. They fell silent. Of course she knew, she'd lost her mother and barely known her father before his death.

Nephi balled his hands on his knees. "Maybe there's something about the water on the morning newscast." He clicked on the screen from the controls at his side.

The normal newscast wasn't on, just a message moving bleakly across the screen.

Due to unauthorized use of water early this morning, water has been shut off on telestial deck until tomorrow. Conserving ship resources is our top priority.

Oh, crap.

"Unauthorized use of water?" Prissa cried. "What does that even mean?"

Oh, crap, crap, crap. "I think it means I baptized Sal last night. Or this morning, I guess." Only three hours ago. He rubbed his forehead.

"You baptized Sal? What are you talking about?"

"She found me after I left Jarom's." His thoughts stuttered briefly over the promised funeral service.

"And you just decided to baptize her?"

"A lot happened before that, but yes." Did one baptismal font really require shutting off the water altogether? Oh, how he wanted to go back to bed.

Prissa tugged her fingers through her unruly curls. "Uh, Nephi—"

Nephi jerked his head off the back of the couch before his eyes drifted shut of their own accord, and checked to see what had upset Prissa now. A new message marched across the ship's logo. *Due to the misuse of water, no food will be delivered to telestial deck today. In addition, work credits are suspended until proper resource balance is restored.*

"That's not fair," Prissa sputtered.

True. They could turn off the fountains on celestial deck for an hour to make up for the water use. Nephi's stomach flipped. "I'm sorry, Prissa. I didn't realize—" He should have realized. He should have known water use was monitored. A headache clawed at the back of his eyeballs.

The apartment door chimed, and Prissa let Sal in. "This is all my fault." She sat on the couch and buried her face in her hands. "What are we going to do?"

"It isn't your fault." Nephi sat beside her and gently took her hands in his.

Sal sat up straight. "I'm going to confess to the bishop. Let them punish me instead of everyone."

"No." The thought of Sal with her hands fixed to a wall while Ammon's rod came down on her back turned him cold. He wouldn't let that happen. "I'll go. It's my responsibility."

"Don't be stupid," Prissa said. Sal flinched. "Nobody's confessing anything. You could both be cast out for heresy for performing a baptism. And anyway, it's not your fault. It's those selfish, greedy celestials. They can't stand to have anything happen that they don't control. Don't give Jeremiah Black the satisfaction of an apology."

"People will suffer," Sal whispered. "I don't want to be responsible for that."

"It's only one day," Prissa said. "We can handle that. We're leftovers. We'll take care of each other." Prissa nodded for emphasis, causing her frizzy hair to bounce.

Sal slumped on the couch, slipping her hands out of Nephi's. "I didn't know this would happen. I feel terrible."

Nephi cocked his head. "If you had known this would happen, would you have refused to be baptized? After everything that happened in the core—would you have been unwilling to make the sacrifice?"

Sal turned a fierce gaze on him. "No. I would have done it. I just would have thought it through a little better."

There she went again, making him smile in spite of himself. "Me too, Sal." He placed his hand on her cheek, and she leaned into his touch. "Prissa is right, you know."

"Of course I'm right," Prissa said. She winked at him, and he dropped his hand from Sal's face.

"We'll help each other," Nephi said. "We won't give in to Black."

"Right." Sal smiled wanly. Nephi stood, taking her hands, and pulling her up.

"Spread the word for everyone to bring any extra food they have to the cafeteria tonight."

"Good idea." Prissa opened the little fridge. "We have a couple of apples and some milk."

"That's a start. You want an apple, Sal?"

"No, thanks." She stifled a yawn. "I'm already late. I'll sneak a few bites from the kitchen. And I'll see what leftovers we can sneak out."

"Great. Oh, I almost forgot. We also need to plan a memorial service."

Both Sal and Prissa stared at him in silence.

"Like the celestials do?" Prissa asked after a moment.

"Maybe not as flamboyant, but yes. For Sarai and her baby. And everyone else we want to remember. Everyone we had to send out the airlock without saying goodbye."

"Mom," Prissa whispered.

"Nephi, that's…that's wonderful," Sal said. "Perfect."

Perfect? That remained to be seen. "Let's get through today first."

Nephi was halfway to aeroponics when a message beeped on his tab. He pulled it out of his pocket and groaned.

Notice: Permanent job reassignment: Filter scrubbing. Report immediately.

Could this day get any worse? He didn't have the energy to face Hyrum and Zeniff again. The headache settled farther into his head. Would a desperate plea to Brother Sorenson do any good? Not likely.

He steeled himself before entering the stinking filter room, but it wasn't Hyrum or Zeniff who greeted him. It was a scowling Enoch.

"Reassigned too, huh? Why am I not surprised?"

"Sorry, buddy," Nephi said. "Guess associating with me doesn't get you into Brother Sorenson's good graces."

Enoch grunted and lugged out a filter. Probably everyone was grumpy about the food and water ban. Not to mention working for no credit. Nephi asked, "Where are Hyrum and Zeniff, anyway?"

"They were reassigned also," Brother Ryan said, coming up behind them.

"Did they go to aeroponics?" Nephi asked.

Brother Ryan tapped his tab. "Hmm." A line appeared on his forehead. "That's not your concern, Brother Packard. I expect you'll both work hard."

"Yes, sir." Nephi said. Enoch grumbled again.

Brother Ryan walked away, but stopped before he left the room. "Listen, boys—" He cleared his throat and stuck his tab into a back pocket. "Don't worry about missing lunch. I'll make sure you don't go hungry."

For a minute, astonishment stole Nephi's voice. "Th-thank you, sir."

Brother Ryan nodded once and left them to their work.

"I'd like to know what this water use crap is all about," Enoch said sourly.

Nephi swallowed a sigh. "Let's talk about it later."

Dinner was a meager affair. The offerings of everyone on Nephi's level only filled one round table. Maybe the other levels had fared better. Nephi set down the sandwich and fruit Brother Ryan had brought for him, not wanting to eat while others went hungry thanks to him. A glass of water would be nice, though. His mouth was as dry as the vacuum of space. Body odor and weariness hung heavily in the air, and the tear-streaked faces of hungry children spiked his guilt up a notch. Sal wasn't there, and Nephi prayed she hadn't been caught sneaking food out. He pulled out his tab and sent her a message. *You okay?*

She replied a few seconds later. *I can't face everyone. This is all my fault.*

This is Black's doing, not yours.

No answer came, and he couldn't blame her. The thought didn't make him feel any better, either.

Enoch nudged him. Hyrum and Zeniff had swaggered in wearing clean clothes, looking not the least bit hungry. Nephi turned his back, but Zeniff's voice rose over the general chatter. "How was the filter room, fellas?" He snorted out a laugh.

Enoch gave Zeniff the thumbs up and a plastic smile. "Fantastic."

"Yeah," Nephi muttered. "Without those two there."

Hyrum and Zeniff bent over the food table, the greedy pigs. Enoch rolled his eyes. "So, you had something you wanted to talk to me about?"

"Yeah." Nephi led Enoch off to a corner. "It's about last night."

"Sarai Jenson? I heard. Was Prissa there?"

"Yes. She was pretty shaken up, but she'll be fine. That's not what I wanted to tell you."

Prissa breezed up before he could continue. "Where's Sal?"

"She's home. Didn't want to see anyone." He sighed.

"I got these for her." She handed Nephi a small, chipped teacup painted with pink and blue flowers and full of cherries. "Sal loves them."

"She does?" He raised an eyebrow. He couldn't help but think she'd love the old teacup too.

125

"Will you take them to her?"

"Sure." He cradled his hands around the cup. It had had gold trim painted around the rim once. Now mostly worn away. He wondered where it had come from. Maybe one of the original families had brought it with them from Earth. It looked old enough. And only celestials ate from china dishes nowadays. Prissa must have found it in the celestials' castoffs.

He wished he could have known those early passengers, learned their hopes and dreams. They had given up everything they knew to give their descendants a home they would never see. A home even Nephi would never see. Why had they made such a sacrifice?

"You're not going to leave me hanging now, are you?" Enoch's voice pulled Nephi from his reverie.

"No." He jerked his head toward the door. "But not here."

Enoch and Prissa followed him into the hall. "So what's up?" Enoch asked.

Nephi glanced down the hallway, and saw no one nearby. "Last night I was in the core with Sal."

"Oh, really?" Enoch wiggled his eyebrows.

"We weren't—you know." Nephi dismissed the implication with a flick of his hand. "The archangel came back."

"Sal saw him too?" Prissa's eyes filled her face.

"She did." The memory of golden fire flooded him with warmth. Too bad she wasn't here to share her own feelings.

"Among other things, Uriel gave me the power to baptize."

"What?" Enoch cried. "Like the bishops?"

"No. Like with the holy priesthood after the order of the Son of God. Something President Black and his council and elders and bishops don't possess."

126

Enoch looked struck speechless.

"It was well after midnight, so I took Sal up to a font and baptized her."

Enoch made an exasperated noise in his throat. "That was the unauthorized water use? What were you thinking?"

His anger took Nephi aback. "I didn't think they'd be so strict about filling a font. I was thinking about doing the will of God."

Enoch's jaw tightened. "I really don't know what to say. It's heresy to baptize her like that." His eyes slid to Prissa, who was glaring at him.

Nephi held up his hands to stave off an argument between them, squelching the disappointment rising inside him. "Okay. I get it. We're all hungry, and I'm exhausted. We'll talk about it later."

Chapter 13

Sal answered the door and looked up at him with eyes red from tears. Great. Something else he'd screwed up. "Want some cherries?" He held out the cup.

"Thanks." She cradled the cup in her hands, staring at the cherries blankly.

"Prissa picked them up for you. I'm just the delivery boy."

"Oh." Her shoulders drooped. "Tell her thanks too."

"That teacup reminded me of you."

She lifted her head to meet his gaze. "Broken?"

"No." His heart dropped. "That's not what I meant. You're not broken."

Sal turned without a word and walked back into her apartment. Nephi followed her in.

"I mean, I thought you would like it. It's unique. It must be old enough to have come from Earth with the First Families. I don't think you're really anything like a teacup."

Sal sat down on the worn, brown couch and Nephi sat beside her. No one else seemed to be home. She ran a finger over the pink and blue flowers painted on the side. "It's pretty."

"Okay, in that way you are like a teacup."

She didn't smile or blush as he hoped. "And I'm broken too," she said. The sorrow in her voice cracked Nephi's heart a little.

"Why do you say that?"

"I've been thinking about my mother a lot today. I miss her so much." The teacup trembled in her hand.

"I understand," Nephi said.

"I know." She faced him. "I know you miss your mom as much as I do. But I don't know if you can understand that there are some things a girl needs to talk to her mom about." The last word broke over her tears. She handed the cup of cherries back to Nephi and stood up. "I'm not really hungry." With that, she disappeared into her room at the back of the apartment. It was separate from her father's and brother's rooms, unlike the tiny space he and Prissa shared.

"Okay. Goodnight," he said to the empty hall. "I'll leave these here for you." He set the teacup on the table.

The sweat and grime of the day clung heavily to him as he made his way home. Small wonder Sal hadn't wanted to be around him. He smelled like rotting algae. His mouth tasted sour and sticky and his insides rumbled. He thumped his fist against his thigh as he walked. Tomorrow would be better. Hopefully. He'd get a shower, anyway. That made everything better.

He opened his door to find Enoch curled up on his couch with Prissa, both oblivious to his arrival. He stepped back into the hall and shut the door, resting his hand against the cool metal. 401 was engraved permanently across the top. He and Prissa had been assigned the small room after their mother died. Things were changing again, faster than he wanted them to. But Prissa was a big girl and Enoch was a good guy, though Nephi had to wonder how Prissa could stand him right now. He surely smelled as bad as Nephi did.

With a sigh, he straightened and headed back toward the lounge. To his relief, it was empty. Although, Sal would have been a nice addition to the emptiness.

Nephi slumped onto a couch and let his arms dangle between his knees. He clasped his hands loosely. His head bent forward.

Lord, nothing went right today. What is it I'm supposed to do? I have no power against Jeremiah Black or anyone else who wants to stand in my way. I can't do this.

With a groan, he stretched out on the couch, covering his eyes with his arm. Why didn't he have more faith? After everything he'd seen, he should have more faith than this. He tried to rekindle the intensity of emotion he'd experienced last night in the core or standing in the baptismal font with Sal. But all he could see was Hyrum's smirk and a room full of hungry, tired, broken people.

"Lord, I believe," Nephi whispered. "Help thou mine unbelief."

Be still, came the answer, silently settling into his troubled heart. *And know that I am God.*

Nephi breathed deeply, letting the peace seep in. A scene unfolded behind his eyelids. He'd never seen anything like it except in pictures—promises of a future only his distant great grandchildren would see. A field of gold swayed around his feet, stalks bending and rippling in the movement of the air. Soft dirt and prickly bits of plants lay under his bare feet. The blue sky above stretched into eternity, dotted with streaks of white clouds, bathed in a light brighter but softer and more pure than any Nephi had known. The air smelled of water and growing things like in the aeroponic garden, but mixed with sharper, mustier scents he couldn't place.

Nephi tipped back his head and let the fragrant breeze ruffle his hair. On the horizon, unfamiliar shapes of structures stood silhouetted against the sky. Homes, Nephi thought. Real houses and barns, and whatever else a community needed to survive. Behind the houses was a larger building soaring above the rest. Nephi didn't know what it was, but his heart felt drawn to it. He couldn't see any people, but he knew they were there. Longing swelled in his chest. He needed to be with them—his family and friends.

He stepped forward through the swaying grain, and realized hard, leather boots had appeared on his feet. His loose clothing was made of thick homespun cloth, nothing like ship-made fabrics. He stopped. This was not his place. Not his time. The *Kingdom of Heaven* would not reach the planet Canaan for hundreds of years yet. This was the world of his descendants. What kind of life did he want them to inherit? He stepped forward again, brushing his hand over the tops of the grain, scattering the seeds.

"Nephi!"

He jerked awake. Prissa stood above him, her hands on her hips. "What are you doing here? Did you even come home last night? I was scared to death when I woke up and you weren't there."

Last night? Nephi sat up, rubbing the remnants of his dream from his eyes. He could still smell the earthy odors and see the brilliant sunshine. "What time is it?"

"It's seven in the morning. You're going to be late. Did you sleep in here?"

"Guess so." He stretched. "I mean, you and Enoch seemed pretty busy."

Prissa's mouth fell open. She turned even redder than Sal. "We weren't...he didn't...stay that late." She folded her arms. "You could have come home."

"I fell asleep." He shrugged.

"You'd better get ready for work. Oh, and message Sal. She was worried. too."

Nephi pushed his hair back. "The water's on?"

"Yep." She gestured to her reasonably tamed curls. "I'm going to get breakfast. I'll see you later."

He waved goodbye and headed to the apartment. He'd slept in his filthy work clothes and wouldn't have time to clean them now. Probably wasn't even worth showering before going to filter scrubbing, but he did it anyway and felt better despite his dirty clothes. He guzzled down three glasses of cold water, and with fifteen minutes to spare, made his way to the back of the kitchen to talk to Sal in person.

The fridge room was deserted. He leaned against a counter, praying Sal would come in before he had to leave. His stomach rumbled. Maybe he should have gone to the cafeteria and messaged her instead. But he wanted to see her. Make sure she was all right.

At last, she came through the swinging doors with a flat of eggs she nearly dropped when she saw him. "Oh, Nephi. You startled me."

"I'm sorry." He took the eggs from her She opened one of the fridges and he put them inside. "Prissa said you were worried about me."

"She said you didn't come home last night. Where were you?"

"Fell asleep in the lounge. Sort of. I'll have to tell you about it later."

The memory of his dream vision stabbed through him, sharp and poignant. "Anyway, I wanted to see if you're feeling better today."

"Yes. I guess. Sleep helps." She looked away.

He reached for her, but stopped, remembering how she'd walked away last night. Sal wrapped her arms around herself and shivered. Then, to his surprise, she turned toward him. He wrapped his arms tight around her, and she clung to him. He brushed his lips across the top of her head. "You worry too much," he murmured.

"I'm sorry."

He pulled her back to look her in the eyes. "You have nothing to be sorry for. That's what I keep trying to tell you."

"Are you sure?"

"Absolutely." He caressed her cheek, and she leaned into his touch. Her expression softened.

The door banged open, and another kitchen worker came in. She shook her head when she saw Nephi and Sal. "Don't you have a job to get to or something?" She rolled her eyes.

"Yes, I do. Thanks for the reminder, Mary." He kissed Sal on the cheek. "I really do have to go. I'll see you at lunch?"

"Okay." She slipped her hand into his. "Thank you," she said softly. "I do feel better."

"Good." He squeezed her hand and watched her disappear behind Mary back into the noisy kitchen.

Oh, he was going to kiss her so hard the next time he got the chance.

The meeting in the cafeteria that evening was packed with people from all over telestial deck. Word was really getting around. He stood up to call the meeting to order. "Brothers and Sisters, welcome."

The chatter of voices slowly quieted. A flash of nerves shot through him as it always did when hundreds of pairs of eyes turned their attention to him. And after losing two nights of studying with Sal, he wasn't even sure what he was going to say.

"I hope everyone got through yesterday okay. That was hard on all of us. But we pulled together and we made it.

That's how it should be. All of us looking out for each other." He brushed his hair out of his eyes. "The Lord wants us to live like that, helping and taking care of each other. He called it Zion." Nephi took his tab out of his pocket. "There is a scripture in the book of Moses that describes Zion." It took him a few seconds to find what he was looking for. It was easy to spot the newcomers when he started to read from the scriptures. They were the ones who looked ready to faint or get up and run.

"Here it is. 'And the Lord called his people Zion because they were of one heart and one mind and dwelt in righteousness, and there was no poor among them.'"

No poor. He thought of all of them dirty and hungry yesterday while the celestials enjoyed their privileges. He thought of a peaceful settlement surrounded by grain fields in the warm, mellow sun.

"Brothers and sisters, I believe this is what the First Families had in mind when they boarded the *Kingdom of Heaven*. They wanted Zion for themselves and for their children down through all our generations. It was their hope for a distant future on Canaan." He looked at Sal, who gave him a wistful smile. "But that's not what they got. Somewhere along the way they went off course. We're still heading for Canaan, but we're far away from Zion."

The audience had fallen silent, watching him with eager eyes. Listening to him. Believing him. It sent a thrill through his veins.

"The notion that we are destined to a certain kingdom at birth is false doctrine, my friends. It is the opposite of what God wants for us, what our ancestors wanted for us, and what we want for our descendants. What kind of life will we give to them? What will they be when they arrive at Canaan? Will the Lord call them Zion?

"It has to start with us. Today. We must unite ourselves in heart and mind, worship God in truth, and take care of one another. We can do it. We must do it. Our Lord will be with us."

He stopped. A murmur ran through the room. What was it they were feeling? Hope? Doubt? Nephi hardly knew himself. It seemed like an impossible task. But his heart burned in his chest with the certainty that he'd spoken the truth.

"I want you all to go home and pray to your Father in Heaven. Ask Him if I'm telling you the truth. Ask Him if you should follow me or follow Jeremiah Black. Ask Him for help with your problems. Tell Him all your needs. Thank Him for what He has given you. I know praying is awkward. We aren't used to it. But keep trying. I promise God will answer. He will hear you. He loves you."

Nephi's gaze caught Jarom Jenson's, his face drawn and sad. "Friends, there is one more thing I want to talk about tonight. We all are sad, I know, at the passing of Sarai Jenson and her son. Death is no stranger to telestial deck. I don't think anyone here hasn't lost a loved one. A parent, a spouse, a child, a grandparent, a friend. To the celestials, our lives don't matter. They would have us believe that our lives don't matter to God, either. But they are wrong. God has taken our loved ones into His bosom where they wait to receive eternal glory.

"The celestials honor their dead with feasts and fine speeches, fancy caskets and solemn ceremonies. I have none of that to offer our dead, but I still want to honor their memory. We have nothing to give but our tears and our prayers and our loving memories, but that is enough." He'd thought about this a lot while scrubbing filters that day.

"I want to hold a memorial service for Sarai Jenson." He met Jarom's eyes and nodded. "And anyone else we want to remember. Let's meet tomorrow night. Right here. Bring a small memento of your loved ones. Something that represents their lives and your love for them. If you don't have anything, you can write your feelings on a piece of paper or scrap of fabric. Then we can gather and keep them all together somewhere special where we can always see them and remember those we have lost.

"They are not gone forever. I promise you that."

His looked over the audience. Some had tears running down their cheeks, but it wasn't sorrow that permeated the atmosphere. It wasn't joy either, but something more mellow and elusive. Maybe it was hope.

Chapter 14

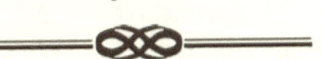

Thomas Sharpe procured a six-foot tall clear plastic cylinder a foot in diameter from the shipworks manufacturing bay where he worked, complete with an end cap for the bottom and a removable lid for the top. Prissa had added a number of rods around the outside, from which dangled her wind chimes and more God's Eyes. It was lovely in an odd, cobbled sort of way. Sal dubbed it the Memory Tree, and she and Nephi placed it in an empty corner of the cafeteria a few minutes before the memorial service began.

"Such a beautiful idea," Sal said, slipping her hand into Nephi's. "Thank you for doing it."

Nephi squeezed her hand in response. "Would you like to get us started?"

She nodded, eyes glimmering with unshed tears, and dropped in her offering, a sketch of her mother drawn on a page from her journal, with a poem written on the back—one she hadn't let Nephi or anyone else read.

Prissa gave a little set of chimes—four metal triangles bound together with braided cords—that represented their family, because their mother had started Prissa making the chimes and sculptures after their father had died.

Soon the tree began to fill with bits of jewelry, clothing, baby booties, hats, drawings, written tributes, blankets, and other small and simple treasures. The three Ashton sisters had nothing to bring, and asked if they could sing their mother's favorite song instead. They stood hand-in-hand around the memory tree and sang a sad, sweet lullaby in haunting harmony. Phoebe brought a small, heart-shaped pillow Nephi and Prissa's mother had made for her.

When at last everyone had placed their remembrances, and the Memory Tree was nearly full, Nephi placed the lid on the top and faced his congregation. "We miss our dear ones," he said. "And they miss us too. But someday we will be together again. We'll live forever in love and light and joy." He could see it as he spoke, though it was more of a feeling than an actual vision. And it was up to him to show everyone the way there.

Sal hung around after everyone else had trickled out. Nephi watched her standing with her arms folded, contemplating the Memory Tree.

"Do you think it helped at all?" Nephi asked her. "Did it bring comfort or only more grief?"

"It helped." Sal faced him. "Being allowed to grieve. Knowing they are with God, that their lives mattered, that our lives matter, too." Her eyes lit up. "Do you realize how monumental that is?"

"Yes." Nephi put his hand on her shoulder. "I think I have some idea."

"Thank you for letting me be part of it."

"Are you kidding? Thank you, Sal. I wouldn't get anywhere without you."

Sal shook her head. "You're amazing up there in front of everyone. Like a whole different person."

"I feel like a different person. Like it's not even me talking at all."

"I'm proud of you," Sal said, turning pink.

Nephi ran his hand down her arm. "Are you ever going to let me kiss you again?"

Her blush deepened. She stepped closer. He bent and kissed her. Her arms encircled his neck. His worries melted away.

"Aw, isn't that sweet?"

Hyrum.

Sal jumped out of Nephi's arms so fast he almost fell over. Nephi grabbed her hand and pulled her to his side while Hyrum and Zeniff snickered. He clenched a fist. "What do you want?"

"We saw the lights on and thought there might be a party," Hyrum said. Zeniff snorted. "We didn't realize you two were fornicating in here."

That was it. But before Nephi could take a step toward Hyrum, Sal laid a gentle, restraining hand on his arm. She shook her head ever so slightly. Nephi relaxed his fist, his heart still pounding.

"The place is all yours, guys," Nephi muttered. He kept himself between Sal and the other two as they moved toward the door.

"What's all that crap?" Zeniff asked, gesturing at the Memory Tree. "Some kinda back-up in the recycling system?" He laughed harshly.

Nephi would have kept on walking, but Sal stopped and turned around. "It's our Memory Tree," she said. "Didn't you hear about it? To remember and honor our loved ones who've died."

Hyrum scoffed. "How very nice."

Nephi tightened his arm around Sal, praying he wasn't making a mistake. "You're welcome to put something in if there's someone you want to remember."

Hyrum's eyes turned cold. "No, thank you. Nobody I want to remember. You, Zeniff?"

"Nope."

The bitterness in the brothers' voices took Nephi aback, and for a second he wanted to find out who had caused them so much pain.

"So, we're just going to keep it here forever?" The sarcasm in Hyrum's voice drove out all of Nephi's compassion.

"That's the plan," Sal said mildly. "Where everyone can see and remember." Nephi could tell from the tension in her shoulders that she was angry, or maybe afraid, but she kept her voice calm.

"Was this your idea, Packard?" Hyrum stared Nephi down, daring him to deny it. Nephi took in Hyrum's and Zeniff's fine new clothes, wondering where they got them.

"A lot of us felt it was high time our families and friends got the respect and remembrance they deserve," Nephi said. "When Sarai Jenson died, we decided to do something about it."

"I think it's nice," Sal said. "Something we should have done a long time ago."

"Well, I think it's an eyesore," Zeniff said. He reached a hand toward it.

"Don't touch it!" Sal stepped forward, her hands bunched. "That belongs to all of telestial deck. Leave it alone."

"Why don't you come and make me, you little whore?" Zeniff said.

Nephi stepped out in front of Sal. "Don't speak to her like that. In fact, don't speak to her at all."

142

"I'll speak to her whenever and however I want. You think you can stop me, you son of a stinking coward?"

Nephi started for him, knocking chairs out of his way, ignoring Sal's protests, consumed in a haze of anger.

Hyrum stepped into his path and shoved him in the chest. "Back off!"

Nephi stumbled into a chair. It was enough to bring him back to sanity. Zeniff glared at him over Hyrum's shoulder, but Hyrum wasn't letting him past, either. "Come on," he growled over his shoulder. "They're not worth the trouble."

Zeniff continued to glare at Nephi all the way out the door, and made a vulgar gesture in Sal's direction as he went past. She turned her face away from him.

Nephi slumped into a chair. Sal came up beside him and laid her small hand on his shoulder. The quiet touch made him want to crawl into the nearest exhaust port and die.

"Nice, huh? Preach about Zion one night, try and beat someone up the next. Not very impressive."

Sal pulled up a chair that squeaked across the tiles and sat down beside him. He lifted his head. "Do you think they'll tell someone about the Memory Tree? Get us in trouble?" Sal said.

"I don't know. Maybe." He put his hand atop hers on the table. "They're still leftovers like us, so who knows."

"Thank you for standing up for me," she said. A smile danced at the corners of her mouth, that rare and dazzling smile he would fling himself into the silent depths of space for.

"Always." He brought her hand up to his lips.

Her smile broke out in full force. It wasn't what he expected to see after such a long and trying evening. He reached for her, threading his fingers through her hair, and pulled her to him.

—⊗—

The next morning, the Memory Tree was gone, along with all the treasured mementos left in it. That was a kick in the gut. Nephi would have suspected Hyrum and Zeniff of hauling it off out of spite, if it weren't for the notice posted on every wall screen in the cafeteria.

The only authorized religious services allowed on ship are those conducted by the High Council in the chapel. Anyone participating in unauthorized religious services will be subject to discipline from the Council. Work credits are suspended for the day.

The scarred skin on Nephi's back twitched and prickled. Someone from telestial deck must have told the High Council about the Memory Tree. None of them ever set foot down here. Hyrum and Zeniff had to be responsible.

He didn't know why they would, though. Did they really hate Nephi bad enough to betray all leftovers? Surely they didn't feel any level of devotion toward President Black.

The bulk of the people in the cafeteria drank their sludge shakes—noticeably thinner this morning—in silence, casting an occasional glance at the spot where the Memory Tree had stood. Some shot glances at Nephi. Maybe they expected him to stand up and say something, but this wasn't the time for it. Half the people here had never been to a meeting and didn't know what the notice was about at all, and thanks to the explicit threat, probably never would.

Nephi moved through the room offering quiet condolences and commiseration. *I'm sorry. I don't know how they found out. I didn't expect this. No, this isn't going to affect our meetings, but we'll have to make some adjustments. Be discreet. You're right—they shouldn't have taken it. I'm sorry. Don't worry, we'll share our extra credits for food today.*

"You should get yourself a shake before they're all gone," Phoebe Sharpe said when Nephi got to her table.

"I've lost my appetite."

"Have a seat, young man," Thomas Sharpe said. Nephi sat. "Do you have any idea how serious this situation is?" Thomas asked. "Black knows about our memorial service. He could haul you or any one of us up for discipline right now."

"If they were going to do that, they already would have."

Thomas scowled. "Something that visible was a mistake."

"Maybe." Nephi pushed his hair out of his face.

"This project of yours isn't sustainable."

"Brother Sharpe, it isn't my project. It's the Lord's."

An awkward silence fell. Thomas bolted down the last of his sludge, avoiding Nephi's eyes. Phoebe patted Nephi on the hand. "Get something to eat."

"I'm not hungry."

Prissa and Enoch sat down at the table. "I hate celestials," Prissa muttered. Enoch looked angry, his jaw tight. He refused to meet Nephi's gaze as well. Fine. He had no more reassurances to offer anyway. "I'll see you guys later."

"We can't keep meeting together as a group," Nephi said that evening.

Sal nodded, pulling her legs up under her. It was just the two of them in the lounge—a relief after the past few days. "If two or three families meet together in an apartment, that wouldn't attract any attention," Sal said.

"True. But I can't go speak to thirty different groups."

"Maybe you could write a message and send it to everyone to read and discuss in their groups."

"Or you could. I'm no good at writing. I'd rather talk."

Sal drew her knees up and rested her cheek on top. "You're better than you think. But I could help if you want."

"Yeah, I want." He winked at her. "What we really need, though, is for everyone to have access to the scriptures. To be able to read and study on their own." He leaned back against the couch with a sigh. "I have no idea how to make that happen." Or if anyone was going to listen to him anymore after today.

"I know someone who can help," Sal said.

"You do?"

"Amaleki Cooper. He's a friend of mine—a computer tech on terrestrial deck."

"Terrestrial deck? How do you know him?"

"I've known him since we were kids," she said. "Our mothers were friends. I don't know how they met. Anyway, I haven't seen him much since my mom died. But he messages me sometimes. I'll bet he could hack the system."

Nephi wrinkled his forehead. "You trust him?"

She thought for a minute. "Yes, I think we can trust him."

Nephi closed his eyes and said a silent prayer. He didn't know if this was the right thing to do, but he trusted Sal. That was enough.

"All right. If you trust him, let's see if he'll meet with us."

"You two are completely out-the-airlock nuts. You know that, right?" Amaleki Cooper put his feet up on the table in the lounge half an hour later. "I mean, ten stripes wasn't enough for you, or something? You buckin' to get cast out too?" He sported spiky blond hair and an attitude, and Nephi already regretted bringing him here.

"Sal-gal," Amaleki said, "you really think this joker saw an angel?"

"Yes, I do. Absolutely. I saw him too."

"Huh. I never took you for the crazy type, you know?"

"She's not crazy." Nephi struggled to control his temper. "Neither am I. Can you help us or not?"

"I can help you." Amaleki folded his hands behind his head. "The question is will I help you? I mean, you want me to put my butt on the line so you can read what only President Black's holy eyes may look upon." His tone made it clear he had little regard for Black's holy eyes. "I'm in no mood for a date with outer darkness, if you know what I mean."

Nephi bristled. "This isn't for me. I've already 'looked upon' the scriptures. I think everyone ought to have that chance."

"Yeah." Amaleki dropped his feet to the floor and leaned forward. "Sal mentioned that. Let me see your tab." He beckoned with his fingers. Nephi hesitated, unwilling to like or trust the man. Sal nudged him. With a frown, he took the tab from his pocket and handed it to Amaleki.

Amaleki tapped the screen and whistled. "You've got everything. Wow, even private message encryption—just like Black himself. Shoot. If you can do this, I don't know what you need me for."

"I didn't do it," Nephi said. "The angel did."

"Then get your angel friend to do it for everyone else."

"The archangel is not at my beck and call." He snatched his tab out of Amaleki's hands. "Just forget it."

"I'll make you a pie," Sal told Amaleki, laying a conciliatory hand on Nephi's arm.

"A pie, huh?" Amaleki stood up. "Now we're talking. Peach?"

"Of course." Sal actually smiled at him. Nephi almost called the whole thing off right there.

"All right, kids, here's the deal. Take it or leave it. I have no particular love for President Black and his High Council, plus I can't resist a good challenge. Or Sal's peach pie. I doubt I can do anything as comprehensive as what you've got—however you got it—but I should be able to open up the scriptures for whoever you want. Just give me a few days. Oh, and my primary concern will be covering my own butt, not yours. I will not hesitate to roll over on you if necessary. Got it?" He held out his hand.

Nephi's teeth clenched, but he shook it. "Got it."

"Thanks, Amaleki," Sal said.

"Anytime Sal-gal." He gave her a hug. "You'll hear from me soon."

Nephi let out his breath as Amaleki left the lounge. "Wow. He's a real charmer."

"He's my friend, Nephi. And he's going to help us." She gave him a stern glare. "He doesn't have to, you know. He could get in real trouble here just like we could."

"I hope he enjoys his pie."

"Honestly, Nephi. What's more important here? The scriptures or your ego?" Sal stalked out of the lounge, leaving Nephi staring after her, kicking himself.

He sent her a message as soon as he got home. *Sorry I'm a jerk. Forgive me?*

He got a response a few minutes later. *Yes. You don't have to be jealous, you know.*

Jealous. He grinned ruefully. And impulsive, lustful, quick to anger… The list went on. Some servant of God he was.

Well, your pies are pretty delicious. I'd put my life on the line for one of them, too. Goodnight, Salome.

Goodnight, Nephi.

He set his tab down on the table. Prissa was gone, but a God's Eye she had made was sitting on the table. He picked it up and studied the variegated pattern radiating out from the center. A mish-mash of colors and prints that somehow turned out beautiful. Maybe that's what God saw when He looked down on his children—a motley mix of personalities and talents, strengths, weaknesses, triumphs, and tragedies. Maybe that's what he saw when He looked at Nephi. A mess He could use somehow. Maybe even make something beautiful out of.

Nephi set the God's Eye down, folded his hands on the table, and began to pray.

Chapter 15

"You know," Nephi said to Enoch over filters a few days later, "talking about girls was more fun when one of them wasn't my little sister."

Enoch wrangled a filter back into place. He tapped his scrubber against his legs. "You trust me, don't you? You know that I treat her only with respect, right?"

"I hope so," Nephi said mildly. "She's awfully young."

"I know she is. I promise you I'm not taking advantage of her. I'll take care of her and protect her just like you would."

"Good."

"So, what's up with you and Sal?"

"Who knows. Sal's heart remains as mysterious as her poetry journal."

"Nah. It's pretty obvious how she feels."

Well, maybe. She could be warm and eager one minute and cold and stand-offish the next. Whatever her feelings were, he doubted they were even clear to Sal, let alone anyone else. Maybe it didn't even matter how she felt. After all, his life was so far from normal it wasn't even funny. Maybe he shouldn't even be trying with her. He bit back a sigh, and hefted his filter into the slot. Nothing was the same anymore. Nothing ever would be.

The tab in his pocket beeped, and he froze. Enoch's head popped up. Messages during the day were rare and usually involved an emergency. Holding his breath, he took out the tab. The message was from Amaleki, which was simultaneously a relief and a cause for alarm.

Okay, here's the thing. Each tab is pre-programmed with a certain level of access—telestial, terrestrial, or celestial. And then there's President Black level, which is what you somehow got on yours. Yeah, I know. Angel and all that.

I did some digging around and figured out how to change telestial level access to include the following—Holy Bible, Book of Mormon, Doctrine and Covenants, Pearl of Great Price. Is that all you wanted? I don't even know. All telestial tabs now have access. I can't get any more specific than that. So, if some leftover peon who isn't listening to your 'message' notices and reports it, you can bet the bull crap is going to hit the fan. I, however, will not be in the line of fire because I am good at covering my tracks. Ha. So someone will have to take the fall, but it won't be me. Until then, knock yourselves out. Oh, and I hope you're paying attention because this message will delete itself in one minute. Don't try to reply. Loved the pie! Cheers, A.C.

Nephi let out his breath. Access to everyone on telestial deck. Good and bad at the same time. What if Hyrum and Zeniff found out, for example? But how would they? No one would notice the increased access unless they went looking for it, and why would Hyrum or Zeniff or anyone else do that? He checked his tab again, and sure enough, Amaleki's message had disappeared.

"Is everything okay?" Enoch asked. "Was it Prissa?"

"Huh?" Nephi dragged his attention back to Enoch. "No. Not Prissa. It was—" He looked around to make sure Brother

Ryan wasn't there. "It was a friend of Sal's—" He stopped, unsure how to continue.

"What's going on?" Enoch asked, eyebrows raised. "Nephi?"

Nephi pulled out another filter for scrubbing. "Check your tab," he said quietly. "You should have access to the scriptures."

"Excuse me?"

"Check and see."

Nephi glanced at the door to make sure Brother Ryan wasn't around. A minute later, he heard a strangled gasp. "What did you do?"

"I made sure we could all read the word of God." Nephi raised his eyes to Enoch's, questioning him in a glance.

Enoch, slightly pale, put his tab in his back pocket and shook his head. "How far are you going to take this, Nephi? Are you willing to put all of us in danger for this? Because that's what you're doing. Just like we all had to pay for you baptizing Sal, and you didn't even have the guts to admit it."

Nephi didn't say anything. He thought of Thomas Sharpe complaining about the Memory Tree and the stern warning about unauthorized religious services. He hadn't spoken to anyone but Sal about religion at all since then. He met Enoch's angry gaze. "What is it you want me to do? Just forget about the archangel? Pretend like nothing ever happened and go on with ordinary life? Tell five hundred people, 'Never mind, I was kidding...?'"

Enoch's features tensed. His fists clenched.

"I won't do that," Nephi said. "You know I won't. You want to play it safe, but safety means remaining in darkness and ignorance and oppression when God has put light and truth and freedom into our hands. God doesn't ask us to stay on the safe path. He wants us on the path that leads home to

Him, no matter how dangerous that path might be. I intend to take this as far as I have to—until everyone on this ship knows the truth."

"Everyone?" Enoch asked flatly.

"Yes, everyone." A thrill went through him, followed closely by his own mind-numbing fear. He wanted to take it back, but he couldn't. Every word was true.

"Might as well cast yourself into outer darkness now, and save Black the trouble," Enoch muttered.

Have a little faith, Nephi wanted to say, but he didn't. How could he expect Enoch to have faith when the whole concept of faith was something foreign and new to all of them? Nephi was only now starting to find that faith for himself, and he'd seen an angel. What did Enoch have to go on besides Nephi's word? No wonder he was scared, and everyone else too. Except Sal. She had more faith than Nephi did, and she'd had it even before he'd seen the angel.

"Maybe," he said to Enoch. "Maybe I will get cast out over this. It doesn't matter. The work is more important than my life."

Enoch let out a frustrated snort. "Why do you think I'm so upset about it? I don't want to see you die, and Prissa doesn't either. You're my closest friend. And you're all the family Prissa has left."

"Enoch." He stopped, unsure how to continue. There was so much to say. "Someday I think you'll understand."

Enoch opened his mouth and shut it again without speaking.

"For now, I need you to trust me, okay? And put your trust in God, too. If you believe what I told you, then you can do that right? The same way I'm willing to trust you with my baby sister?"

Enoch's silence stretched on uncomfortably.

Nephi heard the whoosh of the door opening, and Brother Ryan came back in. He took in the scene. "Is everything okay, fellas?"

"Yes, sir." Nephi resumed scrubbing in silence. If Enoch didn't trust him, then he didn't. But it hurt to think so.

After a quick check of the filters, Brother Ryan left them alone again. Nephi tried to think of something to say to lighten the mood, but he couldn't.

Enoch breathed a loud sigh. "I'm trying, okay? I do believe you. Or at least I want to. I just... I'm sorry."

"That's all I can ask," Nephi said. He hefted a now-clean filter back into place. "That's all God asks of you, too. That you try."

"Should we put the Evans and the Jenkins together?" Sal asked. "I don't know if they're friends."

"Sure." Nephi plucked at a loose thread on the arm of the lounge's couch. If he yanked it free would the whole thing unravel?

"That's forty-two study groups," Sal said. "If they each meet once a week, six each day, you could meet with each group in person once every six weeks."

"Enoch almost popped a rivet when I told him he could read the scriptures."

"Yeah." Sal set down her tab. "My dad too."

They fell silent. A line creased the center of Sal's forehead.

Couldn't he count on anyone? "Are you afraid?" He sounded more angry than he intended, and she flinched.

"I'm not afraid," she snapped. Her hands curled up on her lap. "Well, maybe I am a little," she said more quietly.

"We took a big risk." She kept her head down, not meeting his eyes.

"You think we made a mistake?" Enoch's doubt was one thing, but Sal, too?

"I don't know." Her eyes darted to him for half a second. "The study groups won't work if no one is willing to read the scriptures on their own." Her face had flushed, but not in her cute, shy way.

"Then what do you suggest we do?" Nephi pulled the errant thread out of the couch, leaving a little hole behind. The lumpy padding underneath poked through, and Nephi shoved it down with his finger.

Sal stood up and picked up her tab. Her hands trembled. "I suggest we do what we've planned. I didn't mean to imply otherwise. I was just making an observation about what we'll have to do to make it work."

"Don't be angry, Sal. I'm sorry."

She sniffed and moved her finger over her tab. "I sent you the groups and the schedule," she said coolly. "It's up to you to let everyone know and convince them to try."

"Thanks." Nephi picked up his own tab and glanced at the schedule Sal had created. "This doesn't leave any time for you and me to study alone."

Sal hugged her tab to her chest. "I think that's for the best. Don't you?"

No, he didn't. He tried to say so, but Sal cut him off.

"I put us in a group together, so—" She shrugged. "Goodnight, Nephi."

"Sal, wait." But she was already out the door.

Nephi went back to his apartment, only to find Enoch and Prissa there, playing cards. He was beginning to feel unwelcome in his own home. Enoch didn't even look at him.

"Why don't you get Sal over here and we'll play some games?" Prissa said.

If only life were still that simple. Weariness washed over him. "No, thanks. I'm going to bed."

Chapter 16

It took a couple of weeks to get the study groups settled into a routine—though his followers still looked over their shoulders whenever they opened their tabs. The new access had not been noticed, and, so far, the power of the word of God proved worth the risk. Nephi's life settled into a new routine of filter scrubbing by day, and studying the gospel in the evenings. His little flock was learning, thinking, praying. Nephi began to think seriously about how to move forward, get them baptized, and hold real worship services.

At night, he dreamed. Not ordinary dreams, but more visions of places he'd never seen and never would. Like the field of grain he'd seen before. Sometimes, he stood beside a vast, blue sea with the sand squishing between his toes. A thick, salty tang stung his nose and coated his tongue, and the cold water tugged at his bare feet as the waves came rolling into shore, one after the other.

Or else he'd find himself on a mountain peak overlooking a vista of snow-covered ridges and green valleys with the brisk, fragrant air raising gooseflesh on his arms. At other times, he wandered a dark forest of twisted vines and vegetation and tall trees that hardly let in any light. Sweat clung to his skin, and the cries of unseen animals and calls of bright-colored birds filled the air.

He wondered why he'd be shown such things. It made the *Kingdom of Heaven* feel small and sterile, and he woke with a lonely melancholy, not unlike what he felt when he looked at Sal.

She avoided sharing lunch with him anymore, so he only saw her when their own family group met on Thursdays, and on Sundays in the chapel on the telestial balcony, but she sat with her father, not with him. And she never came over with pie on Sunday afternoons. She was still friendly, still full of insight on study nights, still the amazing girl he'd fallen in love with. Was still in love with, he had to admit. But she kept her distance, so he kept his. After three months, it was like they'd never had a closer relationship at all, and he missed her terribly.

Then one evening coming home from a study group, Hyrum stopped him in the hall. "Come with me." He folded his arms across his chest and glowered.

"No thanks, man." Nephi kept his voice mild. "I'm going to bed."

"I wasn't giving you a choice, Packard." He moved to block Nephi's path.

"Get out of my way," Nephi said. Hyrum was no bigger than he was. Nephi clenched his fist.

Footsteps thunked behind him, and Zeniff said, "Don't start anything, Nephi. Brother Nielsen-Black of the High Council wants to talk to you, that's all. I suggest you cooperate."

A sudden, electric humming raised the hairs on the back of Nephi's neck. He turned to see Zeniff holding a rod charged with a faint, blue glow—the kind of rod Ammon had used to administer the stripes on his back. He cringed involuntarily.

"That's right," Hyrum said. "Just come along nicely and Zeniff won't have to use that thing."

So, they were working for Ammon? It made a terrible kind of sense. "What does Ammon want with me?"

Zeniff brandished the rod. "Don't use his first name."

"Okay." Nephi held up his hands. His fear of the rod made them tremble. He stuck them quickly in his pockets. "I'm coming."

"Yeah, you are," Hyrum sneered. Zeniff laughed. They proceeded down the hall, Hyrum and Zeniff on either side of Nephi. He wrapped his hand around the tab in his pocket, wishing he could send a message to Prissa—on the off-chance that he was never coming back.

An elevator took them up to the park on celestial deck. The lights were turned down this time of night, the good celestials tucked away in their houses. They walked past the big double doors leading to the High Council room and into a hallway next to it, the offices of the High Council.

Hyrum stopped and knocked at the first door and shoved Nephi inside. Ammon sat behind a polished black desk. He wore a smug little grin. "Brother Packard, please have a seat." He gestured to a fine upholstered chair that matched his desk.

"No, thanks." Nephi folded his arms. "I'll stand."

Ammon shrugged. "Suit yourself." He folded his hands on the desk. "My telestial liaisons," he nodded toward Hyrum and Zeniff standing behind Nephi, "have been keeping an eye on you, brother."

Liaisons? Their new assignment was spying for Ammon? Nephi clenched his jaw and didn't speak.

"Seems like you've been visiting your neighbors quite a bit lately."

"That's not a sin, is it?"

"That depends on the nature of the visit, doesn't it?"

"What is it you think I've been doing?" His hands were shaking again. He folded them stiffly behind his back, all too aware of Zeniff with his rod right behind him.

"Give me your tab," Ammon said.

"Why?" Nephi's palms grew sweaty but he kept them clasped. Had Hyrum and Zeniff discovered their expanded access?

"To either confirm or disprove some rumors my liaisons have heard." Ammon held out his hand.

"Heard or started?"

Hyrum shoved Nephi in the back. "Just hand it over!"

Nephi stumbled forward, caught himself on the edge of Ammon's desk, and pushed himself back upright. No telestial would refuse to hand over a tab to one of the High Council. He stayed still. If he could destroy it somehow before Ammon got a hold of it, maybe he wouldn't end up dead.

"Just hand me your tab," Ammon said, "so I can prove your innocence, and this will all be over." He held out his hand, the smug smile back.

Nephi reached into his pocket. Ammon's smile turned vicious. Nephi slipped the tab out. He'd throw it against the wall and break it, he decided. But Zeniff caught his wrist just as he threw, and the tab clattered across the desk, no harm done. Ammon picked it up. "Thank you, Brother Packard."

Nephi held his breath. Zeniff squeezed Nephi's wrist so hard he feared it would break. Ammon examined his tab. His eyes narrowed. "How did you do this?" he demanded.

Nephi stood straighter. "Do what?"

"Gain access to everything in the database?" Ammon threw the tab down on his desk.

Nephi took a deep breath. "An archangel appeared to me. His name is Uriel. He told me God was not pleased with our worship—that we have lost the true gospel. He opened the access on my tab so I could bring that true gospel back."

The room went so silent the only sound was the faint whine of the rod and the gentle hiss of the ventilation. Nephi kept his hands clenched at his sides and his eyes fixed on Ammon's. This was the moment, he thought, when he ought to be so full of the fire of the spirit that he actually glowed, just like in the scriptures, but instead he felt like his insides had turned to jelly, and he could only pray he didn't faint.

Ammon stood up very slowly and rested his hands on the desk. "And you've been spreading this blasphemy across telestial deck?"

Nephi didn't answer. No one else would be cast out with him if he could help it. He clenched his hands tighter to hide the shaking.

"Tomorrow morning, I will bring this to the High Council, and then, my friend, you'll be cast out into outer darkness and all your false doctrines along with you." He smirked. "I wish I could say this pains me, but frankly I can't think of anything I'd rather see. Boys, put him in lock-up."

Hyrum grabbed his arm and yanked him roughly back. Nephi struggled, and Zeniff smacked the rod squarely across his face. Nephi howled in pain. He would have fallen if Hyrum had not been dragging him backward away from Ammon's office. Tears stung the wound unbearably. Had the rod hit his eye? Through the exquisite pain he couldn't tell.

Hyrum pushed him into another room, and Nephi was barely coherent enough to put out his hands and catch himself to prevent his wounded face from smacking the ground. He stayed there on his hands and knees, panting, until he heard a door shutting behind him, and he was alone.

Tears continued to stream into the wound beside his eye and down his cheek. He couldn't stop them or even wipe them away. He gritted his teeth, pressing his palms hard into the cold tiles. After a few minutes, he grew more aware of his surroundings. A bare metal bed frame with no mattress, a small sink, and a toilet. Lock-up. Where he'd spend the last night of his life alone and in pain. At least he could see, but his right eye, nearest the wound, was blurry.

He leaned forward until his forehead pressed against the floor. *Father in Heaven, I have failed Thee. I'm sorry. Please don't let anyone else suffer for my mistakes.*

Not Prissa. Not Enoch. Not Sal. Oh, Sal. He'd thought it was best to keep his distance to let her make the next move if she wanted. But now, all he could think was that he'd wasted all the time they might have been happy together. He'd never see her again. Or Prissa, or anyone else. "Take care of my sister, Enoch," he whispered. Then he stretched out on the floor and closed his eyes. The stripe wound burned and his heart ached. He would see his mother again soon. That was something. Unless God condemned him outright for his failure and sent him straight to outer darkness.

The door opened and the lights came up. Surely it couldn't be morning already. Maybe he'd slept after all. He sat up, expecting Hyrum and Zeniff, or even Ammon, but not—

"Elizabeth?"

She knelt beside him, tossing her loose hair back over her shoulder. Her delicate features were grim. She wore a long, billowy nightgown the color of butter.

"Oh, my. That looks terrible," she said, reaching toward his face. She stopped short of touching him. "I brought what I could for it."

"Th-thank you." He sat up in astonishment as she pulled medical supplies from a large pocket on her nightgown. Wound cleanser and a tube of quick-healing ointment. Stuff they didn't get on telestial deck.

"This might hurt," Elizabeth said.

Nephi closed his eyes and tried not to cringe when she began to clean his wound with the gauze. "Ammon told me you were here," she said as she worked. "Told me everything that happened. Couldn't help but gloat, I guess. He likes to hold you over my head." Bitterness laced her voice.

"I'm sorry, Elizabeth."

"Don't be." She finished with the wound cleanser and smoothed the ointment over the stripe with a gentle touch. "It was my own fault. You know, I actually believed I had done something terribly wrong? I actually believed I could be forgiven, too." She laughed unhappily. "You're lucky, Nephi. The rod barely missed your eye."

"I know." The ointment dulled the pain almost instantly. Nephi opened his eyes to find Elizabeth staring into them.

"I don't want you to die," she whispered. A long moment of silence passed before she tore her gaze away. "Here." She reached into another pocket and handed Nephi a tab. His tab. "How?—"

"I took it from Ammon's office. Take it and go. Hide somewhere.

Nephi turned the tab over in his hands, not wanting to look into her eyes again. "Why would you do this for me?"

She was quiet for a moment. "Did you really see an angel?"

"Yes, I did."

"All my life, I believed I was in good standing with God. That I would live with Him when I died. I thought my grandfather always spoke the truth. I was naïve. But if you really have something different—something real—then…" She stopped and handed him the tube of ointment. "Hurry. Before anyone sees you."

"Will Ammon know it was you who let me go?"

She shrugged. "He'll probably figure it out. It doesn't matter, though. He has to keep me around to legitimize his claim to the presidency." She smoothed her hand over her belly, which protruded slightly. "And now I'm carrying his heir." She smiled sadly. "So I won't be cast out or anything."

"I wouldn't want to cause—"

"Just go. Please." She stood and helped him to his feet.

"Thank you, Elizabeth."

"Thank you for giving me one bright spot in my memories." She leaned forward and kissed him on the cheek. Then she turned away, hurrying out the door and down the hall. Nephi thought about what Sal had said about celestial women and their station, and his heart ached for her. He watched her go until she disappeared around the bend. Then he took off in the other direction.

Chapter 17

Nephi slipped through the darkened halls with fear pounding out the beat of his heart. How long did he have before they discovered he was gone? He wanted to go home, but that's the first place they would look, and he wouldn't endanger Prissa or any of his friends. But where was there to hide on the ship? The empty decks, he decided. No one ever went there except maybe an occasional maintenance crew. If he kept moving, maybe Ammon wouldn't find him.

The empty decks of the *Kingdom of Heaven* were far larger than the sections in use. The ship held only 11,000 people, and would house ten times that before they reached their new home on Canaan. Nephi found an access panel to the core on celestial deck, and pushed himself hand over hand to the unused levels, as far from celestial deck as he could get.

He chose an empty apartment at random. It must have been a terrestrial or even celestial living space. It held a living room, kitchen, two bathrooms and three bedrooms, all of which were larger than the single room he shared with Prissa. There wasn't any furniture but he could turn on the water, and soft lights flickered to life along the floor when he entered. Bless whatever ancestor had decided the ship needed automatic lights everywhere. The air was cold, but bearable. He stretched out on the soft carpet of the farthest back bedroom and fell into a dreamless sleep.

He didn't know how much time had passed when he awoke, but his cheek hurt. He applied some more of the ointment and, having no other choice, relieved himself in one of the toilets. It wouldn't flush, but he'd find a way to deal with that later.

A quick check in the mirror revealed the nasty red stripe that ran down the side of his nose and across his right cheek. Elizabeth was right. It had missed his eye by millimeters. In fact, his vision in that eye was still a little blurry, and that was going to be one hell of a scar across his face. Better than being dead, though.

Only then did he pull out his tab. It was 7:00 in the morning. The wall screen wouldn't turn on, so he had no idea what, if anything, the celestials had to say about him. He had to assume they'd noticed his absence and begun searching. He spared a prayer for Elizabeth, that she wouldn't suffer for her act of mercy, at least no more than she was already suffering. She didn't deserve that. "Bless her, Father," he murmured, pushing back his hair. "She has a good and honest heart. She saved my life."

He huddled, shivering, in a corner and sent a message to Prissa, counting on the fact that the message would be encrypted as Amaleki had said. *"I'm fine. I'm safe for now. Don't worry about me."*

Prissa responded almost at once. *"There are elders down here looking for you. I'm scared."*

"Stay close to Enoch. Tell the elders the truth. You haven't seen me since last night. You don't know where I am."

"They asked if I believe you saw an angel. I said I didn't know what they were talking about. I'm sorry for the lie."

"You did the right thing. Tell everyone not to talk about it."

"No one's going to rat you out. Don't worry about that."

Nephi smiled. Dear girl.

"I'm not worried. I know I can count on you. I love you, sis."

"Love you too, bro. BE CAREFUL!"

Oh, I will, he thought, but didn't send.

Next he messaged Sal with trembling hands. She'd already be up in the kitchens, but he hoped she'd respond anyway.

"Sal, I need your help. Can you come to me? Level 357, section 4, apartment 28."

Long minutes passed, but she didn't respond. He couldn't blame her for that. What kind of a jerk would ignore her for months, then beg for help. He paced around the bedroom. He should have asked Prissa to come. Or Enoch. He still could, he supposed. But he needed Sal as much as he needed food and blankets right now.

The front door opened. Nephi tensed. He should have moved on sooner. Shouldn't have sent messages. He had nothing to use as a weapon, but he wouldn't go down without a fight.

"Nephi?"

Sal. Relief made him lightheaded. *Thank you, Lord.*

"I'm here." He hurried down the hall. She was in the empty kitchen, setting a covered tray on the counter. "I thought you'd be hungry," she said, like nothing had changed between them. "It's so cold in h—"

Nephi cut her off, pulling her into his arms and kissing her. Pain shot through his cheek, and he pulled away, silently cursing Zeniff.

Sal gasped and stepped away from him. "Nephi—oh, you're hurt. I'm sorry."

"Blame Zeniff for that. He took a rod to my face."

"What?" She reached toward his cheek, but stopped short of touching him. "You should have told me. I could have got something for it from Phoebe."

"It's all right. Elizabeth gave me some ointment for it when she got me out of lock-up."

"Elizabeth?" She turned away from him.

"It's a long story." He put his hand on her shoulder.

Sal shrugged it off. "I brought you some food," she said, her back still to him.

"Salome." He took her shoulder and gently turned her around.

"What?"

"Elizabeth felt sorry for me and she let me go. That's all. There's nothing between her and me. That was just a stupid crush. I didn't know what it was like to fall in love until you, Sal." He cupped her cheek in his hand, wanting to kiss her again, but the pain of his wound stopped him.

She regarded him for a long moment, her face inscrutable in the dim light. "I have to go," Sal whispered at last. "I'll be in enough trouble as it is. But I'll find you some blankets or something first. It's so cold." She shivered.

"Don't worry about that. I'll be fine. I'm not staying here anyway. If I keep moving, I'll be harder to find. I hope."

"You think that'll work?"

"Well, I didn't expect to be alive this morning, so it's working so far." He reached for her hand, and she didn't pull away. "Make sure no one talks to Hyrum or Zeniff. They work for Ammon. And don't let the elders intimidate you, either."

"I won't."

"I'll let you know where I am."

"And I'll make sure you get what you need." She raised up onto tip-toes and kissed his uninjured cheek, and then she was gone. Nephi felt more alone in that moment than he ever had before.

Nephi polished off breakfast—a real, celestial breakfast even, with oatmeal, fruit, and scrambled eggs—and washed it down with the water Sal had brought him in a metal pitcher. He gathered up the dishes and took them with him up thirteen levels and over four sections to another apartment, almost identical to the first, with plush carpets and cream-colored walls. He sat in the front room with his back against the wall and imagined what it would be like to live here with Sal as his wife and a houseful of kids running around. He could almost hear them laughing and shouting. He imagined Sal with her belly swollen and round, ripe with a baby inside, reading to their children, praying with them, teaching them to write and read. He could see her in her own private space composing poetry under the soft light of a night lamp.

His heart grew heavy. It could never be. Even if he could marry her, free from the threat of being cast out, they'd live in a tiny, bare-walled, linoleum-floored apartment on telestial deck. It galled him. There were thousands of apartments like this sitting empty while all of telestial deck lived in cramped, Spartan quarters, probably retrofitted from animal pens or something, all to satisfy some false religious doctrine. And here he sat alone, injured, and freezing, and soon-to-be very hungry, too, with no hope he'd ever be able to go home. At that moment he wished he'd never seen an angel at all. It wasn't like he could change anything, anyway.

"I don't think you really mean that."

Nephi leaped out of his skin at the sudden appearance of the angel. "Uriel." He scrambled to his feet. "No, you're right, I don't. I mean—" He ran his hands through his hair. Truth was, he did mean it. *Please just go away. Let me scrub algae filters and marry Sal and live in peace.*

A chill passed through him as he saw the rest of it. *And lose Sal in childbirth and be left to raise our children alone and watch them grow up in grief and hunger and never know the goodness of God.*

He lowered his head. "No. I didn't mean it. But I don't know what to do now."

Uriel stood in the air, which was much more disconcerting in full gravity than in the core. He folded his hands and regarded Nephi in a way that made him want to shrink into the carpet.

"You are going to marry the girl you love just like you want to."

Nephi laughed. "That sounds terrific, but I don't think it's possible at the moment. If we go to our bishop and ask to be married, he'll turn me over to the High Council. I don't know how I'll survive another week, let alone marry Salome. Besides, I don't even know if she wants me."

"Nephi." Uriel's voice shook the walls. Nephi cringed. "You must repent of your unbelief. Do not fear what man can do. Fear God and do as He directs. Otherwise you will lose your place, and though you may think that would make your life easier, believe me, the consequences for eternity are dire."

A cold wave of blackness sent Nephi to his knees. He couldn't breathe for the weight of despair pressing on him. He couldn't go on. Couldn't exist in the awful absence of light.

All at once, the sensation ceased. Nephi slumped onto the carpet, gulping in the air. Bathing in the warmth of Uriel's glow.

"Do you understand?"

"Yes." Shaking, Nephi pushed himself to his feet again. The emotional emptiness had been worse than any pain inflicted by the rod. He kept his eyes on the floor. "Forgive me."

"Ask God to forgive you."

Nephi closed his eyes and pressed his hand to his aching chest.

"You will not marry Salome by the authority of men, but by the power of God."

Nephi raised his head to meet the angel's gaze. "What do you mean?"

"You must be joined to her for eternity, not just this life."

"Like the celestials do."

"Their ceremonies have become corrupted and their ordinances without power. But you can cleanse the temple, purify it, and make it a place where the Spirit of the Lord can dwell. Where the Lord himself can come."

"The temple? The one on celestial deck?"

"It can be made acceptable to God."

Nephi's protest dies on his tongue. "W—when? How?"

"Tomorrow night. I will come to you there."

"And—I'm going to marry Sal then?"

"You must, if you are to continue with this work. You may also bring your family and closest associates."

"What if Sal doesn't want to?"

Uriel shimmered with amusement. "We men are fortunate women are so long-suffering and patient. If she gives herself to you, never forget that she is a beloved daughter of God, and you will be accountable to Him for how well you care for her."

"I'll do my best. But it doesn't look like much of a life right now."

"Perhaps not. But maybe Salome will have more of an eternal perspective than you do."

"Right. Sorry."

"Prepare yourself," Uriel said. The light flared around him, and he was gone.

Nephi shivered in the cold left in the angel's wake. Prepare himself. He wasn't entirely sure what he was supposed to prepare for. He pulled out his tab and searched for everything he could find about temples, studying the way Sal had taught him to months ago. Dear Sal. Goose bumps from more than just the low temperature prickled on his skin. He set the tab down, folded his arms, and began to pray.

Chapter 18

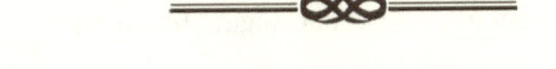

“*I*’*m coming to you,*” he messaged Sal later that night.
  “*Be careful. Ammon hasn't given up the search.*”
  “*I will.*”

In fact, his heart was racing, but not because of Ammon Nielsen-Black. *God, if you want me to marry her, please get me down there safely.*

The corridors of the unused section were empty, thank the Lord. He found a core access panel and slipped inside. For a minute, he floated there, letting the blessedly warm air seep into his bones and drive out the chill of the empty apartment. Then he gathered up his courage and made his way to agri-deck, and from there down the elevator to telestial deck.

He heard footsteps when the elevator door opened, and ducked back inside until they passed. Cautiously, he made his way to the Hunsaker's apartment. Every sound made him jump, and he expected Hyrum or Zeniff to materialize out of nowhere and haul him back to Ammon and stripes. Or death. By the time he reached Sal's place, he could barely breathe.

Sal opened the door, and Nephi stepped in so quickly he almost knocked her down. “Sorry.” He took her shoulders to steady her.

"You made it." She looked him in the eye for a minute as if gauging something. He held his breath. Would she turn him away?

Then her arms slid around him, and all the coldness fled from his bones as he held her. "I was so worried," she whispered.

"It's all right. I'm here."

"You'd better not stay long. I think Ammon has terrestrial men patrolling the halls now to find you."

"I didn't see anyone."

"Thank goodness for that." She hugged him tighter.

"Sal—"

"Oh." She stepped back. "I have some food for you. It's not much. I'll get you some water, too." She went into the little kitchen.

"Sal—"

"Did you see Prissa yet? She's worried sick."

"Not yet. Look, Sal—"

"Here." She set a small sludge shake and a glass of water on the table. "That's all I could get today."

"Sal." He grabbed her hand before she could walk away again. "Stop a minute. I need to talk to you about something."

"What is it?" She had that look on her face like she wanted to run. Like the night he'd kissed her in the kitchens. His courage almost failed him.

"I want to get married."

"Married?" She turned a delightful shade of pink. "To me?"

"To you? Of course to you! You think I'd sneak down here and risk my neck to tell you I wanted to marry someone else?"

"I don't know." Her cheeks grew more fiercely pink.

Nephi took her other hand and stepped closer to her. "Salome, these past few months—I don't know what I was thinking. I've missed you so much. And then I thought I was going to die and my biggest regret was that I'd never see you again. I love you, Sal. I should never have pushed you away. I can't live without you. I can't do this work God has given me without you beside me. I never want to be apart ever again, and I want to marry you more than I want to breathe. Will you be my wife, Salome?"

"I—" She blinked. Then she smiled. "Yes."

He pulled her against him and kissed her. Her arms slid around his neck. She melted into him, and nothing else mattered—not the pain from his wound, not the men searching for him. All that mattered was holding her and feeling her mouth move against his.

They parted after an eternity, but still too soon. Sal gasped. "But, Nephi, how can we marry?" Tears gathered in her eyes.

"Don't worry about that," Nephi said. "Uriel told me we will be married for eternity in the celestials' temple tomorrow night."

"Tomorrow?" A tear escaped down her cheek. "Are you serious?"

"Yes. I should have mentioned that first, huh? Oh—we should talk to your father too. Can you get him? I mean, assuming you do want to marry me."

Sal swiped at her tears. "I—I'll go get him."

Nephi sat down on the couch and tried not to fidget. Sal and her father returned a moment later. Brother Hunsaker was in his pajamas, blinking sleepily. He pushed his glasses up on his nose. Sal sat down next to Nephi and Brother Hunsaker sat in the chair beside them.

"What can I do for you, Nephi? You're taking an awful risk coming down here tonight."

Nephi glanced at Sal. Hadn't she said anything to him? She still looked a little shocked and all the pink had drained from her face.

"I want to talk to you about Sal. I want to marry her. With your blessing, of course."

"Ah." Brother Hunsaker rubbed his eye under his glasses. "I admit, I expected that at some point, but your timing seems...off."

"I know. I thought so too. But the archangel told me Sal and I can be married by the power of God for all eternity. Tomorrow night."

"In the celestials' temple," Sal whispered.

"What? You're kidding, right? You can't get into the celestials' temple."

Sal touched her father's arm. "If Uriel said to do it, then we will do it. There will be a way."

Oh, how Nephi loved that sweet girl.

Brother Hunsaker patted Sal's hand. "Is this what you want, honey? Not because an angel said so, but because you want it in your heart?"

Nephi held his breath, waiting for Sal's response.

"Yes." She turned to Nephi and that rare, breathtaking smile lit up her face. "It's exactly what I want."

"Me too." Nephi took her hand. "Uriel only told me when and where. I already knew it had to be you, Sal. For always."

Brother Hunsaker cleared his throat. "That's wonderful, and I would give you my blessing, but I don't know how all of this will work out. I don't want you to get hurt or punished."

"Brother Hunsaker, you can come to the temple with us. If I understand what I've been studying, you can also be married to your wife for eternity, even though she has already passed. You'll be together again as husband and wife forever when you leave this world to join her."

"How?" he whispered, his eyes gone wide. "How is that possible?"

"By the grace of God," Nephi said. "Through his merciful plan for all His children. Will you come tomorrow?"

Brother Hunsaker nodded. "Yes. I'll come."

"Good." Nephi put his arm around Sal. "Bring Reuben, too. Meet me after lights-out tomorrow on celestial deck in the main park."

"I've never been up there," Sal said. "How will I find you?"

"Don't worry. Any elevator will take you to the park. I'll find you." He kissed her gently on the lips, hoping her father wouldn't object. "I don't know how this is all going to turn out. Maybe not the way we hope. But whatever happens, God will be with us."

Prissa jumped up with a shriek when Nephi came into their little apartment. Enoch remained on the couch, but he smiled. Prissa threw her arms around Nephi. "You're okay. I'm so glad to see you. I was so scared. Oh, what happened to your face?"

"Zeniff. But I'm fine. Everything's going to be fine, okay?"

"Okay." She squeezed him tight. "You can't stay here, though."

"I know, but I wanted to see you. I have good news."

"Good news? What?"

He grinned. "Sal and I are getting married."

Prissa clapped her hands, bouncing on her toes. "I knew it! That's fantastic. But, wait. Now? How will you do that?"

"Uriel came to me and told me to marry her in the celestials' temple. Tomorrow night."

"Seriously?" She giggled.

"Yes, seriously. And I want you there too. You and Enoch both." He turned to his friend. "Bring your family." Then to Prissa, "We should invite Phoebe and Thomas too. But that's all, I think." Their little study group. It seemed appropriate.

Enoch stood up and put his arm around Prissa. "If you're getting married, then I want to marry Prissa there, too."

Prissa's face lit up. "Really?"

"Yes, really." Enoch smiled at her with a tenderness and affection that Nephi had never seen on his face before, but still…

"She's too young."

"I am not." Prissa put her hands on her hips. "I'm almost seventeen."

Enoch frowned. Nephi wondered if Brother Hunsaker had felt this conflicted.

"Enoch, can I talk to Prissa alone for a minute?"

"Sure." He squeezed Prissa's shoulder and gave Nephi a pointed glare as he left.

"I *am* old enough," Prissa said. "And I love him. I'm not a baby."

"I know that. I don't doubt your feelings for him. But do you really understand what you're getting into here?"

"Ha. Do you?"

Nephi chuckled. "No, I suppose I don't. But I want to make sure you're ready to make a lifelong commitment here. An eternal commitment."

Prissa was quiet for a minute, thinking. "I am ready, Nephi. I'm not a little girl. I love Enoch. I've known him all my life, and he's a good man." She reached for her brother's hand. "And with everything…I don't know what's going to happen to you. To any of us. I don't want to be left alone."

Nephi drew a couple of slow breaths, considering, listening to the spirit for the right answer. She had a point. Neither he nor Prissa had truly been children since their mother passed, maybe even since their father's death, and he didn't doubt the sincerity of her affection. Or of Enoch's for that matter.

"If that's truly what you want, I won't object to it."

"Thanks, Nephi." Prissa hugged him again. Then she ran to summon Enoch back inside. "I talked some sense into him," she said.

"Good." Enoch's smile turned goofy. He laced his fingers through Prissa's curls and pulled her in for a kiss.

Nephi cleared his throat. "Seriously, guys? I'm standing right here."

"Aw, c'mon." Enoch let go of Prissa and socked Nephi in the shoulder. "You know what it's like. You're getting married tomorrow too."

"Yes. I know what it's like. That's why you'd better go home now." Nephi socked him back.

"Okay. Okay." He kissed Prissa on the cheek. "I'll see you tomorrow."

"We'll meet on celestial deck after lights-out. I don't have to tell you to be discreet. This will be more than just a wedding. We'll receive great blessings from God, so you need to prepare yourselves with fasting and prayer."

Concern flashed across Enoch's face, and then was gone. "Right. We'll be there." He and Prissa shared another embrace, and he left.

"Oh, Nephi." Prissa collapsed on the couch. "This is so crazy. I can't believe it. I'm so happy."

"I am too." He sat down beside her. "Who'd have thought we'd both get married on the same day?"

"Who'd have thought a lot of things." Prissa sighed. "I wish Mom could be with us tomorrow."

Nephi put his arm around her. "I have a feeling she will be."

"And Dad too?"

"Yes, Dad too," Nephi replied, though the thought troubled him.

The door buzzed, and Prissa jumped up to answer, her eyes dancing. Nephi grabbed her wrist, shaking his head. Her eyes widened at the realization that it might not be Enoch back again.

"Who's there?" she shouted, harsh and frightened. Nephi came to his feet.

"Brother Lewis from terrestrial deck. Let me in, leftover. I need to ask you some questions."

Nephi's jaw tightened. How dare he come harass Prissa late at night when she was alone? He must have seen Enoch leave. Did that mean they'd also seen Nephi arrive? His insides turned to ice. But if this guy had seen him arrive, why wait and ask questions?

He jerked his head toward the back. Prissa nodded. Nephi slid past the curtain and into the bathroom as Prissa yelled, "I'm not opening the door. It's late. I'm alone."

Nephi pressed himself against the door, ready to jump out and defend her if he had to. He pulled out his tab and messaged Enoch. *Get back here now!*

"I've already answered all your questions a hundred times. I don't know where my brother is. I haven't heard from him. I don't know what he did. I don't know anything!"

Her voice broke. That surely wasn't an act. He wanted to go out there and take the guy's head off.

The door opened. Prissa cried out in protest. Nephi stood stiff, torn between saving his sister and not getting caught.

"Is he here?" the terrestrial man asked gruffly.

"No. I told you. I don't know where he is."

"I'll have to verify that for myself."

Nephi tensed, prepared to come out fighting.

"Hey!" It was Enoch. Nephi held his breath. "You get out of here. Stop harassing my fiancé. You have no right—" Enoch bellowed in pain.

"If you don't turn him in, you'll get worse than that, stupid leftovers."

Nephi heard the door close again, and burst out of the bathroom.

"Help!" Prissa called. She had her arms around Enoch, trying to get him onto Nephi's bed. The terrestrial man, thankfully, was no where in sight. Enoch held his right shoulder, grimacing in pain. A familiar red welt peeked out between his fingers.

"He had a rod?" Nephi helped Prissa get him onto the bed.

Enoch nodded, clenching his teeth. He moved his hand away. The fabric of his shirt sleeve had burned away where the rod touched it, but the wound left behind was small, only a couple of inches long.

"I'll get Phoebe," Prissa said.

"Wait." Nephi pulled the tube of ointment from his pocket. "I have this."

Prissa took it from him and carefully rolled up Enoch's sleeve to apply it. Enoch winced, but as soon as the pain relief kicked in, his face relaxed. "That's good stuff."

"Yeah, it is." Nephi touched his cheek just below the still tender mark on his face. "No offense to Phoebe's miracle concoctions, of course."

Prissa rummaged through her drawer and found a strip of linen to tie around Enoch's arm. The same linen she'd used on Nephi's back, no doubt, cleaned and pressed again.

Enoch grunted. "I can't believe you survived ten full-on stripes. That hurt like anything."

"Yeah, I know. Prissa have these guys been bothering you a lot?"

She shrugged. "Yes. But no one's ever come this late at night." She looked back and forth between Nephi and Enoch. "I don't want to be alone."

"No, you shouldn't be," Enoch said. He glanced at Nephi.

"You can stay with Phoebe and Thomas." Nephi said. "Tell them everything. I'm sure Phoebe will have some motherly advice to give you and Sal before the wedding anyway."

Prissa's blush would put Sal to shame.

"Good idea," Enoch said. "Get your things and I'll walk you over there."

"Thank you," Nephi said. "I'll see you both tomorrow night."

"Please be careful," Prissa said, hugging him.

"Don't worry about me. I'm like a ghost in the night. They'll never know I'm there."

She smiled. "You're crazy, you know that?"

"So I've been told."

When Enoch and Prissa had gone, Nephi indulged himself in the luxury of a working toilet and a warm shower. He gathered up a change of clothes, a blanket, some apples and cheese he found in the fridge, and a glass jar with a lid that he filled with water. Then, commending himself into the hands of God, he set off through the darkened hallways.

Chapter 19

The temple stood at the cul-de-sac of the celestial park, far away from any of the elevators or entrances. The doors rose three meters high and employed a holographic display of the heavens. Galaxies, comets, planets, and distant suns swirled across the deep blue surface in an awe-inspiring illusion. Nephi, staring up at them in the dark, could only guess at what lay inside.

The appointed hour had arrived, but Nephi was the only one there. He sat down on a bench and contemplated the fancy door. *Worlds without number have I created...and by the Son I created them, which is mine only begotten.*

Nephi closed his eyes until a gentle touch on his shoulder made him jump. It was Sal, in a simple, blue dress. She didn't look at all like a little girl in it. A smile lit up her face and Nephi's heart both. He stood and took her in his arms and kissed her. "You made it."

"Yes." She laughed softly. Her father and brother stood just behind her. Nephi let her go, but kept hold of her hand.

"That's a pretty dress."

"Thanks. Prissa thought we should have something new. She sewed it out of scraps after work today."

Prissa arrived with the Sharpes a few minutes later. She looked as radiant as Sal in a yellow version of the same dress. Nephi hugged her tight. Enoch and his family were only a moment behind them. His mother, Naomi, twisted a handkerchief between her hands. Her husband, Alma, had his arm around her shoulders.

Nephi beckoned them together. "Thank you all for coming," he whispered. "Your belief in me means more than you can imagine." He squeezed Sal's hand. "I don't know exactly what awaits us beyond these doors, but I believe it will be a sacred and unmatched experience for all of us."

He faced the doors with the others arrayed behind him. For the first time, he wondered if they would open. He'd assumed Uriel would be here to let them in. He took a deep breath and touched the pad beside the door. Nothing happened. He lowered his hand, praying he hadn't set off some kind of alarm.

Sal bit her bottom lip. "How do we get in?"

"I thought Uriel would take care of that," he muttered. Somebody shuffled their feet behind him.

"I don't think we should stand out here for long," Thomas Sharpe said.

"No, you're right." He pushed his hair back. *What now, God?* "I have an idea." Nephi pulled out his tab. They weren't going to like it. He didn't like it himself. It was more risky than trying to pry the doors open, but he couldn't think of anything else to try.

He sent a message to Elizabeth, hoping against hope that she wasn't asleep, that her husband wouldn't intercept it.

"I can't thank you enough for saving my life. I hope you haven't suffered for it. I need your help again. Can you come to the park? I'm near the temple. Please hurry."

He walked back to the bench and sat down, his tab still in his hand.

"What did you do?" Sal whispered, sitting down beside him.

"I asked Elizabeth to come. I think she can let us in."

"You didn't." Sal covered her face with her hands.

"She helped me before. I think she will now. She believes I saw an angel. At least, I think she does." Maybe it had been a bad idea after all. He gently rubbed Sal's back, silently praying.

"Okay." She let her hands drop to her knees. No one else spoke. Prissa leaned on Enoch. His brother and sister sat down in the grass and ran their hands through the blades. Nephi thought he ought to send them to hide somewhere, but they were too far from the elevators now.

Minutes passed. Nephi stood, paced back over to the doors and tried the palm pad again. Nothing. The heavens meandered lazily across the doors. Maybe he'd been judged unworthy after all. His stomach hurt.

"I'm leaving," Thomas Sharpe said.

"No, wait—"

"Nephi!"

He jumped and swiveled toward the voice. Elizabeth emerged from the shadowed depths of the park. *Thank you, Lord.* Sal stood up. Elizabeth stopped short when she saw Sal and the rest of them. "Oh...I..." She pressed a hand to her chest, glancing back and forth between them like she expected to be attacked. She wasn't in pajamas this time, and in the dim light, Nephi could see her mid-section swelling against her shirt. "What do you want?" she asked harshly.

"Elizabeth." Nephi hurried toward her. "We aren't going to hurt you. Thank you for coming."

Nephi glanced over at Sal, who watched the exchange with her eyes wide. He faced Elizabeth. "Can you let us inside the temple?"

"No!" Elizabeth stepped back like he'd struck her.

"No, you can't or no, you won't?"

"I won't." She was angry. "That would be…blasphemous. The temple is sacred."

"Not yet," Nephi said. "But it will be. The angel commanded us to come here tonight. To cleanse the temple and make it holy again."

"How dare you suggest—"

"Elizabeth." Sal stepped forward. "I'm Salome. Look, I know this is frightening. I know it's hard for you. But it's important. I'm so grateful for what you did for Nephi." She took Elizabeth's hand. "You saved his life. You don't know how much that means to me." She glanced at Nephi. "I think, if you want to, you could come with us. Learn the truth."

"That's right," Nephi said.

That took the bluster out of Elizabeth. She sagged, crumpling in on herself. It hurt Nephi to see it. "I can't. I've already been…" she trailed off. "You're getting married, aren't you?"

"Yes."

Elizabeth stood stock still, taking in Nephi and Sal and the rest of them. At last, she met Nephi's eyes. "You're a good man," she said. She threw her shoulders back, marched past Nephi, and slapped her palm against the pad. The doors rose silently. "Whatever you're doing, you'd better be gone before morning. My grandfather comes here every day at six o'clock. And don't leave any traces either."

That surprised Nephi. President Black came here to pray? What did he pray for? Did he get answers? "Thank you," he told Elizabeth. "Are you sure you won't join us?"

She shook her head. "My absence would be noticed. Probably already has." Her eyes met Nephi's, shrouded and inscrutable. "I wish you both much happiness." And then she rushed away.

Sal came forward, slipping her hand into Nephi's. "Hurry, before the door closes."

"Right." They entered the temple together. The others trailed in behind. The lights came up as they stepped over the threshold. Crystal chandeliers cast sparkles across a circular receiving room lined with elegant furniture. Cream-colored couches and arm chairs covered with embossed velvet, and carved, polished end tables made of real wood that boasted actual, living bouquets of flowers. The floor was tiled in white marble with a giant starburst symbol etched in gold across it. Nephi and Prissa's apartment could have fit five times over just in this foyer. A portrait of Joshua Black, the first president, hung prominently on the far wall, surrounded by his successors. On the other end of the circle, above the swirling heavens of the doors was a portrait of Jeremiah Black glowering somberly down at them. Nephi flinched at the sight. Those portraits didn't belong in this place. He could sense it.

Prissa pulled Enoch over to one of the couches and sat down with a sigh. "I've never felt anything so soft in my life."

"We don't belong here," Thomas observed.

True, Nephi did feel rather shabby and out of place amidst the celestial finery. "But we do belong here." He put his arm around Sal. "The Lord commanded us to be here."

"Where is the angel?" Enoch asked. He held Prissa's hand and gave her a look that suggested he'd like to get on with marrying her. Nephi could relate.

"I don't know." He closed his eyes for a minute, breathing in the scent of the flowers, listening to the quiet echoes of the ventilation system around them. "I think we should pray."

The twelve of them knelt in a circle on the cool marble and Nephi offered the prayer.

"Dear Father in Heaven, we have gathered here to this temple at thy command in spite of danger, in spite of our fears. We thank Thee for the knowledge that thou hast sent to us through thy servant Uriel, and for granting us access to Thy holy word. We ask thee to let Thy spirit dwell with us here tonight. Pour Thy promised blessings out upon us. Give us strength and courage to face our enemies. Please let Thy truth prevail. In the name of our Lord Jesus Christ, amen." His heart swelled as he spoke, filled with something sweet and indescribable and more powerful than anything he'd felt before.

The circle echoed his amen, but no one rose. No one spoke, as if doing so would disturb the holiness which had descended upon them. Soft footsteps sounded on the marble, but Nephi felt no fear. Uriel entered the room from a side passage. He actually walked barefoot across the floor rather than floating above it, and only faintly glowed in the prismatic light.

And he wasn't alone. A dark-haired woman, also dressed in white stood beside Uriel. Two more men and two more women came in behind them.

Nephi stood and helped Sal up. The rest of his friends came to their feet as well. A peaceful stillness came over Nephi's heart. His fear of Ammon and Jeremiah Black receded. A feeling of love bubbled up inside him until he couldn't contain it, and it spilled out over everyone in the room. He grabbed Sal's hand. Her eyes were watery.

"Welcome," Uriel said, spreading out his arms. "We have a lot to do tonight, so we'd better get started. Please follow me."

Nephi looked over his little group of friends and family. Thomas' mouth literally hung open. Enoch was pale as the tiles on the floor. Sal positively glowed.

Uriel led them to a doorway which opened to reveal an oddity onboard the *Kingdom of Heaven*. A flight of stairs, leading downward.

At the bottom of the stairs stood another circular room. Sunken into the center of the room was a large round basin full of water with steps leading down into it. A baptismal font. Looking over the edge of the sunken font, Nephi could see a circle of large stone bulls holding the basin in place on their backs. The lighting was more muted here than the room upstairs and the water in the basin stirred faintly with some unseen current. A filtering system, Nephi guessed.

"We will begin here with your baptism," Uriel told them. "Except, of course, dear Salome, who has already received it."

Sal flushed and moved closer to Nephi.

"Then the men will be ordained, and we can rededicate this structure as the house of the Lord before we proceed with other ordinances." Uriel looked the group over, his helpers standing nearby. "You are ready," he said. "Let's begin."

By the time Nephi knelt across the sacred altar from Salome—who shone like a star, or something even more brilliant and pure than that—and made her his bride, he had touched the very heights of heaven, and knew he'd never be the same again.

When all was done, he and Sal and the rest stood in the pinnacle of the temple, the pinnacle of the *Kingdom of Heaven,* really. Uriel called it the celestial room, and Nephi thought it aptly named.

The domed ceiling and curved walls that formed the ship's outer hull were as clear as glass, opening up a real view of the endless heavens they traveled through. Even the floor was clear, and the walls curved down below it and out of sight, so that they were surrounded by the stars. It was dizzying and awe-inspiring all at once.

"I feel so small," Sal whispered. Nephi put his arm around her and pulled her close to his side. He had seen her now for what she truly was, and aside from her height, there was nothing small about her. She was glorious beyond description.

Uriel and his helpers stood facing the group, forming a semi-circle at the front of the room. With the backdrop of the stars, they seemed even more heavenly than they already were. A faint, golden aura surrounded them, and Nephi wondered idly if he and Sal and the rest of the mortal folk looked the same.

"We must leave you," Uriel said. "But first we have been instructed to set you apart, Nephi."

"Set me apart? What is that?"

"You know you have been chosen and called of God as a prophet and a leader of this people. We will, by the power of the priesthood, consecrate you, and set you apart from all others as the bearer of this calling. I will give you the keys of your office, and power to do all that God requires." He gestured to the empty space between them. "Please kneel."

Nephi slipped his arm from around Sal's shoulder with a gentle caress. She smiled rather nervously and caught hold of his hand for a moment as he stepped forward and knelt before the angel.

Uriel and the other angels formed a circle around him. Uriel beckoned to the rest of the mortals, asking them to form another circle around the angels.

"Join hands," Uriel instructed.

Nephi's hairs stood on end there at the center of the two circles. The weight of Uriel's hands came down on his head, then the hands of the other angels. Nephi felt, more than saw, them link themselves together with hands upon shoulders. The spiritual energy prickled his skin, swirled around him, and flowed inside him even before Uriel began to speak. He had become the focal point of a vortex of light and power, more than his being could contain.

Then Uriel began to speak. The words were not English, yet Nephi understood them all the same. He could not repeat the words, nor write them down if he tried, but he could no more forget them than forget his own name. There was power granted, authority given, promises made, and warnings issued.

When all the words had been spoken, the hands lifted, the circles broken, Nephi stayed on his knees, head bowed, and contemplated the glory of the stars below him, above him, and all around him. Who was he that God would notice him in all the wide expanse of the heavens? And yet He had. He had noticed Nephi and Salome and everyone else onboard the *Kingdom of Heaven*. He knew them, He loved them and He wanted them to know Him too. Nephi knelt a minute longer to offer up a prayer of thanks, inadequate to express the depth of his feeling.

At last he rose to a flurry of hugging, handshaking, and back-slapping; he found himself again facing Uriel with Sal close beside him. "I must leave you now," Uriel said, clasping Nephi's hand.

A chilling certainty came to him with those words. "You're not coming back, are you?"

Uriel smiled. "You are ready. You don't need me anymore. Trust the Lord. Learn to rely on Him."

"But—"

"Salome," the angel said, "you must stay beside him."

"I intend to." She threaded her fingers through Nephi's.

Uriel nodded, then turned to his fellow angels. The light around them grew until it blotted out the stars, and in a blink they were gone, and the light with them.

Nephi shuddered. Sal seemed to sense his fear and squeezed his hand. She laid her palm against his chest as if to quiet his heartbeat. "You'll be fine. Uriel trusts you. So do I. And so does God." She looked up at him, her dark eyes earnest and kind, and he knew he was the most blessed man on the ship.

"We should go," Thomas Sharpe said, "You heard how early President Black comes in here."

Coming to pray, Elizabeth had said. But who did the venerable head of the ship pray to? Did he come seeking divine answers or merely to bolster his own ego? It was President Black's portrait that dominated the foyer out front, after all. Unease buzzed along his nerves. "Yes." He bent to kiss Sal's forehead. "Let's go."

Nephi's tab read 3:07am when they emerged into the celestial park, which was still deserted. They took the elevator back down to telestial deck. Nephi hung back until he was certain there was no one patrolling the halls. After a brief debate, Prissa went home with Enoch and Nephi took Sal to his apartment.

He locked the door behind them and turned to see Sal's cheeks turning the perfect shade of pink. "I don't know what I'm doing," she muttered.

Nephi grinned and shrugged. "Despite what you may have heard, neither do I." He gently enfolded her hands in his.

She stepped closer. "Phoebe gave Prissa and me a long lecture yesterday, complete with illustrations, but still..." Her cheeks flamed.

"So you're a step ahead of me already." He slid his arms around her waist. "I didn't get the benefit of a lecture." His heart set to rattling with nervous excitement. "I'm sure we can figure it out."

Her hands came up to tangle in his hair, and he bent to kiss her with more fervor and passion than he'd ever felt before. They belonged to each other forever now—his lover and his queen—and this...this was the most sacred of all the moments he'd experienced so far.

Chapter 20

Nephi paced the apartment from the front door to the end of the kitchen and back. Ten steps each way. Sal had gone to church along with the rest of the ship. For the first time in his life, he wasn't being subjected to the service. Maybe that's what had him so much on edge.

"I'll never go back," he whispered, a liberating thought, but frightening, too.

He turned and took ten steps to the front door. His stomach gurgled. He hadn't eaten since two nights before, when he'd come down to propose to Sal. Ten steps back, and he checked the fridge again. Still empty. He wished Sal would come back. The thought brought a smile to his face.

A beeping from his tab startled him halfway back to the front door. Someone was taking a risk using a tab during church meetings. He pushed the curtain aside and picked his tab up off the bedside table.

It was Sal. *"Black knows someone was in his temple, and he suspects you. He's put a price on your head."*

Nephi groaned. Had Elizabeth ratted him out again? No. He dismissed the thought. More likely they'd left something out of place and Black had noticed. Of course he'd assume it was Nephi.

Another message from Sal came: "*Get back to the unused levels ASAP. I will meet you there.*"

Right. He didn't reply, not wanting to make her tab beep in church. "Thank you, dear one," he said to the tab. He stuck it in his pocket and opened the door, peering out cautiously. Movement caught his eye, a man coming down the hall. He jerked back and lowered the door, engaging the deadbolt with trembling fingers. If there were men searching for him during church, Black wasn't messing around anymore.

Nephi stood with his back pressed against the door. The metal was cool beneath his hands, but irritated the scars on his back. He listened to the *thunk-thunk-thunk* of footsteps coming ever closer. He didn't know if the man had seen him. He held his breath, unwilling to make a sound. Prissa's wind chimes clinked softly. The footsteps stopped. A heavy hand pounded on the door. "Who's in there?"

Nephi cast about for something to defend himself with. The wind chimes might work, if the little metal bits were sharp enough.

"Is anyone there? Nephi Packard, open up!"

I'm not here. No one's here. You only thought you saw something. Please, please go away.

The door shuddered under the man's fist. Nephi tensed, ready to spring for the chimes should the man find a way to breach the deadbolt. After another good pounding, the man moved off, his footsteps trailing into silence. Still, Nephi didn't dare move. It could be a trick to lure him out, after all.

Minutes passed with no more pounding. Nephi relaxed just enough to tiptoe seven steps to the kitchen table and retrieve one of the wind chimes. Once he had it by the yarn hook, he knew it was too flimsy to do any good. He wrapped the yarn around his hand anyway, and stood ready to swing.

Time ticked away. Nephi sat down on the couch but kept hold of his makeshift weapon. Getting out of here now would be impossible. *Lord, what do I do?*

His tab beeped again with a message from Thomas. *"Where are you?"*

"Stuck in my apartment. Don't dare leave."

"Stay there. Black has dismissed church. Offered a thousand credits to anyone who turns you in."

A thousand? Nephi would just about turn himself in for that. He barely earned a thousand credits in a year.

"He's taken Sal, Prissa, and Enoch to be questioned by the High Council."

No. If Black gave any of them the rod… Nephi would turn himself in for sure to save them from that.

"Stay put," Thomas sent, as if he'd read Nephi's thoughts. *"I'll come to you."*

"Take care. Someone may be watching my door. Tried to get in earlier."

"Understood."

Nephi put his tab in his pocket and pushed his hair out of his eyes. There was no way out of the mess he could see except out the airlock. Even if he managed to sneak back into the unused sections, they'd find him eventually. And how was he supposed to accomplish his mission while in hiding?

"Father, you have given me a work to do. You have given me the power to do it. Please provide the way."

The door chimed, and Nephi flinched. "It's me," Thomas said in a low voice. Nephi stood and opened the door, jumping out of sight as it slid upward.

Thomas came inside and lowered the door. "You are in a world of trouble, son."

"We knew that before today. What's happening to Sal and Prissa and Enoch?"

"I don't know. They were escorted out of the chapel by some elders who told us they were going before the High Council. Phoebe went to see the bishop to protest, but I doubt he'll do anything. President Black is apoplectic over the temple, and he worked everyone into a real frenzy."

"Everyone?" Nephi sat down on the couch.

"Near enough."

"What about those who came to my meetings and believed what I taught them? You think they'd turn me in?"

"For a thousand credits?" Thomas shrugged. "Luckily no one actually knows where you are. But they'll be looking. We need to get you out of here."

Nephi shook his head. "I'll never make it. I can't hide anymore."

"You're not going to turn yourself in," Thomas said sternly.

"I might for a thousand credits." He chuckled, but Thomas wasn't smiling. Maybe it wasn't all that funny.

"Seriously, though, it's pointless to try. The ship's not so big that I could keep out of sight indefinitely. Besides, I have a life to live. Work to do. You were there last night. You know what God has called me to do. I can't teach the truth from a hiding place."

"You can't teach it if you're dead, either." Thomas sat down beside him, his eyebrows pulled together in a scowl.

"This is bigger than my life," Nephi said quietly. "If I'm dead, you all can carry on without me. But if I'm hiding to save myself then I'm nothing but a coward. God doesn't need a coward to lead his people."

Thomas didn't answer. Lines of worry deepened on his face.

Nephi's stomach grumbled loudly in the silence. "Do you think you could get me something to eat? I'm starving."

Thomas stood. "That's something I can do. We'll talk about this later. Just stay put for now."

"Thank you."

When Thomas left, Nephi went behind the curtain and sat on his bed—the bed he'd shared with Sal just a few hours before. He longed to run to the High Council room and get her away. Prissa and Enoch too. But for all his bold words, he wasn't ready to rush into a trap. He needed a plan.

He stretched out on the bed, draped his hand over his eyes, and tried to think. They only thing that came to his mind was Sal, and before he knew what had happened, he jerked back awake. The smell of food drifted through the apartment—warm bread and succulent meat drove him to his feet and out the curtain. His stomach growled so fiercely, he didn't even care if it were Jeremiah Black himself come to lure him out. At least he'd die with his belly full.

It wasn't Black standing at the kitchen table, or even Thomas. It was Sal. He scooped her up in his arms, food forgotten. *Thank you, Lord.*

"Are you all right? Did they hurt you?"

"No," she mumbled into Nephi's shoulder. He loosened his hold on her and she stepped back just enough to look at him. "I don't think so anyway. Except for this." She pointed to a small patch of irritated skin on the inside of her forearm, near her wrist.

"What's that?" Nephi cradled her arm and ran his finger over the spot. Tiny bumps prickled beneath his finger.

"They injected us all with something. I believe it was a micro-chip intended to track our location." She rubbed her wrist with her thumb like it pained her.

"So, they know you're here?"

"Maybe."

"It's okay," Prissa said from the couch. "We're here too."

Nephi jumped. "You startled me."

"Yeah, you only have eyes for Sal. I get it." Prissa grinned and snuggled into Enoch's shoulder.

"You guys got injected too?"

"Yep." Enoch held up his right arm. His injection site looked even worse than Sal's.

Nephi drew his eyebrows together. "Did the High Council question you?"

"Yes." Prissa rolled her eyes. "The same old same old. No, we haven't seen you. No, we don't know anything about an angel. No, we don't know how you got into the temple." She sighed. "I'm tired of lying, Nephi."

"I know." He sat down at the table and started in on the roast beef sandwich Sal had brought. His stomach sighed in contentment. "Like I told Thomas," he said, "I think it's time to stop hiding."

"He told me." Sal took the chair beside him. "What are you going to do?" She laid her hand on his arm. Goose bumps danced across his skin. He rested his hand on hers.

"We have to stand up to Black and Ammon and the High Council. Speak the truth and insist they let us worship God as we choose."

"That will never happen," Enoch said.

"You don't know that," Sal said. "We have God on our side, after all." Nephi squeezed her hand and smiled.

"That's great," Prissa said. "But how will it stop Black from casting you out?"

Nephi took another bite of his sandwich, enjoying the spices on his tongue, the juice running down his throat, the crunchy crust of the bread. Simple pleasures he could no longer take for granted. Like the feel of Sal's hand on his arm. He didn't want to die.

"What I need is for everyone who believes me, who believes in the truth, to defend me. Protect me. Refuse to let the celestials get near me. Will they do that, do you think?"

"Yes." Sal stood up, her eyes alight. "We're behind you all the way."

"I know you are, Sal. But everyone else? A thousand credits is a tempting sum."

"Your followers are loyal, Nephi. You're offering them something much more precious than a thousand credits," Sal said.

"Even after President Black's sermon today?" Prissa said. "He had even me scared." She scooted closer to Enoch.

"What do you mean?" Nephi took another bite of his sandwich.

"It was pretty bad," Sal said. "He described all the tortures of hell we would endure if we didn't follow him. It was gruesome and graphic. Frightening, like Prissa said. But anyone who has studied with you and heard the truth will know it's all nonsense."

"Huh." Nephi set down his sandwich. A lifetime of indoctrination might not be so easy to overcome. "Maybe we should get everyone together so we can reassure them and enlist their help."

"Probably won't want the three of us rounding anyone up," Enoch said, pointing to the rash on his arm. "If they're tracking us—not just listening in on our conversations or something."

A rush of fear passed through Nephi. "Do you think they could be listening?"

"With the device on the inside of us?" Sal said. "I wouldn't think so."

"If they were listening, they'd have broken the door down already, right?" Prissa said.

The door chimed and Nephi almost came out of his skin. The four of them stared, unmoving. It chimed again. Nephi bolted for the back, not that it would save him.

"Wh—who's there?" Prissa said, clearing her throat. Nephi couldn't breathe.

"It's me. Phoebe."

Nephi came out from behind the curtain. Thomas came in behind his wife.

"What happened?" Phoebe asked.

"They injected us with a micro-chip or something," Prissa said. "Sal thinks they want to track us."

Phoebe examined the rashy spot on Prissa's wrist. "You all had a reaction like this?"

"Yep." Enoch held up his arm. Sal nodded too.

"Well—" Phoebe frowned. "I can treat the rash at least."

"Phoebe," Nephi said, "I need you and Thomas to get Enoch's family and Sal's and start gathering all my supporters to the cafeteria for a meeting. There's something I need to say."

"Nephi—"

He held up a hand to stop her. "I've already been through it with Thomas and these three, too. My mind is made up. If you trust me, please do this for me."

Phoebe looked into his eyes for several long seconds. Nephi met her gaze without looking away. "I trust you," she said at last. "You know I do." She let go of Prissa's arm. "We'll get everyone together. And I'll be back with ointment for you three." She shook her head. "But, please, don't get yourself cast out." Her eyes turned misty and she surprised Nephi by wrapping him in a motherly embrace. She'd never done such a thing before to his memory, but in that moment, he felt his own mother's arms around him, and his eyes got misty too.

"I'll do my best."

"Good." Phoebe let go and patted his shoulders, blinking. "You and Prissa are like a son and daughter to me. You know that, right?"

"I know," Nephi said. "And I know how thankful our mother would be for that."

Phoebe nodded. "She'd be so proud of you right now."

Nephi's throat tightened. "It—means a lot to hear you say so."

Phoebe smiled, but her chin quivered. "We'd better get busy."

The cafeteria was stuffed to the walls when Nephi came in flanked by Thomas and Sherem Hunsaker like bodyguards beside him. He hadn't imagined the room could hold so many people.

"This is more than I was expecting," Nephi murmured.

"Yes," Thomas said. "President Black's hell-fire sermon may have had the opposite of its intended effect, at least on telestial deck. Besides, word has spread. More people are reading the scriptures, thinking, praying. You've had quite an effect on the leftovers. They want the truth. They want to be free."

"Oh." Nephi pressed his hand to his chest as if that could calm the upwelling of emotion there. God would do his work. A tingling like electricity shuddered through him. "What about the terrestrial men and elders who were sent here on patrol?" he asked.

"Jarom Jenson and his friends invited them off telestial deck."

Nephi gave him an incredulous look. "They left?"

"Strong young men armed with kitchen knives and farming tools can be quite persuasive," Thomas said.

Nephi's eyebrows shot up. "They did that?"

"Yes, they did. Black's not going to take it well, I think, but for now, they're gone."

"Okay." Nephi blew out his breath. "Guess we'd better make this quick."

Hard to be quick, though, when it seemed everyone in the room wanted to pat his back or shake his hand. He did the best he could to greet everyone as he made his way up to the front of the room.

"My friends, thank you all so much for coming tonight. I can't tell you how much it means to me to see so many of you here." Of course, the three people he'd most like to have with him were sitting alone in separate apartments for fear of being tracked.

"I know President Black said some frightening things today and made terrible threats. He also put out a pretty large reward for me, so the fact that I'm standing here says a lot about the character of leftovers. Again, I thank you."

A cheer went up. Nephi's face warmed. He must look just like Sal. He held up his hands for quiet, but it was some time in coming. Nephi watched the entrance nervously, waiting for the crowd to settle down.

"Truly, each of you is loved and valued by our Heavenly Father, no matter what the celestials say. I know this is true."

More cheering. Even longer this time. He hadn't intended this to be some sort of rally. Better cut to the chase or they'd be here all night.

"Brothers and Sisters, the time has come for me to stop hiding. For all of us to stop hiding and demand that President Black treat us as human beings and allow us to worship God as we choose."

That didn't help. The noise rose to a deafening thunder echoing around the cafeteria. At least he knew they were on his side.

Nephi climbed onto a table and cupped his hands around his mouth. "Brothers and Sisters! Please give me your attention."

They quieted, but the air remained charged with anticipation. "I need your help. I need all of you to protect me from President Black, and to protect each other. Do not speak to the men looking for me. Do not allow them on telestial deck or the work decks if you can. Many of you know Hyrum and Zeniff Bradshaw. They work for Ammon Nielsen-Black. Do not trust them or give them any information. Don't let these men intimidate you."

The room had fallen silent as he spoke. An electric excitement danced up and down his skin. "Look at this scar on my face." Nephi lifted his chin. "Look at the scars on my back." He turned and pulled his shirt over his head. He hadn't planned that, but it felt right. A murmur ran through the group. He faced them, pulling on his shirt again. "These stripes are a symbol of everything we are fighting for. We will not let President Black and his celestials do this to us ever again!"

This time he didn't try to quell the pandemonium. He reveled in it. The excitement and energy in their cheering wrapped around him, buoying him up, standing his hairs on end. They could do this, and not Black nor anyone else could stop them.

Chapter 21

"I heard from Amaleki," Sal said the next morning. They'd spent the night in her bedroom at her father's place, which at least was private, with its own door—a place that wouldn't look suspicious to anyone tracking her. Black had not responded to Jarom's forcible removal of his men. Morning news had mentioned only the reward for his capture and his status as a faithless heretic. Maybe Black thought someone would take the reward or maybe he hoped Nephi would get complacent. Whatever Black's reasoning, Nephi knew he ought to be grateful for any amount of safety he could get. But he couldn't help but feel that today's quiet was the prelude to something truly horrible.

Sal rubbed her thumb over her wrist. Phoebe's ointment had cleared up the rash, but Sal still fidgeted over the spot. Nephi took her hands so she wouldn't.

"What'd Amaleki say?"

"He doesn't know how to disable them except to maybe short them out with an electrical shock or something." She shivered.

"That's not a good option."

"No." Worry creased her forehead. "They could be surgically removed, but only in the celestials' hospital."

Nephi pulled her into his arms. "Don't worry. I won't let Black or anyone else hurt you."

"What if tracking me isn't all it's for? What if it's some kind of weapon that's going to go off and kill us both?"

Nephi's arms tightened reflexively. What if it was? "It will be all right," he whispered again.

"How can you be sure?" She lifted her head to look at him.

"I can't, I suppose. But I'm hopeful." He smiled, hoping it looked convincing. "We have to trust God."

Sal stepped back. "I'm trying."

"I know you are. You're much better at it than me." He took her hand.

"I've been thinking," Sal said. "About the meeting last night." She turned pink.

"I wish you could have come."

"Me too. But I was thinking that, if you really want to stand up to Black, then you ought to send him a message. A…manifesto of sorts. Tell him what you saw. What the angel said. What we believe. What we want him to give us."

His hand tightened around hers. How would Black react to such a message? The cheering and excitement of last night's meeting echoed again in his head and sent shivers through his body. It was time to come out of the shadows. "You're right, Sal. I'll do it. I'll need your help though." He cupped her cheek in his hand and brought his lips to hers, wishing she didn't have to go to work, but it wasn't meant to be.

Sal sighed, perhaps thinking the same thing. "I'd better go. I think Sister McKutcheon is keeping an eye on me in particular."

"Okay." He kissed her again and reluctantly let her go.

"Yeah." Her worried look returned. "You get started on the message to President Black, and I'll help you with it tonight." She rubbed her thumb over her wrist again.

"Don't worry so much." Nephi ran his hand down her arm. "We'll figure out some way to get rid of the chip."

"Okay." She offered him a wan smile, and disappeared out the door.

Loneliness enveloped him then. He sat down on the couch and thought about what sort of message he might write. Maybe start with the appearance of Uriel and go from there? But he found it so hard to find the words. Sal was so much better at that sort of thing. He couldn't think. The Hunsaker's apartment, though larger than his, seemed suddenly too confining. The core, he thought. That's where he'd always done his best thinking. And he sure didn't want to sit alone in his apartment and wait to get caught.

The engineers were the only ones who ever went into the core, and they were never there during lunch time. The only other person he'd ever seen in the core was Elizabeth, and she surely wouldn't be there now. Cautiously, he opened the door and peered out. The hallway was deserted. He made his way toward the nearest access panel, glancing warily over his shoulder every few steps, expecting an army of elders to descend on him at any moment. But no one appeared.

He stopped in front of the access panel, and stuck his hands in his pocket. It held his paper copy of the Book of Mormon. Sal had given it back to him that morning with no explanation other than she thought he needed it. He ran his thumb across the soft, worn cover and ruffled the thin, crinkling pages, thinking of the night he'd spent reading it for the first time. The wonder and excitement. The burning of the Spirit in his chest. A fresh supply of courage rose inside. That was exactly the reason he had to compose a statement to President Black. Sal had a called it manifesto, which sounded much bigger and more important than he felt.

Checking to be sure no one was coming, Nephi opened the panel and stepped into the core. Weightlessness enveloped him in its comforting embrace. He closed his eyes, trying to recreate in his mind the appearance of the angel.

The light got so bright, I thought it would burn out my eyeballs.

Ugh. No good. He couldn't imagine how he'd be able to express the wonder, the warmth, the peace. Sal was the poet, not him.

"Should have known I'd run into you here."

Nephi's heart tried to leap out of his ribs. He opened his eyes to see Elizabeth floating above him. She was upside down to his perspective, her hair loose and waving around her head like a silky halo. He laughed to himself at the thought. None of the real angels he'd seen had halos.

"What are you doing in here?" Nephi asked, flipped himself around to face her.

Elizabeth shrugged. "It's a good place to think. What are you doing here?"

"The same." Which, he realized was probably a stupid risk. Anyone could get into the core from almost any deck on the ship. "I should go."

"You just got here. Don't leave on my account. I'll go." Her face, once so innocent and bright, was burdened now with a sense of sadness and loss. Maybe the core was the only place she could really be at peace.

"You can stay. Really. It's not safe for me in here."

Elizabeth chuckled unhappily. "I'm not going to turn you in."

"I didn't think you would." An awkward silence fell. "Look, I wanted to thank you for opening the doors for us. I hope you didn't get in trouble for it."

She shrugged. "If they suspect me, I don't know about it. I've been avoiding everyone since then. You know, I didn't even go to church Sunday. First time in my life."

"Huh. Neither did I."

"I don't think anyone even noticed I wasn't there."

"I'm sorry, Elizabeth."

She raised her eyebrows. "Why? Because I got stuck in a miserable marriage? Because I'm irrelevant to my family? Because everything I believed in was a lie? None of that is your fault." She closed her eyes, and wiped away the tears building in the corners. "Would I have been happier if I hadn't met you? If we hadn't—" She stopped and shook her head, causing her hair to shiver and sway. "I guess we'll never know, will we?" She reached for a rung on the central pillar. "Goodbye, Nephi. I hope I didn't sign your death warrant, letting you into the temple like that."

"I'm not afraid of President Black."

"Really? Then you're braver than me." She started up—or down—the pillar.

"Wait." Nephi stuck his hand in his pocket and took out the Book of Mormon. "I want you to have this." A strange impulse, but it felt like the right thing to do. He sent it floating her direction.

Elizabeth caught the book, and her eyes widened. "Where did you get it?"

"From the archangel. You should read it."

A ghost of a smile touched her face, reminding Nephi of the first time he'd seen her in the core. "My grandfather let me see his scriptures once when I was a child," she said, "but I never got to touch them."

"Just don't get caught," Nephi said, grinning.

She didn't return the smile, but her features lightened some. "Thank you. I won't get caught." She climbed the ladder with the book clutched tight in her hand.

Nephi waited until she was gone before he launched himself toward his own deck and went home.

Prissa was the first to come home that evening. She flounced onto the couch and folded her arms. "Sister Pratt in sewing wouldn't pay me today. Says she can't until you're found."

"What? That's ridiculous."

Prissa shrugged. "Enoch had enough to get me dinner. But then he went home. He thinks we shouldn't be together too much if we're being tracked."

"He's right." Nephi sat beside her and bumped her shoulder.

"Well, I hate it." She sighed. "I didn't think marriage would be like this."

"You've only been married two days. I'm sure it isn't really like this." In truth, he didn't know what marriage was like. He could hardly remember his parents together before his father killed himself. He ruffled Prissa's hair. "You'll probably get sick of him after a few years anyway."

"I doubt it." She pouted extravagantly.

"I was joking." A thought niggled at the back of his brain. Something about the future of their families. But before he could catch hold of it, the door opened and Sal stumbled inside, her face the picture of panic and despair.

Nephi came to his feet, the sudden fear sending pinpricks up and down his limbs. He caught Sal in his arms. "What's wrong? What happened?"

"T-Thomas," she sputtered. Her breath came out in tiny hiccupping sobs. Nephi went cold from head to toe.

"What happened to Thomas?"

Several seconds passed with Sal shuddering in his arms. Prissa stood and grabbed his shoulder. No doubt the horror on her face matched his own. They waited in dread-filled silence until Sal regained her composure. She looked up at him almost calmly except for her trembling hands against his chest.

"Thomas was shot. He's dead."

"Shot? You mean—like with a gun?" *There were guns on the ship?* He'd only ever read about them.

Sal nodded. "O-one of the elders shot him in the chest when Thomas tried to stop him at the elevator."

Nephi felt like he'd been shot in the chest. He'd have fallen over, but he couldn't. He was holding up Sal and Prissa, too.

"Where did they get guns?" Prissa's voice rose hysterically.

"The guns are in permanent storage," Sal said. Her voice broke. "They're intended for Canaan. If the colonists encounter dangerous creatures or need to hunt for food, or—" She choked on another sob.

"Or stop insurrections," Nephi whispered. His heart dropped into his shoes.

"It's not the first time the guns have been used," Sal said. "They were used during the plague."

The plague that had led to the creation of telestial deck. *Damn.*

"Where's Phoebe?" Prissa squeaked. "We should be with her."

"No." Sal stepped back. "No. Nephi, you have to hide. They have guns and they're coming for you."

"I'm not leaving you two alone."

"Don't be so stubborn," Prissa stomped her foot. "We'll be worse off if you're dead."

"No, you wouldn't." Isn't that what he'd told Thomas yesterday? If he'd taken Thomas' advice and gone back up to the unused section, would Thomas still be alive? Probably.

"Yes, we would, and we're not arguing about it." Sal pushed him toward the back of the apartment. "They could be here any second. Now hide."

"Where?" A glance around the tiny space didn't reveal any possibilities.

"Under the bed," Prissa said.

"I won't fit."

"Perfect. Then they won't look for you there."

"Wait—"

But they were already hoisting up either end of his bed. "Lie down on the floor," Sal ordered.

"Yes, ma'am." He lay on his back and scooted under the raised bed as close to the wall as he could get. "Okay. Lower it. Gently."

He held his breath as the bed came down over him. The thin slats pressed against his body. He tried to squish himself tighter against the unforgiving floor. He turned his head to the side. The mattress smelled musty and dust tickled his nose. He couldn't move at all. He could hardly breathe. A sharp bit of something on one of the slats dug into his shoulder. The scar on his face burned while those on his back began to itch.

"The feet are still a couple of centimeters above the floor," Sal said.

Great. Maybe they'd let him out of here.

"Just pull the blanket down farther over the side. It won't be that noticeable," Prissa said. There was some shifting above him. "There. Perfect."

The door chimed. "They're here." Prissa's voice was low.

"Nephi, don't make a sound," Sal whispered. He clamped his lips together, breathing shallowly and—he hoped—silently.

"Where's Nephi?" It was Enoch. No one answered, so he had to assume the girls had pointed out his hiding spot.

"Hang tough, friend," Enoch murmured. "We'll get rid of them."

Get rid of armed men who'd already proven they weren't afraid to kill? *Oh, Thomas.*

The dust tickled his nose something awful, but he couldn't move his hand up to scratch it. He wriggled it back and forth in a desperate attempt to avoid sneezing.

The door opened again with no chime. Prissa let out a shriek. Nephi stopped breathing.

"We know you're in here, Packard. Come out now."

"He's not here." Sal's voice was firm and did not quaver. *Good girl.*

There was the sound of something hard striking flesh. Sal cried out in pain, and Prissa screamed. It was all Nephi could do to lie still and not throw off the bed and strangle the guy.

"That was uncalled for," Enoch said, his voice angry.

"She's lying," the elder said.

"She's not. See for yourselves."

Nephi's fists clenched. Two pairs of heavy steps moved into the bedroom. He heard Prissa's bed rattle. Then someone kicked his bed, hard. The sharp bit sliced across his shoulder. He bit his tongue to keep from crying out.

The bathroom door opened. He heard more banging and the footsteps moved up front again. "Wherever he is, we will find him, and we won't let you leftovers stand in our way. No one defies President Black. No one mocks him and gets away with it, understand?"

No one answered. The door opened and shut again. Nephi heard a flurry of movement. "I'll get you some ice for that," Prissa said.

"Sal, are you okay?" Nephi said.

"Just be quiet," she snapped. "They could be back. They could be listening."

Fine. He waited for the bed to rise, but it didn't. "Stay put," Enoch said. "I want to make sure they're really gone."

"Take your time," Nephi said through clenched teeth. "It's super comfortable under here."

Minutes passed with no one talking. Sweat dripped into Nephi's eyes. He squeezed them shut and tried to ignore the pain, the sweat, the itchiness. After a few more minutes, he couldn't take anymore. "Okay, guys. Enough is enough. Let me out of here."

Sal mumbled something under her breath, but after a few seconds the bed lifted enough for him to roll out from under. He groaned, pushing himself up from the floor.

"You're bleeding," Sal said.

Nephi touched his shoulder. Sure enough, his shirt was ripped and blood seeped through the fabric. He looked at Sal and gasped at the goose egg and ugly bruise forming on the side of her face.

"Oh, Sal." He reached for her.

"He hit me with the gun." She stepped into his arms. "But at least he didn't shoot me, like Thomas."

Nephi held her close as she quivered. *Dear God,* he prayed, *what do I do now?* "Where do they keep the guns? I think we're going to need some of our own."

Chapter 22

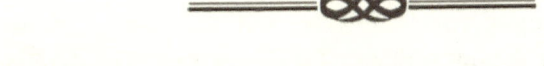

They went through the core in the dead of night—Nephi, Enoch's brother Micah, Sal's brother Reuben, her father Sherem, and Jarom Jenson. Nephi's tab showed the location of permanent storage, an entire deck devoted to all the necessary supplies their descendants would need when they finally reached Canaan.

The others weren't used to zero G like Nephi was. He laughed in spite of himself, watching them flail around. Some stealthy crew they were. "Push off the pillar like this." Nephi demonstrated.

"You're going up feet first," Reuben said. He groaned. "I think I'm going to hork."

"No. Don't." Nephi flipped himself over and took the boy by the shoulders. "Just breathe. You're fine. We can go up if you want. It's a matter of perspective. In my head, I was dropping by my feet. Whatever you're comfortable with is fine. Though, I guess we should all choose the same."

Reuben closed his eyes and shook his head.

Micah maneuvered himself beside his friend. "Come on, Reub. You can do this. It's amazing. Like you can fly or something."

Reuben cracked open one eye. "That doesn't make me feel better."

"It really is fun." Nephi winked. "Even Sal likes it."

"She does?" Both eyes came open. That sealed it for Reuben. Nephi recognized the I'm-not-letting-my-sister-have-anything-on-me look in his eyes. Reuben took a deep breath. "O-okay. I'm ready."

"Good. Follow me." He launched himself up—or down—or whichever. Being in the core never got old. Even the weight of Thomas's death felt easier to bear in here.

It wasn't long before they reached the right landing. Nephi flew over easily and caught the railing. He reached down to help Sherem up. Micah and Jarom made it fine on their own, but Reuben misjudged and floated too far under the landing for Nephi to reach him.

Nephi flipped off the landing in time to see Reuben crash into the wall. He winced. "You okay?"

"That hurt." Reuben spun away from the wall, rubbing his head. His momentum carried him sideways, around the pillar instead of back toward it. Nephi caught a rung and directed himself after Reuben. He grabbed the boy by the shoulder, sending them both into a dizzying tumble.

"Oh, no." Reuben's face went pale. "Oh, no. Oh, no. Oh, no."

"Close your eyes," Nephi said. "Breathe. That's good. I've got you. Don't worry."

It took a minute to get close enough to the pillar to catch another rung. Reuben kept his eyes tight shut. Nephi maneuvered them both back around and over to the landing.

"You can open your eyes," Nephi said.

Reuben blushed just like Sal. "You should have left me home," he muttered.

"Nah. It's fine. We're here now. Let's go."

Jarom opened the access hatch, and the six of them stepped onto permanent storage deck. Dim lights along the floor came on as they moved—just like on the unused levels.

Nephi used the screen of his tab like a flashlight, shining on the touchpads along the wall to find the room they sought. The deck felt endless. According to the info on his tab, the rooms held seeds, embryos of animals, building materials and equipment, tools, textiles, generators, and yes, weapons. All held in sacred trust for the arrival at Canaan. A full half of the deck was dedicated to a large hangar filled with landers ready to transport people and goods to their new home.

Images bubbled in Nephi's mind as they passed each door—images of homes and gardens, children running through the cut grass under a warm, golden sun. Images so vivid they brought him to a halt mid-stride and took his breath away.

"What's wrong?" Jarom whispered.

"What?" Nephi blinked. "Oh. Nothing. Keep moving." The vision still clung to him—the sights, the sounds, the smells. So much so that the dim, lifeless hallway felt more like an illusion.

"Nephi." Sherem whispered, and put a hand on his shoulder. "Look." A guard waited at the door to the weapons rooms. A young elder with barely enough scruff on his face to be considered a beard. And he was sound asleep. A gun lay on the floor near his hand.

Nephi froze and the rest behind him.

"Do we shoot him?" Jarom whispered in his ear.

Nephi shook his head. Bloodshed was not a part of the plan. He motioned everyone quietly back until they were well out of ear-shot. "One of us will have to get his gun before he wakes up," Nephi whispered. "He can open the door for us if it's locked. Then we'll tie him up and leave him somewhere. Agreed?"

Everyone nodded. "Jarom and I will go," Nephi said. "One of you go back and get some rope. The rest wait here. All right? Let's go."

Nephi and Jarom crept down the hallway and back in sight of the sleeping elder. Nephi hung back as Jarom moved silently forward on his bare feet. He stopped inches away and bent slowly toward the gun. The elder jerked awake. Jarom dove for the gun, but the elder was quicker. Nephi lunged forward and tackled the guard.

The gun went off.

"Jarom!" Nephi cried, fearing the worst. He got hold of the elder's wrists and slammed his gun hand against the ground until it came loose.

Jarom scooped it up, much to Nephi's relief. The shot had not hit anyone.

The young elder struggled under Nephi's grip. Jarom waved the gun around menacingly, but fear reflected in his eyes. Nephi felt it too. Their utter inexperience was going to get someone killed.

He came to his feet, hauling the elder up with him, his hands squeezed tight against the young man's wrists. "Open the door and we won't hurt you."

"Heretic!" The elder spit in Nephi's face. "Filthy leftover!"

Nephi tightened his grip and ground his teeth together with the effort of not slamming the guy into the wall. Where were the others with the rope?

"Do it!" Jarom shouted, pointing the gun over Nephi's shoulder and into the elder's face.

"All right. I will," The elder's voice cracked. "Don't shoot." His hate-filled glare could have melted Nephi's bones.

"Turn around slowly with your hands in the air and open the door," Nephi said.

The elder turned, keeping his death glare on Nephi as long as possible.

Jarom rammed the gun into the elder's back, and Nephi winced. He gave Jarom a warning look. *Please don't kill the guy.*

The elder touched the keypad and the door slid open. Nephi stepped past him over the threshold, and the lights came on, revealing a narrow room filled with row upon row of weapons hanging on racks, and shelves stuffed with ammunition. It looked like someone wanted to wage a war, not hunt for food. A shiver passed through him.

Jarom forced the elder into the weapons room behind Nephi. "Don't move," he growled. The elder stood quivering with his hands still raised. At last, Sherem and the others showed up with a coil of strong, slender rope.

"You won't get away with this, stupid leftovers," the elder groused as Jarom and Micah bound him hand and foot at the back of the weapons room.

"Let's hurry. We may have alerted someone to our presence," Nephi said. He bypassed the longer rifles and went in search of smaller guns, more easily concealed. He didn't know their names or how they functioned, but the info was there on his tab to study later.

He loaded up as many guns as he could reasonably carry into his drawstring bag. Sherem did the same. Micah and Reuben collected ammunition, and Jarom stood guard at the door.

It took only a minute or two before their bags were full and heavy. Nephi motioned the others back toward the door.

"Someone's coming," Jarom hissed over his shoulder. "The lights are coming on."

Nephi's heart stuttered. "This way." He led them toward the core access panel on the opposite side of the deck. It was a ways to run, but it was away from their pursuers. The guns and ammo made a terrible racket as they moved. Nephi swung his bag around front and held it against his chest. That was quieter and didn't bother his scars, but it was more awkward too. He did the best he could. Fear of being caught proved a great motivator.

A glance back showed him that Reuben was falling behind, breathing hard, and stumbling with his heavy bag. He had to be hurting still from hitting the wall in the core. Nephi dropped back beside him, as did Reuben's father.

"Come on," Nephi said. "Push a little harder. We're almost there. You can do this."

Sherem took Reuben's arm and pulled him forward. "You can make it, son."

Reuben huffed out his breath. "I can't. I can't. I'm too scared." The whites of his eyes stood out brightly against his olive skin, wide with fear.

"We're going to make it back to the core," Nephi said. "We'll take care of each other. Keep going."

Echoes of heavy footfalls rose from farther down the hall. The elders were catching up.

"Faster," Nephi urged.

Reuben lurched forward, tripped over his own feet and crashed to the floor. Nephi grabbed his arm and helped him up.

"Stop!" The celestials were still far behind, but not far enough.

"Run," Nephi whispered in Reuben's ear. "Don't look back."

A gunshot cracked behind them. Reuben cried out in pain and staggered to his knees. Blood blossomed on his shoulder, seeping down his arm.

Sherem dropped beside his son and pressed his hand against the wound. Reuben gasped. The color drained from his face. His features contorted.

Nephi took off his bag and threw it aside. Then he slipped Reuben's bag off and scooped the boy up in his arms.

"I've got him," Nephi told Sherem. "Let's go."

"The guns—"

"Leave them. Just run."

The elders fired another shot that hit the wall just behind them. Nephi gathered all his strength into a tremendous burst of speed. Reuben moaned and whimpered. His blood stained Nephi's shirt as well as his own. "Hang on," Nephi said. "We'll get you home. I promise."

Another gunshot zinged wildly over their heads.

"There's the access panel!" Nephi shouted. Jarom, in the lead, opened the panel and held his fingers on the control pad until everyone had gone through. When Nephi and Reuben were in, Jarom shut the door. Micah used one of the stolen guns like a hammer to destroy the control pad on the inside. But it wouldn't take the elders long to get around to the other access panel.

"We can't stay in the core," Nephi said, adjusting Reuben to a more comfortable position. The boy had fallen unconscious, and Nephi prayed to God he'd make it home where they could get Phoebe to treat him.

"Everyone jump," Nephi said. "Jarom, you pick a deck—maybe three or four down—or up—from here. We'll get out there and take the elevators home."

Nephi held tight to Reuben as he stepped off the platform. Reuben's blood lifted from his body and hung in the air. It couldn't be helped. Reuben had lost so much already, speed was more important than stealth now.

Jarom grabbed the railing of a platform. Nephi wasn't even sure which deck it was. The others landed easily enough, but it was awkward business for Nephi with Reuben in his arms. He caught the railing, but the extra weight threw off his aim for the platform. He swung beneath it, nearly losing his grip.

Sherem caught him by the wrist and pulled them back in the right direction. As soon as Nephi hit the platform, he let Reuben fall into his father's arms, and landed hard on his knees. Jarom helped him up.

"Hurry!" Nephi shepherded the men onto the deck Jarom had chosen—one of the manufacturing decks. He smashed the door controls as Micah had done.

Sherem had taken his shirt off and was wrapping it around Reuben's shoulder. Already the blood had seeped through it. Reuben tossed and moaned, his eyes still closed.

"I'll carry him," Nephi said.

Jarom shot the controls of the elevator as soon as they got out on telestial deck. Nephi handed Reuben off to his father. "I'll take down the other elevators," Jarom said. The repair bots would have that fixed up by morning, but it would help for now.

"Take a gun for your family," Nephi told Micah, "and take one to Prissa too."

Micah nodded. He and Jarom took off down the hall. Nephi waited there for a moment, heart still hammering. "Oh, God," he prayed aloud, "send thy angels to watch over us this night. Protect thy people." Then he ran toward the Hunsakers.

Nephi, Sal, and Sherem waited in tense silence while Phoebe worked on Reuben. Three bags of firearms and one bag of ammo sat in the center of the floor. Nephi studied the instructions for loading and firing the things, but he didn't touch any of them. The sight of the weapons made him ill. No one else made a move to handle them, either.

Sal laid her head on Nephi's shoulder with a sigh. He set down his tab and put his arm around her. *It will be all right.* That's what he wanted to say, but couldn't. He didn't know if it was true. He should have known. He should have had the faith to make it so. But he didn't. The feeling of power and certainty he'd felt in the temple had fled and couldn't be recaptured. Even when he and Sherem had administered a healing blessing to Reuben, Nephi hadn't felt anything.

He reached for Sal's hand, warm against the cold in his heart. She had drifted off. A blessing indeed. Her father stood up to pace.

No one spoke. Nephi rested his head on Sal's. Weariness made his eyelids heavy. Phoebe's voice dragged him back to consciousness. Sherem paused in his pacing. Sal jerked awake and came halfway off the couch.

"We got the bullet out of him," Phoebe said, "and I sewed him up as best I could. Here." She handed the tube of celestial healing ointment to Nephi. "That was very helpful."

"Keep it," Nephi told her. "I don't need it anymore."

"I gave him some sleeping tea," she said, pocketing the ointment. "He's weak from blood loss, but he should recover just fine. I can't tell yet how much the wound will affect the use of his arm." She shrugged. "We'll have to wait and see."

Sherem took Phoebe's hand. "Thank you so much for saving him. I don't know what I'd do if I lost him." He stopped. "I'm so sorry about Thomas," he whispered.

The last of Phoebe's strength seemed to drain out of her then. She visibly sagged, and to Nephi her face looked ten years older. The reality of Thomas's death pricked him keenly.

"Me too," Phoebe said, her voice barely audible, and Nephi tried to remember if he'd ever heard her speak so softly before. Prissa reached up from behind and laid her hand on Phoebe's shoulder.

"You're exhausted," Sherem said. "Please sit down. We'll try and find you something to eat." Phoebe started to say no, but her head drooped and her shoulders hunched forward. She nodded. "Better than going home, I suppose."

Nephi's heart cracked in two.

Sal came to her feet. "Here, sit down. I'll get you something."

"Thank you." Phoebe sat beside Nephi and leaned back into the couch with her eyes closed. A tear tracked slowly down her cheek. Nephi took her hand.

"Phoebe, I'm so sorry. I should have turned myself in."

"No." Phoebe opened her eyes. "I wouldn't trade your life for his. We need you."

"But—"

She held up her hand to stop him. "Nephi, two days ago, Thomas and I were sealed for eternity by an angel of God. I believe in those promises. And that was all because of you. I would never have thought it was possible." She brushed the tear from her cheek. Sal handed her a chipped mug full of warm milk—the very cup Nephi had given to Sal. Nephi's stomach gurgled at the sight of it, but now didn't seem the appropriate time to ask for one of his own.

Phoebe took a long sip of her milk. "I will say this, though." Her voice grew stronger. "Those guns—" she gestured toward them—"are not the answer."

Nephi grimaced. He didn't like it, either, but they had risked their lives and nearly lost Reuben's trying to get them. "We have to be able to defend ourselves so no one else dies." He rubbed his eyes.

"No one else? I barely got to Reuben in time." She shook her head. "I know where you're coming from, but—this isn't the answer." She took a sip of milk before she continued. "I saw the man—the boy, really—who shot Thomas. He was distraught at what he'd done. I feel badly for having screamed at him. He wasn't a killer, Nephi. No one on this ship has ever witnessed that kind of violence, let alone perpetrated it. If we start a war, we'll lose everything that matters to us. There will be no future for this ship."

"The guns are probably the only reason the celestials aren't banging down our doors already," Nephi said.

"You may be right. Jeremiah Black is smart enough not to want a war, either." Phoebe handed her cup to Nephi, the cup that had reminded him of all their ancestors had hoped for them. She stood. "Violence is not the path to peace."

"We may not have a choice." Nephi set the cup down and stood.

"There is always a choice." Phoebe gave him a look so firm, so familiar, so...motherly, Nephi almost burst into tears.

She'd always been there for him. Always. Now it was up to him to do the same for her. For everyone who had decided to follow him. Whether with guns or without, he vowed then and there that he would do whatever it took to protect his little flock.

Chapter 23

Morning came too soon. Sal slid out of bed to get ready for work. She had to be exhausted. She'd been up every hour or so to check on Reuben. Nephi buried his face in his pillow and tried to pretend life hadn't slipped so far out of control. He'd never thought he'd actually wish to be scrubbing algae filters, but boy he did today.

Sal finished dressing and went out to the living room, but moments later she was back. "Black did it again. No credits for working. Says it'll be that way until you are caught." She sat on the edge of the bed. "And the reward still stands, plus a hundred credits each for my dad, Reuben, Micah, and Jarom."

Nephi sat up and pushed his hair out of his face. "Guess it's time, isn't it?"

"Did you finish writing it?"

"I started it—sort of—before everything fell apart last night." Nephi threw back the covers and scooted himself off the end of the bed. He retrieved his pants from the floor. Specks of blood dotted the legs. His tab was in the pocket. He handed it to Sal.

She studied it for a moment. Nephi cringed, watching her read over the document he'd created. He'd only managed a couple of paragraphs. "I don't use words as well as you do."

Sal glanced up. "It isn't bad. It just needs a little switching around and polishing."

"And you'll write the rest of it?"

"No." She stood up and handed him the tab. "It has to come from you or it won't sound authentic. You write. I'll polish."

She put her hands on his shoulders and leaned over to kiss him. "I have to go."

He caught her hands. "Are you really going to cook for celestials and terrestrials and get nothing for it? We aren't slaves, you know."

"In the kitchen, at least I can collect the leftovers and scraps to share. We all need it, but I'm worried about Reuben, mostly." She threaded her fingers through his. "So it's not for nothing."

Nephi stood. Sal slipped her arms around him, leaning her head on his chest. "And besides, what would happen if we refused to work? It's in our best interest to keep the ship running, right?"

"Maybe. Maybe not. Maybe we ought to shake things up."

"More so than we already have?"

"Yeah. Maybe." He pressed his lips to her forehead. An idea began to take shape in his head. "You go on. I'll finish the manifesto, and we'll see, okay?"

"Be careful." She kissed him goodbye and he prayed it wasn't for the last time.

Nephi put on a clean shirt his father-in-law had lent him and went down the hall to check on Reuben.

Sherem was with him. Reuben was awake and sitting up in bed. The bandage around his shoulder was tinged pink from the wound. "Nephi." Reuben raked his good hand through his dark hair. "I'm really sorry."

"Don't worry about it." Nephi patted his leg through the blanket. "I'm just glad you're going to be okay. You were very brave."

"No, I wasn't. I didn't even make it out with the ammo."

"That wasn't your fault. It was the fault of the man who shot you, not to mention President Black who ordered it. You did your best. You stared your fears right in the face and pressed forward in spite of them. That's nothing to be ashamed of." Nephi reached out to ruffle Reuben's hair the way he would Prissa, but stopped. The kid probably wouldn't appreciate that. Instead, Nephi slapped his good shoulder. "Your job now is to rest and do whatever Phoebe tells you to until you're back in fighting shape, got it?"

"Got it." A half smile wisped across his face, like Nephi had so often seen on Sal's. "But what will happen when I don't show up for work?"

"You won't get paid," Nephi said. "But you wouldn't get paid even if you did show up." He shrugged.

Sherem stood up. "Get some rest, son. I have to go, but Phoebe will be along to check on you soon. And Sal will bring you something to eat."

Reuben nodded and lay back on the bed, shifting as he struggled to get comfortable. Nephi and Sherem stepped out of the room.

"What do we do now?" Sherem asked.

"I'm going to fix this," Nephi said. "Starting with writing a manifesto to deliver to President Black." He sighed. "He can't let all of telestial deck starve if he wants to keep the ship running." His tab beeped.

"Who's that?" Sherem asked.

Nephi took the tab from his pocket. It was Enoch. *"Meet me in the filter room. It's safe. I promise."*

Frowning, Nephi showed it to Sherem. "Could this be fake?"

233

Sherem shrugged. "Maybe if someone stole his tab? I wouldn't go if I were you."

Nephi frowned at his tab, studying the message as if the truth would reveal itself on the screen.

"Stay here." Sherem patted his shoulder. "Don't take any chances. Tell Enoch to meet you here."

Nephi nodded without speaking. Sherem left. Nephi sent a message to Enoch. *"Come to me."*

The reply was almost immediate. *"Can't. You know why. This isn't a trick. Trust me."*

Nephi turned his eyes to the ceiling. *Well, Lord, what should I do?*

Go.

He put the tab away and stepped into the front room. All the stolen weapons were still there in the middle of the floor. He hefted one of the guns, cold and heavy in his hands. No matter what Phoebe said, he needed some protection here. On his tab, he looked up the directions for loading it with twelve slender bullets from the ammo bag. He made sure the safety was on, and tucked it into his pocket. It was designed to fire swiftly and silently with computer-guided sights. It was a miracle, really, that no one but Reuben had been hit. *Thank you, Father.* Still, Nephi really didn't want a chance to try it out.

With another prayer for safety and guidance, he stepped into the hallway. No one was in sight. Work shifts had begun. Children would be in their classes. Even without credits, everyone was going about their business. But how many of them were looking to turn him in?

He moved to the elevator quickly and quietly, with his hand in his pocket, wrapped firmly around the grip of his gun.

The elevator stood empty, and he made his way down to filter scrubbing without running into a soul. He thought about what Phoebe had said—that the elders didn't want to kill, and perhaps knowing Nephi had weapons himself made them even more reluctant. Lucky for him, whatever the reason.

He hesitated outside the filter room, and opted to knock rather than try the control pad. The door slid up and a grim-faced Enoch ushered him inside. The smell made him gag. He'd never get used to it.

"What did you want to tell me?" Nephi asked, and sucked in his breath when he saw Brother Ryan standing there, arms folded.

"Don't worry, Nephi. I'm not here to turn you in. I want to help you," Brother Ryan said.

Nephi glanced at Enoch, who nodded. "We can trust him."

"You've always been good to me, Brother Ryan" Nephi said. "I'd like to trust you."

"I hope you will. I don't agree with President Black's methods here. And besides—" Ryan cleared his throat. "I'm curious to learn more about what you're teaching."

"I'd be happy to teach you," Nephi said, warily. "But first I need to make sure everyone gets fed today."

Brother Ryan nodded. "Several other supervisors feel as I do, about the work credits situation, anyway. We're willing to make sure all the left—er, that is all of telestial deck gets food until this is resolved."

"That would be greatly appreciated, Brother Ryan, but won't it get you and the others in trouble with Black?"

"We'll be discreet. It…may not be much."

"We never get much," Enoch grumbled under his breath.

"True. Whatever you can do will be welcome," Nephi told Brother Ryan.

"Sister McKutcheon in the kitchens is willing to do what she can. Several other supervisors have agreed to use their own credits for extra food."

"That's very generous." More generous than he'd ever expected the supervisors to be. Though he doubted Brother Sorensen would do anything for leftovers. *Can't win 'em all.*

"But how long can it go on?" Enoch asked. "We need a long term solution." He shot Nephi a concerned look.

"I'm working on that," Nephi said. "Brother Ryan, tell the other supervisors thank you. God is pleased with your generosity and kindness. I want to invite all of you to a meeting tomorrow morning before work in the level three cafeteria on telestial deck. I intend to deliver a message to President Black. Your support would be appreciated."

"A message?" Brother Ryan's forehead creased. "I…I will see what I can do."

"Good. I have an idea, but I'll need the help of the supervisors to pull it off." He pressed his hand against the lump of the gun in his pocket and shuddered. Hopefully, it wouldn't come to violence.

Brother Ryan nodded. "It isn't right for anyone to go hungry. And I'm curious about your religious ideas too. I will come, and I'll bring as many others as I can."

"Again, thank you. If you don't mind, I think I'll stay down here to work on this message." He wrinkled his nose. "It may be safer than upstairs."

"And as a bonus, you can join me in scrubbing." Enoch clapped him on the shoulder.

A laugh broke free from his throat for the first time in ages, it seemed. "Sure, why not? Maybe it'll help me think."

"So you want a siege?" Sal asked. She held a tub of lettuce she had taken from the fridge.

"Is that what it's called?"

"Yes. Well—sort of."

"I guess so, then. I just think we ought to keep what we need instead of sending it all to the celestials and letting Black decide what if anything we get back."

A single line crossed Sal's forehead. "So, did you write it yet?"

"Yes. Mostly. In between scrubbing filters." He kissed her nose. "I hope you can make it sound intelligent."

"I can try." Her dazzling smile flickered for a moment. Oh, how he loved that smile.

"Fear not, Sal. This will work."

"I hope so." She touched his cheek. Love and worry intermingled in her gaze. He kissed her and let her go. She had lettuce to chop, and he had to make sure people got fed.

In the end, the supervisors sympathetic to their plight fed the leftovers without making a big deal out of it. They still had leftover sludge shakes, but it was better than not eating at all. Nephi had Jarom post guards at the elevators just in case, and spent dinner visiting each cafeteria on telestial deck to talk to everyone he could about his vision, his teachings, the scriptures. People who'd expected to go hungry were so thankful for any food at all that he had to give Black himself credit for Nephi gaining supporters. "We'll meet in the level three cafeteria in the morning," he whispered to them. "Please come, and don't be afraid. God will be with us."

Later that night in their bedroom at the Hunsakers, Sal handed him his tab with the final draft of his manifesto. It was nothing short of miraculous how she'd taken his clumsy words and lined them up into something magnificent, capturing the awe and glory of Uriel's appearance, the wonder of his message, and Nephi's bold declaration that the telestials would no longer be treated as inferiors—that anyone who wanted could learn what he had to teach.

"It's perfect," he said. "I don't know how you do it."

"A mystery which shall never be revealed." She smiled dryly and leaned on his shoulder.

"You still haven't let me read your poetry."

Her cheeks colored. "Yeah. Maybe someday. But not tonight."

Nephi set down his tab. "Sal," he whispered, "I keep seeing something. A place. All the time. In my dreams. Even when I'm awake."

Sal shifted to be closer to him. "What sort of place?"

"A world. With oceans and mountains and sunshine. With fields and homes. I feel like I'm right there. I can even smell it."

"Is it Canaan?"

"Could be. But why would God show that to me?"

"Don't know. Maybe it's Heaven."

"Heaven, huh? It might be."

"You're lucky," Sal said as her eyes drifted closed. "I can barely imagine such a place." Her head slipped off him onto the pillow. She had fallen asleep.

Nephi kissed her forehead and rolled over. The soft hiss of the air circulation put him in mind of a warm wind passing through fields of ripening grain. What could it mean?

It was a long time before he let sleep claim him.

Chapter 24

"Look what I made you." Prissa beamed early the next morning, presenting Nephi with a crisp white dress shirt with shiny buttons all down the front and a stiff collar encircling the neck, and a pair of brown pants. Nephi lifted a sleeve and rubbed the soft fabric between his fingers. He hadn't had an actual new shirt for ages.

"Wow, Prissa. Thanks. It's perfect."

Sal wore the midnight blue dress she had worn on their wedding night. Prissa punched Nephi in the shoulder. "Hardly. It's just sewn from scraps that Sister Pratt let me have. You should get changed. People are already starting to gather in the cafeteria."

"Already?" Nephi held up the shirt and gathered his courage. He could do this.

"Oh, yes. This is going to be something else." Prissa grinned.

Prissa wasn't exaggerating about the crowd. People lined either side of the hallway leading to the already full cafeteria. Nephi kept his hand on Sal's back and smiled and nodded at his cheering supporters.

The cafeteria itself was full to bursting even more so than the other night. True to his word, even Brother Ryan and some of the terrestrial supervisors had come. Nephi grasped Sal's hand, and they squeezed through the bodies toward the front. Everyone tried to get out of their way, but there was no room to maneuver at all. The room had grown uncomfortably warm.

When they made it up to the front, he hoisted Sal up onto a table, then climbed up himself. The crowd erupted, stamping their feet and slapping the tables. Nephi held up both hands for silence. "Brothers and Sisters, I thank you for coming. Today is a historic day. Today we tell President Black and his celestials that we will be treated as equals. That we will worship God in our own way. That he can no longer withhold the truth from us."

The cheering echoed around him, resounding in his bones. He slipped his fingers through Sal's and raised both their arms in the air.

"Nephi," she whispered, giving her head a little shake. He lowered their arms, winking at her. "You're right. Sorry," he whispered. "Brothers and Sisters, let's start with a prayer. The crowd fell quiet. "Salome, my wife—" he grinned at her— "will offer the prayer." She cast him a nervous glance, but she nodded. It had taken some convincing to get her to agree, but her sweet and sincere prayer brought a reverent hush to the room.

"My friends, I have written a message, a manifesto, to President Black. I am ready to send this statement now. To President Black and to all of you. To everyone on the ship. Read it and ponder it and pray about it. Decide if you believe in what I've taught. If you believe in the Lord and His promises. My hope is to soon begin baptizing all those who wish it."

A murmur of surprise and joy rippled through the room. Families and friends embraced, wiping tears from their cheeks. A lump formed in Nephi's throat.

"I want to bear witness, that everything in this manifesto is the truth. I did see an angel. He gave me the Book of Mormon and other scriptures. He gave me a call from God to restore the truth to the *Kingdom of Heaven*. A few days ago, Sal and I were married in the celestials' temple for all eternity. You can enjoy that blessing too, and there are even greater blessings awaiting us, brothers and sisters. This is only the beginning. We may have to fight for those blessings. We may have to prove to the Lord that we are willing to sacrifice for them. But those blessings will be ours and our children's. It's what our ancestors wanted for us. We will see their dream come true. Not the nightmare President Black and his predecessors created. It is time."

The crowd fell unnervingly silent. Nephi brought up his manifesto on his tab. All he had to do now was tap the send button. His finger quivered. Every man, woman, and child on the ship would soon know his story. He looked at Sal. She nodded, her face serious. She slipped her arm through his.

Courage, Nephi reminded himself. He punched his finger down on the tab. It was done. "Here we go," he said without raising his voice. A moment later, a cacophony of beeping tabs filled the cafeteria. Sal took his free hand and squeezed it hard. Nephi felt himself slip over the edge he'd been teetering on for weeks. No going back now. Not ever. He gathered his scattered thoughts back together.

"Brothers and sisters, I want you to go to work. Carry on as usual. We have to keep the ship running, but we will keep what we need without giving it to the celestials. Black won't have the power to threaten us with starvation again. We won't lack for food or clothes or anything else we need. It may take a few days to get organized. Don't let anything President Black says or does intimidate you. We're in this together. We'll watch out for each other."

The people—his people—clapped and cheered, whistled and stamped, until he climbed down from the table and helped Sal down, and they joined the press of bodies leaving the cafeteria. Nephi put his arm around Sal's waist to keep her close.

Sherem and Enoch managed to get on either side of Nephi and Sal. Though the guns were hidden, Nephi knew they had them. He had one in his pocket too.

"That was quite a speech," Sherem said.

"Thanks." Nephi looked at Enoch, who didn't speak. His face was grim. Nephi elbowed him in the ribs. "Cheer up, buddy. This is our moment of triumph."

"I know." Enoch looked over his shoulder.

"Is Prissa okay?" Nephi asked.

"She's fine." Enoch forced a smile.

"Good. Then I'll meet you in filter-scrubbing as soon as I change out of these…" He stopped. Two familiar figures caught his eye, moving along with the crowd. "What are Hyrum and Zeniff doing here?"

Sal drew in a sharp breath.

"Where?" Enoch asked.

"Over there." He pointed to the two men in their fine black shirts.

Enoch swore under his breath. "I'll find out."

"No." Nephi put a hand on Enoch's shoulder. "You'll never get through the crowd before they're gone. It doesn't matter. They didn't hear anything that Black and his High Council won't know about anyway." He frowned at their retreating backs. "Just have Jarom and his boys keep an eye out for them."

"All right." Enoch sounded unhappy, but the crowd was too thick to do anything else about it.

"Check on Prissa before you come down to filters," Nephi said. "I'll meet you there."

Nephi had been scrubbing filters for only a few minutes when the all-hands-assemble alarm sounded. He froze with Enoch beside him. Brother Ryan emerged from his office, looking harried. "Seems President Black wants to deliver his response in person. I think it would be best to go."

Nephi considered it. He'd love to get back in his new clothes and march right into the chapel. Not a great idea. But everyone else, though...

"He's right. You, especially, Enoch."

"Darn tracker."

"Look after the girls for me, and don't fear Black's threats."

"Where will you go?"

Nephi shrugged. "I doubt anyone's going to look for me down here. What with the smell and all."

"True." Enoch screwed up his face in disgust. "Carry on, then. Less work for me, right?"

"Right."

For a moment, they exchanged a look fraught with unspoken tension. Nephi clapped his hand onto Enoch's shoulder. Words crowded his throat and died on his tongue. All he managed was, "Watch out for the girls." Though, he'd already said that.

"Watch out for yourself," Enoch said.

Brother Ryan motioned Enoch toward the door. "We'd better hurry."

"Okay."

The door slid shut behind them. Nephi stood alone with the all-hands-assemble still sounding through the empty room, echoing in his head. He lifted his scrubber and resumed his work. The cloying, rotting scent of the algae lingered. He could taste it, bitter and sickening in the back of his throat.

When the signal finally stopped, the sudden quiet left his ears ringing. What was Black telling them? Condemning Nephi as a heretic, no doubt. What promises or threats might the old man make? And as much support as Nephi had gathered, he couldn't help but worry that old habits and ingrained beliefs would push them back to Black. He scrubbed harder.

His tab beeped, startling him. It was Sal. *"Black is confiscating our tabs. Don't reply. It's too late."*

Confiscating tabs? That would make communicating difficult. Impossible, really. And they couldn't—

The soft sigh of the door rising interrupted his thoughts. He tossed away the scrubber and pulled the small gun from his pocket as Hyrum came into view, holding a gun of his own. Zeniff came in behind him carrying a charged rod.

"Well, look at this. Just like old times, huh?" Nephi's voice didn't even quaver. That surprised him.

Hyrum snorted. "How about you come with us, and no one has to get hurt."

"No one?" Nephi held his gun steady, aimed at Hyrum's heart. Hyrum didn't need to know Nephi had never fired it. "I think being executed might hurt a little."

"For you, yes. But maybe you'd like to avoid other people getting hurt."

Nephi tensed, but didn't waver. *Nothing but an empty threat,* he told himself. It had to be. "Don't come any closer."

Hyrum stopped. "Do you even know how to use that thing?"

"Do you?"

"You're about to find out." Hyrum sneered.

"You won't shoot me. Black wants a big, public execution."

"Maybe so, but that doesn't mean I can't maim you."

Zeniff chuckled at that.

Nephi saw Hyrum's hand move. He jumped aside as Hyrum pulled the trigger. The shot hit the wall behind him, and a stream of green ooze from the dirty filters trickled out the hole. Nephi kicked over the algae filter in front of him. It rolled into Hyrum, who fell, cursing.

Nephi dodged around Hyrum, heading for the door. Zeniff lunged for him with the rod. Nephi fired in Zeniff's direction without even looking. The door slid upward. Zeniff cried out. Hyrum bellowed, and everything froze.

Nephi turned around. Zeniff lay on the ground, blood pouring from his gut. In that moment, Nephi understood exactly what Phoebe had been talking about. Violence was not the path to peace. Sour bile burned his throat. Hyrum stood, staring at his brother. He seemed to have forgotten about Nephi.

Nephi glanced at the empty hallway. To freedom. Or at least safety, however temporary.

But Zeniff was dying. Nephi was sure of it. Just as he was sure that he could save him. That he *had* to save him.

He knelt beside Zeniff. Hyrum cried out in wordless protest.

Nephi held up his hand. "I can help him."

"You shot him."

"I know." He hoped Hyrum wouldn't return the favor. He seemed too shaken by Zeniff's wound to shoot anyone else.

Nephi's hands shook as he lifted Zeniff's head onto his lap. They trembled as he laid them on Zeniff's head.

"What are you doing?" Hyrum demanded.

"I'm going to bless him."

"You?" Hyrum scoffed.

"Yes. It's the only thing I can do."

"You could've avoided shooting him in the first place."

"And you could've avoided betraying your friends," Nephi grunted. "Just be quiet." He settled his hands on Zeniff's head. "Zeniff Bradshaw," he began, "in the name of Jesus Christ and by the power of His priesthood, I say unto you, be healed."

Hyrum sucked his breath through his teeth.

"Zeniff, I promise you a full and complete recovery, and I exhort you to seek guidance from your Father in Heaven. Let Him direct your paths. Amen."

Nephi lifted his head. Hyrum was staring at him in stunned silence. Zeniff's eyes were closed, but his breathing was even and steady. Nephi thought the wound had stopped bleeding. He eased Zeniff's head back to the floor and stood. He picked up the rod Zeniff had dropped. "He'll be all right, but I recommend getting him to a doctor. A celestial one, if Ammon allows it, but Phoebe Sharpe will do if he won't."

Hyrum didn't answer, but nodded, his mouth tight.

"And I suggest you take the same advice I gave your brother. We don't have to be enemies, you know."

Hyrum's eyes narrowed. His hand tightened on the grip of his gun. Nephi edged toward the door. "Think about it. We could let bygones be bygones."

Hyrum didn't answer. His expression darkened into anger. Nephi stepped into the hallway, hit the door panel, and ran. He'd left his gun there beside Zeniff, but that hardly mattered. He doubted he'd be able to use it again anyway.

Footsteps sounded behind him. Hyrum, or someone else? Nephi broke into a sprint and dove into the closest elevator, pressing buttons at random until he found himself once again in the freezing darkness of the unused decks with no food, no water, no warmth, no idea what was happening, and no way to contact anyone.

Chapter 25

Nephi drew his knees up to his chest and rested his head on top of them. Hyrum's veiled threats now rose ominously in his mind. His chest constricted. "Lord, protect them."

That's when the messages began to pour in on his tab. From Prissa and Enoch and more. *"Where are you?"* they said, and *"Come home. It's safe now."* And from Sal, *"Where are you, my love? Please come home. I'm frightened."*

But it couldn't be from her, could it? She said Black had taken all the tabs. None of these could be real. He stood and paced the bare floors. His tab continued to beep. *"Nephi, please answer. I need to know you're okay."*

It couldn't be her. He tossed the tab away and pushed back his hair. Where was Sal, anyway? He wished he knew if Black had done anything more than take her tab. He fought to get his breathing under control. He paced hard enough to wear a hole in the soft carpet of the unused apartment. He was well and truly trapped now. Before, Black had been toying with him. Now he was going in for the kill. All the bold words of Nephi's manifesto seemed empty puffs of air.

What would his followers think to see him so easily displaced? Powerless to change a thing? How many would abandon him as quickly as they'd followed him?

In the furthest corner of the apartment, he stopped his pacing and fell to his knees. "Lord, I have failed Thee. I thought I was strong and unstoppable. I thought the cheering meant I couldn't lose. I was too proud, and now Thomas is dead. Reuben is hurt. And Zeniff. Oh, God, forgive me. I shot Zeniff." His clasped hands trembled. "I am a weak and foolish man, and I am not worthy of the trust you placed in me. I am not worthy to ask Thee for another chance." Tears wet his cheeks. His head sagged. "Forgive me. I got it all wrong."

He shivered. The darkness pressed around him. Surely God had forsaken him.

Nephi.

He didn't hear the voice with his ears so much as he felt it in his bones.

Nephi, I have heard thee, and if thou wilt repent, I will forgive thee.

Nephi gasped, overwhelmed by the love and acceptance flowing into him. Undeserved. How many times already had he screwed up and needed to repent? God's patience must be limitless.

Inasmuch as President Black and those who follow him have rejected my word and do not turn from their unrighteous paths, I will separate thee from them, and thou shalt find the place I have prepared for thee.

A vision broke upon him. The world he'd been seeing for weeks. The empty room vanished. He stood again among ripening stalks of grain with heavy, yellow heads that dipped in the breeze. He watched the sun set into a shimmering ocean, and squished the sand beneath his toes. He looked down from a tall, snowy mountain peak at the infinite stretches of land below. Scenes flashed past him—homes and other buildings, roads and pathways, boats on the water, even small ships in the sky. Though he saw each scene for only a moment, the sights and sounds and smells burned into his memory with perfect clarity. At last he understood.

This was no vision of heaven or the distant promised land toward which they traveled. No, this was a new place. His place. The place the Lord had prepared for His children. "How will we get there?" he wondered. They'd have to leave the ship. A shiver went through him. He was back in the golden field again, and someone was calling his name.

"Nephi? Nephi, wake up."

His eyes opened to the dimly lit apartment bedroom. He lay on his back, and the cold penetrated to the core.

"Nephi." He turned toward the voice. A person knelt beside him.

"Sal?" He tried to sit up, but couldn't get his body to cooperate.

"No, sorry. It's me, Elizabeth. Your wife asked me to find you."

"Where's Sal?" He reached out a hand, and Elizabeth helped him sit up.

"She and the other telestials are being held under guard in the chapel until they swear an oath of loyalty to my grandfather."

Nephi rubbed his forehead, trying to take that in. His brain still reeled from the revelation that God had another place for them. It was beyond imagining. "How...how did she get in touch with you?"

"Before her tab was confiscated, she sent a message to a terrestrial named Amaleki Cooper asking him to get in touch with me."

"And he did it, huh?" How many favors did he owe the guy now? Or maybe Sal had promised him another pie.

251

"Yes. Sal wanted to make sure you were all right and knew what was happening." She paused. "She seems like a remarkable person."

"She is." His voice turned gruff with emotion. "I'm lucky to have her."

"I'm happy for you," Elizabeth whispered, though she didn't sound happy at all. In the darkness it was hard to read her expression.

Nephi cleared his throat. "How did you find me? Must not be much of a hiding spot." He meant it as a joke, but his voice fell flat.

"Well, I've been searching for hours. Here, I brought you some food."

He heard a rustling as she removed a pack from her back and set it heavily on the floor beside him. The thought of Elizabeth Black sneaking around the kitchens stealing food made him chuckle to himself. Then again, maybe she had just walked in and asked for it.

"I didn't realize how cold it is up here. I would have found a blanket."

"I'll survive." He opened the pack and took out an orange, heavy and fragrant, and broke open the peel with his thumbnail. "Thanks." He peeled the orange and broke off a section. Juice beaded up on the skin. His stomach gurgled in anticipation. "This is much better than I usually get." He popped it in his mouth. "What will Black do with the leftovers he's holding?"

"Hard to say," Elizabeth said. "He can't lock them up forever. Normal operations will come to a standstill without them."

Nephi suppressed a snort. Naturally, a celestial wouldn't think of working herself. But Elizabeth had done too much for him to say so out loud. "He'll let them go, then?"

"I suspect he'll punish them with a stripe or two, and force cooperation under threat of more."

Nephi grimaced. The scars on his back burned against his skin. He longed to charge down there and set them all free with the fiery sword of God, but that was not to be. "If you can, get word to them to comply with Black. God has another plan in mind for us."

"I'll see what I can do," Elizabeth said.

"Don't put yourself in danger."

"You should worry about you. If I found you, Ammon can too, and he has a lot more manpower.

"I'll be careful."

Elizabeth sighed. "I read the Book of Mormon you gave me." She opened a pouch on the side of the backpack and took out the book. Her fingers worried over the leather cover. "I didn't think I should leave it lying around, so... here." She handed it to him. "And thanks."

"You're welcome." It felt good to have it back again. "What did you think?"

"Nephi, I believe in what you're teaching, and in this book. It's what I always believed without realizing it. But I don't think there is anything I can do about it. I can't openly defy my grandfather or my father. And Ammon... Well, I have to consider this baby now too."

"Does he hurt you?" Nephi asked. "Ammon?"

Elizabeth's jaw tightened. "Sometimes." She wrapped her arms around herself. "He thinks I'm still in love with you." She lowered her head. "Sometimes he accuses me of carrying your child, not his. He says he won't let some bastard son become president someday. He...he scares me."

Nephi's hand clenched. "I wish I could change things."

"So do I. Elizabeth said. "But it isn't your fault." Her hand rested against her belly. Nephi waited for her to say something more. The air had grown heavy between them. Elizabeth raised her hand as if she would touch his face. Nephi held his breath, unmoving. Her hand dropped to her side again.

"I think I know how to convince my grandfather and my father and Ammon to stop searching for you."

"How?"

She drew in a deep breath. "I'll tell them I watched you cast yourself into outer darkness. Out the airlock."

"No." *I'm not my father.*

"They'll stop looking for you. Grandfather won't punish your followers anymore. Do you have a better idea? Like I said, Ammon will find you. He's crazy with jealousy. He'll make you suffer and those you love."

Nephi turned away from her. It was a good idea—but what then? Stay in hiding forever? Let the work stop?

Prepare for the blessings that await you.

His breath stopped. Of course. This would give him the time he needed to plan and prepare. But to let everyone think he'd killed himself? Could he do that? Even after everything he'd seen, the anger and pain from his father's suicide lingered inside him.

He faced Elizabeth. "All right. Do it. But you must tell my wife and sister that I'm not dead. I couldn't bear to hurt them like that. I know...I know how painful it is."

"I can't tell anyone, Nephi. You can't take that chance."

"Just Salome and Priscilla. Please. Otherwise I can't go through with it."

Elizabeth nodded, tight-lipped. "I'll need something identifiably yours to prove my story."

Nephi's eyes fell on the Book of Mormon he still held in his hands. He couldn't part with it, but maybe... Trembling, he opened it up and tore out the title page. "This."

Elizabeth took it from him. "Until Grandfather and Ammon believe you're really dead, contact no one. For your safety and mine. A month at least."

Nephi nodded.

In her absence the dark apartment seemed colder than ever.

Chapter 26

Nephi's days fell into a numbing routine, moving between decks from one apartment to another, trying not to leave an obvious trail behind. He didn't even know where he was anymore. In the unchanging darkness, the days blurred together, but according to his tab, two weeks had passed, and despite his careful rationing, his food had run out. But besides that, his heart could no longer bear the ache of missing Sal and Prissa and the rest. Mostly Sal.

Still, the hours had not been empty. While he sat in the dark, hungry and alone, he studied, delving deeper and deeper into the archives on his tab. At one point, he stumbled on a painting of the prophet Joseph Smith, and smiled to realize he knew him after all.

And with all of that study, God had opened a floodgate of knowledge and inspiration. More than his being could contain. And so he wrote. It seemed all his hours were consumed with writing everything he'd seen, everything he'd learned. Pages and pages of it waited on his tab, and he hoped he could get it to Sal, so she could make it all shine. How he longed for her. Enough time had passed. He had so much to tell her. To tell everyone.

He sat against a wall, and contemplated the next step. "Lord, guide my actions. Bring them into harmony with thy will."

He checked his tab. 3am. That seemed to him the best time to sneak onto telestial deck. He shouldered the empty pack, picked up the rod he'd taken from Zeniff, and commending himself to God, stepped into the hall. This part he'd done a hundred times before, but instead of going to another unused level, he took the elevator to one of the industrial floors, and found a core access panel. He activated the rod, and opened the panel.

The core appeared empty, but an uneasiness crept over him. Did they truly believe he was dead, or did Ammon have someone watching the core? He thought about contacting Elizabeth and asking for her help again. But not in the middle of the night. Besides, she'd already risked enough for him, and he couldn't ask any more of her. No, it wasn't Elizabeth he needed now.

With another prayer, he dropped into the core. The lights came on. No one was there. He moved quickly to agri-deck, and with a short jaunt on the elevator he was home. As the elevator door slid upward, Nephi held the rod ready to strike, but no one was there.

Holding his breath, he slid through the hall, trying to stick to the shadows just in case. He passed his own apartment and wondered if Prissa and Enoch were inside. He didn't stop to find out. Sal's apartment was close. No one was in the hallway. He ran to the door, relieved that it still opened at his touch.

His heart began to pound in the darkened living room. Would she be here? Five steps down the narrow hall to the bedroom they had shared for such a short time. He raised the door.

She was there. Asleep. The soft glow of a night lamp illuminated her still form. His heart leaped. He almost felt bad about waking her up. Almost. He sat down on the edge of the bed and ran his hand along her shoulder and down her arm. She sat up, a scream cut short in her throat. She scrambled away from him.

"Sal, it's me."

She pulled the blanket up to her chin and pressed herself against the wall.

"Sal?"

"Nephi?" It came out a breathless whisper tinged with doubt.

"Who else would sneak into your bedroom in the middle of the night?"

Her hands loosed their death grip on the blanket. "Nephi."

He reached for her, and she fell into his arms. His mouth found hers, hungrier for her touch than he was for food. His hands cradled her face, gently brushing away the tears wetting her cheeks.

"Tell me this isn't a dream," Sal breathed.

"It's not a dream." He kissed her neck and down into the hollow of her throat.

"You're alive."

"Yes. A little hungry, but very much alive."

Sal leaned forward, gathering up the front of his shirt in her hands, and buried her face in his chest. "They said you were dead."

"I know." Nephi wrapped his arms tight around her. "Didn't Elizabeth tell you? She promised me she would."

Sal lifted her head. "Nephi, Elizabeth is dead."

"What? How?"

"The note. It was from both of you, they said. And the rumors! That you two were lovers and killed yourselves together. That it was your child she carried. Or that you were jealous of her marriage and murdered her and killed yourself." Tears rolled unchecked down her cheeks so fast she could hardly breathe.

Nephi pulled her close against him again. "Oh no. Sal, none of that is true. None of it. You know that, right?"

"I didn't…I couldn't…" she hiccupped, sobbing.

"I'm sorry, Sal. So, so sorry. I made her promise she would contact you. I didn't think she'd take her own life. I can't believe she did."

He rubbed circles across Sal's back as she cried. "I didn't want you to think I'd done that. But you did. I'm so sorry." His heart ached, and he found himself crying too, wetting Sal's hair with his tears. Not in a million years would he have wanted to cause her such pain.

At last her tears slowed. She lifted her head and rested her hand against Nephi's cheek. "I'm glad you're alive." And there was that smile.

"So am I."

He kissed her then, laying her back against the pillows, savoring every touch, every sigh, every scent of her skin and hair, every breath, and every heartbeat. It was some time before his brain returned to reality again, with Sal curled up sleepily in his arms.

"Elizabeth told me you sent her."

Sal shifted to look at him. "I messaged Amaleki and deleted it before they took our tabs. I didn't know if he got it or if he'd care. They held us in the chapel until they told us you were dead, and that we should forget all you said and get back to normal again."

"And everything went back to normal?" That was some relief, anyway.

"Hardly normal. We still don't have tabs. The supervisors don't allow any conversation while we work. We aren't allowed out of our apartments after eight in the evening. The elders check every night to make sure we're all where we're supposed to be. We have to stay in the chapel for hours on Sunday while the bishops lecture us about our proper place and duty, and they cut our daily credits in half."

"How can you live on that?"

"It's hard." She sighed. "We're hungry. Reuben's shoulder hasn't healed properly because he was forced back to work and hasn't had enough food."

"That's awful." He held her tighter.

"Anyone who protests or refuses to work is punished with stripes or cast out for a second offense."

"Has anyone been cast out?" Nephi asked, shocked.

"No. After a dozen or so people got stripes, everyone fell in line."

Anger wrapped a firm hand around his chest. "How's Prissa? And Enoch?"

"Oh, Nephi. You have to go see her. She was devastated. She and Enoch asked to be married by the bishop so they could move in together, but they were denied."

"Why?"

"The bishop said because of her age, but I think someone wanted to punish them for supporting you. Prissa moved in with Phoebe. She and Enoch are together as much as they can be, but like I said, it's hard now. Especially when we still have trackers in our wrists."

"They're still tracking you?"

"It's safe to assume so." She sighed. "Prissa is more depressed than I've ever seen her. It hurts me."

"I don't know if I can safely go see her. You'll tell her I'm alive, won't you?"

"I'll tell her."

"How have you been holding up?"

She shook her head. "Until now? Not very well, I'm afraid."

He kissed her softly. "I'm so sorry, Sal. I thought about you every minute. If I had known..."

"But you didn't. I tried so hard not to lose faith, but I don't see how we'll ever be free of President Black. Not when he holds all the power." Tears filled her eyes again. "Forgive me."

Nephi sat up, bringing Sal with him. "There's nothing to forgive. Black doesn't hold all the power, you know. The Lord has chosen a different path for us."

"What path?"

"You know the place I told you about? The one I kept seeing?"

"Heaven?"

"Not quite. God has prepared a home for us. Another world. Sal, we have to leave the ship. It's the only way."

"Leave? That's...well, that's impossible."

"With God, nothing is impossible."

"But how? Where is this world? How do we get there? Black won't just let us leave, you know." She covered her mouth with her hand, as if to stop any more from coming out. Nephi moved her hand away to kiss her again.

"I know," he said as he pulled away. "I don't have those answers. Not yet. I'm going to need a lot of help coming up with a plan. But, oh, Sal—I've seen so many things. Here." He fished his tab out of the pile of clothes on the floor. "Have a look. I wrote it all down." He opened his notes and handed it to her.

Sal began to read. Nephi watched anxiously. Her forehead creased. Her eyes raced over the words. After a minute, her expression turned to one of surprise, then wonder. "Oh, my." She looked up at Nephi. "God told you all this?"

"Yes. I was hoping you'd have a chance to make it sound good for me, like you did with the manifesto."

She ran her finger over the screen, scrolling through the pages and pages he'd written. "I don't think you need me for this," she said. "It's all so beautiful. So pure and clear." She cradled the tab against her with a sigh. "I wish I had time to read it all." She held it out to Nephi.

"Why don't you keep it for now." He pushed it back toward her. "Read it through, and tell me what you think."

Her eyes lit up. "Really? You won't need it?"

He shrugged. "If you can do without a tab, so can I. I'm going up to the kitchens now before anyone is in there, so I can load up on food again. I think we have a lot of planning to do."

Sal stood up and hugged him. "I don't want you to go."

"Believe me, I don't want to." He caressed her back.

"Just promise you'll sneak into my bedroom at night more often."

"Without a doubt."

"No." Sal stepped out of his arms, her face serious. "No. Don't. It's too risky."

"I'm willing to take the chance."

"It's not worth it. We have important work to do. We shouldn't jeopardize it selfishly."

Nephi cradled her cheek in his hand, feeling with a pang the truth of her words. He'd been down here too long already.

"Soon we'll never have to be apart," he said. "I promise you."

She closed her eyes and leaned into his touch. "Soon," she whispered.

"We need some way to communicate." Nephi let his hand drop from her cheek. "Or we'll never find our new home."

Sal sat down on the edge of the bed. "Black has gone to great lengths to make sure we can't," she said. "Not by tabs. Not even by talking."

Nephi sat beside her. "He won't win. There has to be another way."

Sal's forehead creased as she thought. Her eyes widened. "What about this?" She opened her nightstand drawer and removed the red journal.

"Your journal?"

"There are still a lot of blank pages. We could write notes to each other—although we'd have to use some kind of code in case it's found.

"What kind of code?"

"Oh, you know, we'll give ourselves code names and be discreet about how we word things. Something like that. And we need to think of some way to deliver them."

Nephi mulled over the possibilities. Little repair bots went all over the ship, but there was no way he knew of to direct one of them to a specific person. Maybe if they found a spot to hide notes where the other person could find them without being suspicious. "Where could we stash notes for each other that we could both get to, and no one else would find?"

Sal bit the inside of her lip. "An elevator, maybe?"

"Too public. And how would we know if we got the right car?" An idea came to him. "What about in the core? On one of the landings?"

Sal shook her head. "I can't go into the core. The tracker, remember?"

"You wouldn't have to enter the core. Just leave it on the landing from the access panel on the kitchen level. That won't arouse suspicion."

"But it might be easy to spot there." She pressed the journal against her chest.

Nephi thought. "Could you get one of the metal bins from the kitchens? That would blend in with the landing. If you leave it just inside the panel where gravity is still strong, it won't float and shouldn't attract attention."

"Okay, let's try it." She grimaced. "We should also tear out and destroy each message once we've read it."

"No way. We don't need to rip your journal up. We'll just write in it and leave the journal on the landing. I'd hate to ruin your beautiful book."

"It won't ruin it. Just remove the pages carefully. We can't risk it otherwise." She ran her hand over the book's soft cover with a sigh. Then she looked at him sideways. "Are you using this as an excuse to read the rest?"

Nephi grinned. "That idea may have crossed my mind." He nudged her with his elbow. "You know I wouldn't read anything without your permission."

"I know." A trace of a smile touched her face. "You may as well read it. I mean, Hyrum already did, so why not?" She rolled her eyes.

Nephi kissed her cheek. "I look forward to it. But you should keep it for now."

A familiar feeling came over him, then. The feeling of God speaking to him as he had up in the lonesome darkness, except this time a string of numbers came into his head instead of images or words. "Let me see the journal," he told Sal.

She handed it over, a questioning look on her face. Nephi took the pencil from the binding and wrote down the numbers on the first blank page.

265

"What is that?" Sal bent over him curiously.

"I'm not sure, but the Lord just sent it to me, plain as anything." He wrinkled up his forehead.

"It looks like planetary coordinates," Sal said.

"See if you can contact Amaleki. Maybe he knows what it means."

"I don't know if that's possible. We aren't allowed to speak to anyone on the higher decks. Only our supervisors, and only during work hours."

"What about the supervisors who were sympathetic to us? Could one of them help?"

"They've all been replaced." She shook her head. "And some—like Brother Ryan and his family—were demoted to telestial deck."

"What?" Nephi scoffed. "I thought Black preached that God decided which deck we belong to before we were born."

Sal shrugged. "Unless the president decides otherwise."

"Well—" Nephi raked back his hair. "Amaleki is the only one with the computer expertise to help us find our promised land. Maybe it's worth the risk to use my tab. Amaleki did say my messages are encrypted." He paused. "And we need to figure out what we need to support a viable colony, and how we can get a hold of it."

Sal rested her hand on his knee, a gesture of assurance that warmed him and calmed his jittery nerves. He kissed her again. "We should be able to find all of it in permanent storage," he said thoughtfully. "Do you know what happened to the guns?"

"Yes." She stood up and lifted the door of her tiny closet. "The elders ransacked yours and Prissa's place," she said, pulling her few belongings out. "They searched here too, and at Enoch's and Jarom Jenson's." She worked loose a tile in the back corner of the closet and lifted it out. Nephi peered over her shoulder. There were the bags of guns and ammunition. "But they didn't find them here."

"Good work. We may need them yet." Nephi shuddered, though, at the memory of shooting Zeniff. He stood and pulled the closet door shut again. He took Sal's hand.

"You should go." Her voice broke. "The morning shift in the kitchens starts soon."

Right. He swept her into his arms, holding her trembling form against him. "Don't lose hope," he whispered in her ear. "Don't lose faith. God is with us."

"I know." Her voice grew firm. "You're alive. That's good enough for me."

Nephi kissed her once more, slowly, then let her go. "I'll be watching for the journal."

"I'll do my best."

"Spread the word. I'm not dead. God has a plan for us." He picked up the empty backpack. Excitement and fear burned like fire against his skin. "Tell them not to despair. We will be free."

Chapter 27

It took more than a week for Sal's journal to appear on the landing in the core. Doubt had crept in to replace Nephi's certainty. Thoughts drifted to the enormity of the task. Hope was undermined by loneliness. Since Nephi didn't have his tab to record his impressions, God didn't seem inclined to send more revelation, and Nephi thought his insides would crumble under the weight of silence.

But now a small, stainless steel bin waited below him, bringing him a flicker of hope. He cast off his sorrow as he propelled himself through the core to reach it. His tab was there too, underneath the journal. So, she was done with it already. He smiled to think of her bent over it, reading his words. Would she believe they came from God?

He picked up both the journal and the tab and stuck them in his pocket. He couldn't linger here, no matter how much he wanted to. Sal was so close, just beyond the access panel. He let his hand rest against it for a few seconds before launching himself back into the core.

In an empty apartment, he used the tab as a light to read the journal, opening up to the page where Sal had left a pencil for him. The first note was not from Sal at all. Prissa had written to him in blocky, print handwriting.

Angie Lofthouse

"You oozing algae ball! How could you let us think you were dead for so long? I was so upset. But I am glad you are alive. I can't be with my husband(!!!) and that stinks so bad I can't stand it. Sal says you have some big plan, or God does, so I'll do whatever you want me to, big brother. Because I love you even if that was a rotten thing to do, letting us be sad for so long. I guess you couldn't help it.

"I love you too, Prissa." He shook his head, chuckling. Below that was Sal's tidy, practiced script.

"There is only limited room in here, so I'll try to be brief. All those things you wrote—I can hardly believe it. They're so beautiful and marvelous. Thank you for sharing them with me. Okay. I contacted computer man. Black suspects him of opening up our tabs, but he couldn't prove it. So, instead of punishing him, Black removed him from the computer techs. He's angry about that. But he's curious enough about the coordinates to try. He agreed to sneak into the computer lab and see what the coordinates show him. He thinks we're nuts, of course. If there is a world closer than Canaan, why aren't we headed there? He has a point, but I also think that however our ancestors were able to search for new worlds to inhabit, they probably missed some. Anyway—he'll do it tomorrow night. I guess that's all for now. The word is spreading. I miss you. All my love."

"I miss you too, my dearest." Nephi ran his fingers across the page. The ball was rolling. Nephi carefully removed the page with the precious notes, and picked up the pencil to answer. He hadn't written anything by hand since he'd been in school, nine years ago. His handwriting was even worse than Prissa's, but he did his best.

"Thank you, my heart. You are amazing. Let me know what computer man finds. And tell Curls I love her. I love you,

too. I'm lonely here without you. I will start planning how to achieve our ends. Keep the faith. Love, Me."

The words seemed inadequate to express what he felt. Sal knew how to use them far better than he did. Speaking of which…

He used the pencil to mark the page, and turned to the front of Sal's journal. She'd been keeping it a long time, since just after her mother had died. There were sketches of her mother, of the baby sister she'd never known, of her father and brother, and others. Some Nephi recognized and some he didn't.

And there was poetry. Many poems spoke of loss and sorrow, but many rang with hope and beauty and love. They chronicled her grieving and her questioning and her laughter and joy. There were poems about him, too, and his visions, and her feelings for him. It was a glimpse into her heart like he'd never had before, and he loved her all the more for it and wished he could give her the same.

He flipped back to his note and added, *"P.S. Just like I thought. Everything in here is as beautiful as you are."*

Then, reluctantly, he returned the journal to the core.

Three days later, the journal was back. *"He found it. You were right. Of course you were. I never doubted that. The coordinates lead to a moon circling a gas giant in a binary star system. It's not as ideal as Canaan, but we can live there. The Kingdom of Heaven will be in the best position to reach it three months from now. If we can get off the ship then, it will take another five months to get there.*

Five months. He bowed his head and thanked God they could reach their new home. But a five month journey would still be tricky. They'd have to use the landers, there were no other space-faring vessels onboard, but those weren't designed for months-long travel, only short trips. There were no water recycling systems or food-growing areas like on the ship. They would have to bring enough food and water for the journey, as well as all they would need once they landed. Not to mention the small problem of gathering those supplies and launching the landers without President Black putting a stop to it.

He rubbed his eyes and read the rest of Sal's message. *"Computer man was impressed. I think he wants to know more about your teachings. He'll send all the info to your tab, so watch for that. I don't understand most of it, but he said we would need it to program a course into the landers. It's so hard to talk to anyone about it. The new supervisors watch and listen to everything we do. There is almost no chance for private conversation. It's frustrating. How can we plan anything? I suppose that's what Black wants. There must be a way. Secret meetings in the middle of the night might work. Of course, the three of us with the you-know-what would be left out. But we could get the info from others.*

Nephi leaned back against the wall, discouraged. The obstacles loomed in his mind, threatening to crush his hope into dust. It didn't help that everything he'd tried thus far had led to failure. To suffering and even death. He closed his eyes, envisioning Thomas' stern face which had always hidden his kind and loving heart. He ached thinking of the man. Dark thoughts wrapped icy fingers around his throat.

You can't lead these people to a new home. What makes you think you can? Leaving the ship is impossible. A death sentence. Give up now before anyone else gets hurt.

How many of his friends had endured stripes for following him? Brother Ryan had been removed from terrestrial deck, and all the leftovers now suffered more deprivations, thanks to him.

I ought to just turn myself in, pretend nothing happened, and let life go back to normal.

The dark and cold around him seeped into his chest. Yes, it would be for the best. Black would still cast him out. But then Prissa and Enoch could marry. Everyone would have enough food, more or less. They'd keep their heads down and not get punished. Death wouldn't come from gunshot wounds anymore. It would hurt Sal, but not forever. She'd be better off without him in the long run. Maybe Amaleki would marry her and take her up to terrestrial deck. Most everyone thought he was dead anyway. Maybe he ought to just skip President Black and make Elizabeth's lie the truth.

Nephi leaned against a wall, gasping for breath. Weight pressed on him, crushing his chest. He tried to pray, but no words would come. *Give in. Give up. Surrender to the pain.* He'd never been so helpless. So alone. Despair waited to swallow him whole.

His knees buckled, and he collapsed. Sal's journal rested under his hand. The soft fabric of the cover provided his only bit of comfort. *Sal.* With effort, he pulled himself up, flipped open the journal and found the sketch she had drawn depicting him and Uriel in the core. He ran his fingers across the drawing and remembered. He had felt this darkness before. In the core when Uriel appeared to him. How had he forgotten?

"Lord," he whispered, hands trembling around the journal, "please save me from this darkness. Deliver me."

A warmth spread through him. The pressure in his chest and around his throat lightened. He flipped to one of Sal's poems—an expression of faith and devotion and joy at the promises of God.

I will see the sunshine
In some eternal world.
I will bathe in the glory of the Lord
And dance among the stars forever.

He closed his eyes, breathing deeply, at last free from the darkness. Suddenly, he understood something of what his father must have felt. Elizabeth too. He bowed his head. "Thank you, Lord. And Sal. Thanks to her, too." He flipped over the page to respond to her note.

"We will meet in the core at 1am two days from now. Five people—those who can lead the rest. And I'll get all the information to you in person. You mean more to me than words can say. You saved me tonight with your poems and pictures. I hope we don't use up all the pages in here, because I know you have more beauty to create."

He closed the book and held it between his hands for a long time before he stood, on shaking legs, and returned it to the core.

Nephi found the core empty at the appointed time for the meeting. He let himself freefall into the space and tried not to worry. No journal waited for him on the kitchen level landing, either. He caught a rung on the central pillar and swung hard the other direction. How long had it been since he'd last been in the core merely for the joy of it? Before he met Elizabeth, for sure. He missed the sense of freedom the core had always given him, when ironically, he'd never been free then at all.

He wasn't exactly free now, in hiding and alone, but President Black and his twisted version of religion no longer controlled his life or his destiny. Ammon may want him dead, but he couldn't dictate Nephi's actions.

But that freedom had come with a weight of responsibility, too—the burden of knowledge, the gravity of his commitments to God. And yet it was responsibility, knowledge, and covenants that would make him truly free. He wouldn't trade that for a few minutes of carefree floating—or even for a lifetime of it.

A panel opened and sent a thrill of fear through him. He spun around the pillar until he caught sight of them. Phoebe, Jarom Jenson, Sherem Hunsaker, Enoch's father Alma, and Brother Ryan stood uncertainly on the agri-deck landing. Nephi dove—or perhaps flew—toward them. He grasped the rail and vaulted onto the landing.

Phoebe gasped. "You don't expect us to go out there, do you?"

"It is a bit crowded here on the landing." Nephi grinned and wrapped her in a bear hug. "I've missed you so much."

"I missed you, too." Phoebe's eyes went all watery. "Especially when I thought you were dead."

Nephi let her go. "I'm sorry about that. I didn't know what else to do. And I didn't dare come out of hiding." He looked around at the six of them squished onto the landing. "Still don't dare, I suppose."

"You're doing the right thing," Phoebe said, her hand on his shoulder. "And we're here to help."

"I am thankful for that," Nephi said. "For all of you coming here in light of what Black has done." He looked at Brother Ryan. "I'm so sorry you got removed from your deck."

"If what Enoch has been teaching me is true, it doesn't matter what deck President Black assigns me to, right?"

"Not in the eternal world. But terrestrial deck has a higher standard of living in the here and now."

"Some things are more valuable than comfort in the here and now," Brother Ryan said.

"True." Nephi's throat tightened. "And I am grateful for your sacrifice. God will surely repay you all you have lost, and more."

"I have no doubt of it."

Nephi slapped Brother Ryan on the back and he winced. Nephi pulled his hand away. "You got stripes?"

Brother Ryan nodded. "They're healing, thanks to Phoebe." He nodded in her direction.

"Same here," Jarom said, bitterness tinging his voice.

Sherem put his on Jarom's shoulder. "We bear them as a badge of honor," he said. "Like you said before. They are a symbol of what we fight for."

"That's a hard badge to bear." Nephi stretched the scars across his back.

"We bear it together," Sherem said. "That makes it easier."

Until that moment, Nephi hadn't realized what a weight he'd had to carry alone. But now he knew others shared that burden, and he could go on. They would succeed. He cleared his throat. "Okay. I assume Sal told you what the Lord wants us to do."

"It sounds impossible," Phoebe said. "But I have learned not to use that word when it comes to you."

Nephi smiled. "Right you are, Phoebe. With God, nothing is impossible." He took out his tab and showed them Amaleki's information about the moon—their future home. One by one they passed around the tab, most of them looking as perplexed as Nephi felt.

"It doesn't all make a lot of sense to me, either. But Amaleki says it's a livable world. Air, water, plants, animals, the whole works."

"And it's a moon?" Brother Ryan asked. "Fascinating."

"Yes. The Lord showed it to me in vision. I thought I was looking at Heaven."

"How will we get there?" Phoebe asked. A straightforward question unclouded by doubt. Nephi could have hugged her again.

"That's where things get tricky. In three months, we'll reach the best position to launch toward the moon. The journey will take five months from that point. Our only option is to use the some of the colony landers and supplies."

"Black won't give those up willingly," Jarom said.

"No, and I don't intend to ask him. This is God's will and we will take what we need. The *Kingdom of Heaven* will have hundreds of years to make up whatever we take from them. Are we agreed?"

The five of them nodded. "Agreed," Sherem said.

"Good. First we need to find out how many people are willing to come. We'll take anyone who wants to go, but we'll need a fairly accurate headcount so we know how many landers to take. How much food, water, oxygen reserves, and everything else we need for the five months out, and all we need to survive when we reach our new home. When we have a good idea about that, we can work on actually putting it all together."

"I hope you don't expect this to be easy," Phoebe said.

"No, I don't. It isn't meant to be easy. It's meant to test us. But God will provide the way."

He looked each of them in the eyes. "This will require our full commitment, our heart, might, mind, and strength. I'm sure this journey will be difficult. Settling a new world is dangerous. You guys understand that as well as I do. There will be sacrifices required of us." He glanced at Phoebe. "In fact, they have already begun."

Nephi took Phoebe's hand on his left and Brother Ryan's on his right. "Let's pray together."

The others joined hands in the circle. Nephi bowed his head and let the clamor of worry and stress fall away so all he could hear was the voice of the Spirit. Then into the sacred silence that descended, Nephi began to pray.

Chapter 28

Weeks passed with a flurry of notes in the journal. Notes from Sal and Prissa and Enoch. Notes from his five captains, as he had come to think of them, and weekly midnight meetings in the core. A plan had taken shape, though it was certainly easier to talk about than to make reality. First, they needed access to permanent storage and the landers in particular. That's where Amaleki came in. After much prayer and considering, Nephi took the chance of contacting him with his tab. Sal, was right. Amaleki was interested in hearing what Nephi had to say, and while he didn't say he'd go with them when they left, he did agree to bypass the locks on permanent storage to help them.

They would take eight landers, with fifty to sixty people in each. Since the landers were designed to hold two hundred, plus cargo, they would have plenty of space for extra supplies and extra systems they hoped to rig up—systems for air and water cycling, sanitation, and aeroponics. There would even be space for some small semblance of privacy within families, if they slept in rotations. And, by the grace of God, the landers were already equipped with artificial gravity. Brother Ryan guessed it was to make cargo hauling easier. Nephi didn't care why it was there. It made the journey possible, and for that he thanked the Lord day and night.

Now they had two months remaining to get everything ready—in secret. Without alerting the celestials. Nephi found it both exhilarating and terrifying at the same time. But something bothered him still. The spirit pricked him over it enough that he risked everything to sneak down to the filter room in the middle of the day. Banking on the fact that the supervisor wouldn't spend much time hanging around the smelly filters, Nephi took a breathless elevator ride down and sprinted around the level in an ironic reversal of his escape two months before.

The door to the filter room opened and Nephi flinched at the memory of Zeniff bleeding on the floor. A clatter pulled him from his reverie. Enoch had dropped his scrubber.

"Nephi! What are you doing in here? You want to get killed?"

"Is your boss around?" He checked the room, heart rate spiking.

"No, but he could be any time. He checks in pretty often." Enoch scowled. "I might as well be a prisoner."

"That's why I'm here," Nephi said. "I wanted to see you. Talk to you. I know you're unhappy."

"Really?" Enoch snorted. "Why would I be unhappy? Just because I can't live with my wife. Can't help my friends. Can't be a part of your grand scheme." He stooped to pick up his scrubber and walked back to the filter he'd been working on.

Nephi followed him, praying the supervisor wouldn't walk in. "You think I don't know how tough it is? I'm not living with my wife, either. I'm not living anywhere. I have to spend my days in freezing darkness. I never get to see my best friend."

Enoch frowned at the filter. "I know, okay? I'm sorry."

"Me too," Nephi said. "This isn't exactly the life we were planning on, is it?"

Enoch met Nephi's gaze, but didn't respond.

"It's only two more months. Then we'll be free. And even if you can't do much now, I still need you. I need your leadership and your willing hands. We're going to need everyone to survive on this new world."

"If we even get there."

"You don't think we will?" It hurt more than he wanted to admit, that doubt.

Enoch dropped his gaze again. "I don't know. It doesn't seem possible."

Nephi walked to the tool rack and pulled off a scrubber. He sat down opposite Enoch and began to scrub. "Yep. It's completely crazy. But so is seeing an angel. So is breaking into the celestials' temple. Crazy hasn't stopped us yet, has it?"

"Not yet." A small, not quite happy smile touched Enoch's lips.

"And it's not going to now. We can do this. We will do this. It's a matter of faith, that's all."

For a dozen long seconds, the only sound was the soft scratch of the scrubbers. Then Enoch set his down. "I'm trying. I really am. But this thing in my wrist, you know? I hate it."

"I do too. But it won't be that way forever. Can you hang on? Can I count on you? I need you, and I need to know you're behind us on this."

Enoch closed his eyes and sighed. "I'm with you, Nephi. All the way."

Nephi stood. "Good. Things will get better eventually, I promise."

Enoch nodded, unsmiling. "You'd better get out of here."

"But I was really enjoying the scrubbing." Nephi grinned, but it didn't last. "Two more months. Then we're free."

He slipped back out the door, jogged lightly down the hall, and reached the elevator just as an angry voice rang out. "Hey, you there! You're not supposed to be down here."

But Nephi was gone before the owner of the voice could catch up.

Nephi and his captains led groups of sixteen on midnight runs every night to permanent storage. Never the same group twice. Nephi didn't want the supervisors noticing a rash of sleep deprivation among the leftovers. They worked in two-man teams, preparing the landers.

First up was creating a water recycling system from the landers' existing, tiny plumbing system. All the necessary parts were in permanent storage, and Nephi's tab provided the designs. It took a few days to get that done.

The landers all contained large water tanks intended to bring fresh water down to get the new colony started, and even better, were meant to be filled from the huge reservoirs of water at the top and bottom of the core, which wouldn't be monitored as closely as the ship's main water supplies. A system to pipe the water into the landers was already in place, and Nephi's crews filled the tanks without anyone the wiser. They built aeroponic growing areas, space to keep animal embryos, and semi-private living spaces in the cabin for the families who would make the journey.

After that, it was just a matter of pilfering the supplies, farm and construction machinery, generators, fuel, and emergency food supplements. Everything they could think of to take with them. The info on Nephi's tab helped tremendously with that.

Three weeks before their scheduled departure, all that remained was getting food for the weeks before their aeroponic systems began producing. Acting on a prompting, Nephi found a room full of silver-wrapped packages labeled MRE, which turned out to be food, though not much better than a sludge shake. The MREs would do, but it was looking like a hungry journey ahead. They would do it, though, one way or another.

Nephi made his way to the core at midnight, mentally checking off items on the night's to-do list. Foremost now was figuring out how to launch the things without anyone knowing until it was too late. Black couldn't do anything to them once they were free of the ship, but getting free of the ship would be the hard part. He suspected they would need Amaleki's help again, if he was willing or even able to give it.

"Good evening, folks. We have plenty to do tonight. I believe Prissa got us some more fabric to use for curtains in the living area." He stopped when he saw only Sherem and Reuben on the landing.

"What's wrong?"

"It's Sal," Sherem said.

Nephi's heart stuttered against his ribs. "What happened? Is she okay?"

Reuben shook his head. Sherem's shoulders slumped. "I think Black figured out you're not dead. Someone must have said something to the wrong person. Ammon's men came for Salome after work. We didn't know where she'd gone. They brought her back an hour ago. She's hurt bad. She's with Phoebe and Prissa now. They'll take care of her."

"I'm going to see her. You two take over tonight." He opened the access panel.

"Nephi, it could be a trap. Maybe you should—"

"I'm going to see her." He stepped onto agri-deck and didn't look back. He ran, his footsteps echoing his heartbeat, barely registering his surroundings, blinded by fear. His feet took him to Phoebe's apartment without conscious effort. Waiting for someone to open the door was agony.

Prissa's eyes went wide when she saw him standing in the hall. "You shouldn't be down here."

"Like hell I shouldn't." He pushed past her more roughly than he intended. Phoebe's apartment for two was nicer than his and Prissa's, with a decent size sitting room and an actual wall separating it from the bedroom beyond. Nephi flung open the door, leaving Prissa out front.

Sal lay in one of the beds, on her side. Swollen, purple bruises covered her face. Phoebe knelt beside her, cleaning a wound on her head.

Anger flared through him. He would kill whoever had done this to her. He knelt beside her and reached for her hand. That's when he noticed the bandage wrapped around her shoulders and torso. "Stripes?"

Phoebe nodded. "That's not all," she whispered.

"What?" His hand tightened around Sal's.

"Nephi?" Sal stirred. She tried to open her eyes, but couldn't.

"I'm here, Sal." He brought her hand to his lips.

"Nephi." She tried to sit up but cried out with pain.

"Just lie still. It's all right." His hand hovered over her, trying to find someplace his touch wouldn't hurt her. He settled for her hip.

She winced. "Nephi," she choked out, anguished. "They took our baby. They took it. I couldn't stop them."

"Our baby?" He shot a questioning look at Phoebe.

"I couldn't stop them," Sal moaned. She sobbed, tears squeezing past her battered eyes to wet the bruises on her cheeks.

"She was pregnant," Phoebe whispered. "The High Council ordered it terminated." She balled up her hands. "They wouldn't recognize your marriage, of course."

"I'm so sorry," Sal sobbed. "I tried to stop them."

"Shh. It's not your fault." Nephi grasped both her hands and bent his head over them. "How did they know?" he asked Phoebe softly.

"Probably through her tracker."

Sorrow burned Nephi's throat. His gut twisted and the room spun. He wanted to hold his beloved, but even that comfort was denied him. His thoughts swam around the dizzying sense of loss for something he hadn't even known he had. A child. Gone. His tears dripped onto their joined hands.

Gradually, Sal's sobs quieted. Her breathing slowed. Nephi felt a hand on his shoulder and lifted his head. "I gave her some sleeping tea," Phoebe said. Nephi nodded. He kissed Sal's hands and rested them on the bed. With effort he came to his feet. Grief and anger wrapped chains around him.

"Why?" he asked Phoebe. "Why would they kill our baby?" His voice came out heavy and raw.

"It certainly isn't standard procedure. Usually an unwed pregnancy results in a few stripes and forced marriage. Not this." She put her hands on Nephi's shoulder. "They didn't just terminate her pregnancy. They gave her a hysterectomy, too."

"What's that?"

"They took out her womb, Nephi. She'll never have children now."

His insides crumbled. "Does she know?"

Phoebe shook her head. "She was too distraught about the baby. I couldn't tell her." Her chin quivered. "This seems too cruel and malicious even for Jeremiah Black."

"Maybe he wasn't behind it." Nephi felt his face contort with the rage inside him. "Ammon Nielsen-Black is behind this. He is that cruel and malicious."

"Nephi." Phoebe's voice grew firm. "You aren't going to ruin everything we've worked for by taking revenge."

Nephi tensed. She'd read his mind before he knew it himself. He clenched his hands to stop the shaking. "I won't," he said through his teeth.

"Leave the justice to God," Phoebe said.

Nephi took a deep breath in an attempt to calm himself. He ran his hand over the scruffy beard he hadn't had a chance to shave off lately. "I know. I know. You're right." He gazed down at Sal in her drug-induced, peaceful slumber. "Will she recover?"

"She'll heal, but it will take time. Emotionally? That will take a lot longer. It will affect her the rest of her life."

"Oh, Sal." If only he could take her pain away. "I want to be here when you tell her."

"I'll try," Phoebe said. "We may not be able to keep it from her. She'll know something's wrong."

"I understand." He sat down on the edge of the bed. "I'll stay until she wakes up. You'd better tell her then."

"You should go, Nephi. It isn't safe."

"I don't care. I'm not leaving her. Not yet."

The front door chimed, followed by a loud knock. Nephi froze, his spine rigid. Both he and Phoebe faced the bedroom door.

They heard Prissa answer the door. "Enoch."

Nephi relaxed. He started for the door.

"Is Nephi here?"

Something in the tenor of Enoch's voice made Nephi pause, his hand stretched toward the door handle.

"He's with Sal. I'll get him."

"Wait."

Nephi glanced at Phoebe. Something was definitely wrong. He considered ducking under the empty bed.

Prissa let out a shriek. "You brought them here?"

"Hide," Phoebe whispered.

Nephi looked down at Sal, still asleep, and made a split-second decision. He opened the door and stepped into the front room. And came face to face with Ammon Nielsen-Black and a cadre of elders armed with guns and rods. Hyrum was with them, but Nephi didn't see Zeniff.

"How could you?" Prissa screamed. Enoch had her by the arms to keep her from punching him.

"I did it for you." Enoch shot a glance at Nephi and looked at the ground. "If I didn't, they'd have done the same to you as they did to Sal. You're pregnant, too. I couldn't let that happen. I had no choice."

"You had a choice!" Prissa tried to twist out of his grip. "You didn't have to turn him in. I hate you!" Her face had gone bright red. Enoch looked stunned.

"Prissa stop." Nephi said. "You'll wake Sal."

Prissa stopped struggling, but she didn't turn off her death glare. Enoch dropped her arms, and she ran to Phoebe.

"So," Ammon stepped toward Nephi. "You're ready to accept your fate?"

"You almost killed my wife," Nephi said. He didn't move.

"She's not your wife. You're a heretic and a fornicator. Whatever happened to that girl, you brought it upon her."

Nephi's gut twisted at the truth in those words.

"Now it's time to face your judgment."

An uncanny sense of calm settled over Nephi. He lifted his arms and allowed Ammon to bind them without speaking.

"No!" Prissa threw herself toward him, but Phoebe held her back.

"Be brave, "Nephi said. "And please tell Sal I love her. Forever."

"Come on." Ammon grabbed Nephi's arm and jerked him forward. The elders flanked them on either side.

"Nephi." Enoch stepped toward him when they approached the door. "I'm sorry. You would have done the same thing in my place. To protect Prissa." He set his jaw, daring Nephi to deny it.

Nephi stared his best friend in the eye. "You're right. I would have."

Then Ammon and the elders herded him out into the hall.

Chapter 29

Nephi found it absurdly amusing that the first thing Ammon had done to him was to take him by his hair and forcibly shave off his beard. As if facial hair were the worst of his crimes. He'd wanted to get rid of the itchy monstrosity for days anyway. The rest of what Ammon had done to him was much less amusing. Aching and bruised, he lay bound hand and foot on the bare cot of the lock-up cell and waited for the summons to appear before the High Council.

He prayed as he lay there aching—prayed for Sal and Prissa and Phoebe and even for Enoch. For all his followers, but not for himself. He had accepted his fate with an ease that surprised him. It really would be all right, as he'd told Prissa—as he'd told Thomas Sharpe months ago. The work would go on without him. It would have to.

The cell door opened, framing Ammon and Hyrum in the bright hallway beyond.

"Morning already?" Nephi made no attempt to sit up.

"We have convened the High Council for your disciplinary court," Ammon said.

"Lovely."

Hyrum came over and pulled him upright, then bent and removed the bands from Nephi's feet.

"How's Zeniff?" Nephi asked under his breath. A genuine question.

"None of your business." Hyrum hauled him to his feet and led him from the room. They marched through the back corridors of celestial deck, past the penance rooms and offices of the High Council, and through the back door of the High Council room, where fifteen men in their beards and fine celestial suits waited to pass judgment on him. Again.

It surprised Nephi they'd even bother with the formality of a disciplinary court. Black must want a big, public spectacle to make sure everybody knew for certain Nephi was dead this time.

He lifted his chin and straightened his shoulders as much as his restraints allowed. Hyrum brought him to the empty space at the foot of the table and left. Ammon took his place at Jeremiah Black's side.

President Black folded his hands on the table. His eyes held no anger, no triumph, only calm, unflappable superiority. "You've certainly stirred things up around here, young man."

"I hope so," Nephi said. "High time they got stirred."

"Unfortunately, Brother Packard, your ideas are dangerous to the stability of this ship and its mission."

"Dangerous to your position onboard, maybe."

Black spread his hands flat. "You have no idea how the power structure on this ship works or why it works. But, then, I wouldn't expect you to."

Nephi shifted his feet. "Because I'm a mere telestial leftover and can't grasp these grand concepts?"

"That's right. You would have done well to remember your place after the first time you were in here."

Already, Nephi's battered body ached from standing. Talking hurt so much he thought his jaw must be dislocated. He fell silent. A hint of a smile formed on Black's face. "Read the charges."

Lamoni Black stood. "Nephi Packard, you are accused of the sins of blasphemy, heresy, desecration, fornication, theft, attempted murder of Zeniff Bradshaw, and evading discipline. Will you now confess your faults before this council?"

Nephi swallowed and licked his swollen lips. "Yes. I have committed blasphemy in speaking the truth. Heresy in showing you as you really are. I entered your corrupted temple and sanctified it. I shot Zeniff to protect my own life, and stole food to keep myself alive while avoiding your unjust discipline. And though we may not be married in your eyes, Salome and I are sealed together by the power of God. One day you will answer to the Almighty for how you ravaged her."

"That's enough," Ammon said, rising. "We've heard enough."

"Yes, we have," Black said. "Proceed with the sentencing."

Counselor Black cleared his throat. "Nephi Packard, for the sins enumerated here and many others, you are sentenced to be cast out of this ship and your name blotted out of our records. You have forfeited your kingdom and glory and are consigned to outer darkness for eternity."

Nephi almost laughed at that. As if the High Council had any say in his eternal destiny.

"This sentence will be carried out at six o'clock this evening in view of the full population of the *Kingdom of Heaven*. Before being cast out, you will confess your sins publicly and denounce your heretical teachings as the lies they are. In so doing, God may exercise some small measure of mercy according to His eternal will." Lamoni sat back down, not looking at Nephi.

President Black stood, unruffled. "Brother Packard, it saddens me that you have chosen damnation. I only hope your punishment will serve as a warning to any you may have seduced with your wicked philosophies. It will be a relief to put this behind us at last." He nodded to the High Council and left.

"You may cast me out," Nephi said quietly. President Black paused, half-turned toward the door. "You may silence my voice." He stood taller despite the pain from his bonds. "But the truth will no longer be restrained. You cannot keep us in our place anymore. Even if I'm gone, the work of God will move forward."

Black shook his head. "Deceived to the end, I see. It's tempting to leave you alive long enough to see your little rebellion collapse. It won't take long." His smug smile returned. "And if you think your insane plan to leave the ship will save you, you're even more ignorant than I thought."

So, he knew about that? Of course he did. He'd taken Nephi's tab. His heart withered inside him, but he kept his head up, and didn't drop his gaze from Black's.

"Take him away," Black said. "And make the announcement. Attendance in the chapel is mandatory." He leaned toward Nephi. "You will renounce all your lies or your most loyal supporters will suffer a fate similar to the whore you call a wife. I will have order on this ship by whatever means necessary."

Nephi tasted bile. Someone grabbed his arm. Hyrum had returned. Ammon made no attempt to disguise his gloating as he accompanied Nephi and Hyrum back to the prison cell.

"Enjoy your last few hours, Nephi," Ammon said. "You could pray for mercy, but I doubt you'll get any." Then the prison door snicked shut and Nephi was alone.

He lay on the cot on his back, bound hand and foot once again, and stared at the ceiling, not thinking, not feeling. He couldn't tell how many hours had passed. Whether his execution was near or still far off. He didn't know what he'd say when Black made him speak. He couldn't deny what he knew was true, but he didn't want Prissa or Phoebe or any of his friends to suffer, either. So he stopped thinking about it altogether. If he was honest with himself, he'd acknowledge that he was scared. Terrified. He didn't want to die. Did that make him a coward? Did it make him faithless and unbelieving? Did it mean he'd been wrong about everything?

No. No, he couldn't be wrong. If he had to die, then so be it. Joseph Smith had died, hadn't he? Surely Sal and the rest would go on one way or another. He had to believe that. He blinked at the silent ceiling, wishing Uriel would appear with an army of angels and make it all go away, but that wasn't going to happen.

The door to the cell opened. It was time already, then. Nephi turned his head. His breath caught when he saw not Ammon or Hyrum or any of the elders, but Prissa and Phoebe supporting Sal between them.

Nephi struggled to sit. Prissa helped him up while Phoebe lowered Sal onto the cot beside him. "You should be in bed," Nephi said. But the sight of her was pure water to his barren heart.

"I had to see you, didn't I? Given the chance." Sal reached for his bound hands. Her face looked better. Less swollen.

She could open her eyes again, more or less. She tried to smile at him. "We're both a sight, aren't we?"

Nephi squeezed her hand between his. "How did you get up here? Black's not allowing visitors, is he?"

"No," Phoebe said. "Hyrum brought us."

"Hyrum?" Nephi blinked, confused. Maybe he hadn't heard correctly. "Hyrum Bradshaw brought you to see me?"

"Yes," Phoebe said. "He said he'd been ordered to take me to a holding cell, but that he'd take us all to see you first—if I came without a fuss. He's waiting outside in the hall. He said he'd get Prissa and Sal home safely, too. A holding cell seems a small price to pay."

"It won't be small," Nephi said grimly. "Black plans to torture you if I don't deny everything."

Sal sucked in her breath, and Prissa's hand flew to her mouth, but Phoebe was unfazed. "Don't worry about me. And don't even think about denying any of it, understand?" Phoebe knelt in front of him. "Nephi, there's something I need to tell you. I should have done it a long time ago. It's about your father.

The room went still "What about him?" Nephi said in a hush.

"He didn't take his own life as you were told."

Prissa uttered a strangled gasp.

"No. President Black cast him out in secret. Your father—he had questions. Questions about God and the scriptures, about President Black's authority and the inequality on the ship."

Nephi couldn't breathe. Phoebe continued. "The High Council gave him stripes for heresy when he asked his questions a little too loudly, but your father refused to recant.

"I was with him, treating his stripe wounds, when the elders came for him again." She bowed her head and rested her hand on Nephi's shackled wrists. "Black said your father had cast himself out in despair because Black feared his heresy would spread. And I…I didn't tell anyone the truth. I agreed with Black, I guess. I thought your father's ideas were dangerous. I didn't want anyone else to end up dead." Her chin quivered. "I'm sorry. I was wrong. But you should know your father would be so proud of you, Nephi. He would be so happy about what you've done here."

Nephi closed his eyes, and saw again his father bathed in light, beckoning him, pleading with him. A drop of healing balm entered his broken heart. *Oh, Dad.*

"Thank you, Phoebe." Then with sudden, perfect clarity, Nephi knew what he had to say. "Black knows about the landers. He knows about the plan. He has my tab. But today he's distracted with casting me out. You need to go. Leave now before he can undo all of our work."

"I won't leave you." Sal laid her head on his shoulder.

"You can do it, love. You can go on without me. You have to, Sal. You can keep this whole thing going forward. We've lost our tabs. We don't have the scriptures, but we still have the Book of Mormon Uriel gave me. It's with my things in the unused sections. Send someone to find it. I can tell you where it is. It won't be everything, but it will be enough. You can teach the people. You can lead them."

"I can't," she whispered.

"Yes, you can. Start with what you've already written in your journal. Write down everything you can remember. Everything the spirit tells you to write."

"Nephi—" Sal's head dropped. Her back shuddered with tears.

"Don't cry, Salome. I'll always be near you. I promise. And one day, like I said before, we'll never be apart again."

"We can't leave," Sal sniffed. "We aren't in position. We'll spend so much fuel making course corrections, we won't be able to safely land."

"God will make a way."

Prissa sat down on his other side and wrapped her arms around him. "Oh, Nephi." She buried her face against his chest. "I can't bear it."

"Priscilla, listen to me. You have to forgive Enoch."

"Never." She didn't lift her head.

"He did it for you. Because he loves you. And your child."

"I don't care. I never want to talk to him ever again."

"That will do nothing but make you both miserable."

"So you want me to stay here and become a terrestrial? Because that's part of the deal they made. To move us to terrestrial deck."

"No. I want you to make sure he comes with you. And that he knows I forgive him, even if you can't."

"I don't want you to die," Prissa said. "It was hard enough the first time."

Phoebe leaned forward and wrapped her arms around all three of them. Sal's and Prissa's arms came around him too, until he was enfolded in their embrace. He clenched his shackled fists. "Be strong for me, okay? And keep going, no matter what." He could hardly breathe around the lump in his throat. "I have been incredibly blessed to have you three in my life. Promise me you'll take care of each other."

"We will," Prissa said.

Sal leaned her head against his. "I love you, Nephi."

"I'll love you forever," he whispered in her ear.

"Prissa, you make sure Sal gets to the landers. Get someone to carry her. You're going to see our new home, Sal. You'll live there for many happy years. I promise."

The cell door opened. Hyrum cleared his throat. "I'm sorry. We have to leave."

Prissa and Phoebe stood. Sal stayed leaning against Nephi. She really wasn't in any shape to be moved. He kept hold of her hand.

"Set Nephi free," Prissa said to Hyrum, her hands on her hips.

"I can't do that," Hyrum said.

"Why not?"

"I'd be cast out myself." He met Nephi's eyes. "I will do what I can for Sister Sharpe. I figure I owe you for saving Zeniff. Of course, you shot him first, but... I've never seen anything like that when you blessed him." He paused. "But that's all I can do for you. I'm sorry."

"It's more than enough. Thank you for bringing my family here."

Hyrum nodded. "Let's go."

Prissa let out a strangled sob. Sal scooted closer to Nephi. "I won't leave you." She gasped.

"Are you in pain?"

"It doesn't matter."

"You need to rest. Save your strength." If she'd even survive the journey. Despite his promise to her, he wasn't sure.

Phoebe helped Sal up. Sal hardly had the strength to stand. Prissa stepped up, still hiccupping out tears, and supported Sal on the other side.

"Nephi," Phoebe said. "I don't want you to think about me at all, okay? We will both do what we must. We all will, right ladies?"

Prissa nodded, unable to speak. Sal didn't appear to have heard. She was losing consciousness. Hyrum scooped up her limp form. Nephi had to bite his tongue to keep his protest back. "We have to go before anyone sees us," Hyrum said.

Prissa watched Nephi over her shoulder until the door slid shut between them and he was alone again. In the quiet swish of the air current, he thought he heard in his memory the echoes of Prissa's wind chimes. He could hear Phoebe's solid lecturing and see Sal's rare and radiant smile. He bent his head and wept.

Chapter 30

Hyrum came back some time later with a bundle of clean clothes. "They want you cleaned up," he said, not meeting Nephi's gaze.

"Don't like the blood-stained, in-hiding-for-weeks look, huh?"

Hyrum didn't respond. He released Nephi's leg bonds and helped him to his feet. The room swayed a little. Nephi staggered, but Hyrum kept him upright. They came out into the hall.

"Is Zeniff okay?" Nephi asked.

"He's healing," Hyrum muttered. "But he's changed."

"Changed how?"

"He won't work for Ammon anymore, for one thing."

"But you will?"

"I have my reasons." Hyrum yanked him forward. Nephi stumbled but stayed upright.

"Are you sure they're the right reasons?"

"Look, I brought your family to see you. I don't owe you anything anymore."

"Even if you did, it wouldn't matter in a few minutes anyway."

"Shut up." Hyrum jabbed his finger against a door pad. The door opened on a real bathroom with a shower and soap and everything. Hyrum opened the wrist cuffs and handed Nephi the clothes. "Make it quick."

Nephi took his time. Why hurry to his execution? He turned the water as hot as he could stand, and let it wash the filth from his abused body. It stung in places, but he didn't care. He scrubbed from top to toe until all the blood and grime and sweat had been rinsed down the drain. The water ran cold, and Hyrum pounded on the door before Nephi finally got out and dried off.

He pulled on the clothes Hyrum had brought—a shapeless pair of drawstring pants and a loose, long-sleeved top, both of the same, plain, cream-colored cotton. They were softer than his usual work clothes. His damp hair hung almost to his shoulder after all the time he'd neglected to cut it. He squeezed the water out and ran his fingers through it, then looked himself over in the mirror. So. That's what his body would look like floating through the cosmos until the end of time. Whenever that was. Probably he wouldn't care what happened to his body once he left it. Maybe his parents would be there to greet him. That would be nice.

And, really, Sal and Prissa and the rest would go on without him as well as they could. Maybe they'd get to the new world God had shown him, or maybe that was a dream for future generations.

Even if they accomplished nothing but planting the seed of truth in the hearts of his people, it would be enough. If they passed those seeds on to their children—who knew what might blossom someday.

He examined the simple, plain clothing and realized it was likely what all the deceased wore when sent on their final journey. No need to waste perfectly good clothing after all. He gave his reflection a rueful smile.

Hyrum pounded again. "Don't make me come in there, Packard."

"I'm ready," Nephi said. As ready as he'd ever be. He came out of the bathroom, and Hyrum put the band around his wrists again. They walked to the airlock in silence. Nothing more to say. They passed nameless doors and empty corridors and were soon far away from the busy residential and work areas, into a part of the ship with only metal on the walls and floors that echoed beneath their footsteps.

The High Council stood in a semi-circle in front of the thick, steel door—the only one on the ship that didn't raise itself up, but had to be physically opened and sealed by means of a wheel placed at the door's center. Ammon stood at the wheel, a delighted gleam in his eyes.

Nephi's heart began to pound, asserting its unwillingness to give up beating. They stopped in front of Jeremiah Black, at the center of the half-circle, and Hyrum withdrew into the line of armed elders arrayed on either side of the airlock door. One of the elders held a camera rather than a gun, recording the scene. The people must be all gathered in the chapel now. That would be a good time for his followers to make a break for the landers. *Lord, save thy people,* he prayed silently. *I've done what I can to teach them what you asked. Please guide them, give them courage and strength. Let the work go on when I'm gone.*

"Nephi Packard," Black said, "you have been found guilty of heresy, blasphemy, desecration, attempted murder, fornication, theft, and other sins, and have been sentenced to be cast into outer darkness. Will you now confess your sins before the body of the *Kingdom of Heaven* and thereby attain some measure of mercy on your soul?"

Nephi looked Black in the eye. "I will."

"Good choice," Black murmured.

The cameraman focused in on Nephi. He lifted his chin, hoping his fear didn't show. *Forgive me, Phoebe.* But this is what she'd told him to do. "My brothers and sisters," he said, "you may already have heard the story of how the archangel Uriel appeared to me in the ship's core, how he gave me the Book of Mormon and access to other scriptures. He gave me the task of spreading the truth of the gospel, especially the truth that we are all equal in the eyes of God and loved by Him."

Black gave him a dark look.

"Jeremiah Black is asking me to tell you all of that is a lie. That I made it up to try and get above my station. He would have me confess that my teachings are false and his are true."

Black relaxed a little.

"I must confess that under the laws of this ship, I am guilty of all the sins I am accused of. But under the eyes of the Almighty God, I am an innocent man. I have spoken the truth, and I will not deny what I have seen with my own eyes. I cannot lie to God, and I have not and will not lie to you. Each of you must consider what you've heard and decide what is true and what is right."

Black made a swiping motion across his throat, and the cameraman turned on him instead. "You're mercy is forfeit. You are consigned to eternal torment. Your followers will be punished appropriately." He spoke to Ammon. "Proceed."

Ammon at least had the decency not to gloat on camera. With a somber expression, he twisted the metal wheel and pulled open the thick door to the airlock. He removed Nephi's cuffs, one small bit of dignity, he supposed.

Nephi squared his shoulders and stepped into the airlock of his own volition. No one would force him to accept his fate. He hoped he looked brave, but in truth his heart was about to burst out of his chest. His breath came out in hard, panicked gasps.

The door clanged shut behind him like his death knell. He swallowed hard and tried to slow his breathing. The opposite hatch had a large window revealing the black of space and a million brilliant stars. Nephi stood with his legs apart and his hands clasped behind his back and contemplated the stars. It reminded him of the celestial room, when Uriel had set him apart as a prophet. And now he was to die for it. How long would he have, he wondered, to appreciate the heavenly view before the vacuum of space took his life? He forced himself to keep his eyes open so he wouldn't miss a second of it.

More breaths passed. His heartbeat slowed. Why had they not cast him out already? Prolonging the suspense, perhaps? He kept his eyes fixed forward. Black, his ilk, and most especially Ammon, would not get the pleasure of seeing him flinch or fidget. Soon, he would face his God and give an accounting of all he had done. In the end, it didn't seem like much. He did wish he'd been able to see Sal one last time. To hold her like she deserved to be held.

Still the hatch did not open. The silence of the airlock pressed around him and made breathing more difficult. A wickedly clever way to make being cast out more agonizing. But, really, what were they waiting for?

He turned around slowly, which seemed more dignified than just looking over his shoulder. Figures moved outside the little round window in the door, but of course he could hear no sound in here. He stepped to the window for a closer look.

He gaped at the scene before him.

His friends had come to save him.

Jarom, Sherem, Alma, Reuben, Micah—and was that Zeniff? It was—had the elders and the High Council disarmed and standing at gunpoint with their arms in the air.

God bless them!

And there in the center of it all was Hyrum, with his gun pressed to President Black's temple. Nephi's head swam. Splatters of red dotted the bottom of the window. So, there had been shooting after all.

Movement caught the corner of his eye. He jerked his head, and saw Ammon moving toward him. Nephi sensed what was coming. Instinctively, he wrapped his arms through the wheel on the door. The far hatch into space popped open. Nephi filled his lungs with air and held his breath. The force of depressurization nearly ripped him off the wheel. He thought his arms might tear right out of their sockets, but he held on with all his strength. Still, he felt his grip slipping. He squeezed his eyes shut. This was not how he'd intended to bravely face his death, but the sight of his friends fighting for him had hardened his resolve to live. *Oh, please, God. Not now. Not when I'm so close to freedom."*

The hatch whooshed closed again. Nephi slumped against the door. He didn't dare let out his breath. The airlock door swung open, and dragged Nephi partway out into the hall, gratefully sucking in air. *Thank you, Lord. Thank you, thank you, thank you.*

He turned his head and flinched. Ammon Nielsen-Black lay dead beside him, a bullet hole through his head. Nephi gagged, his stomach aching. Someone grabbed his arm and hauled him to his feet.

"Enoch?"

"I couldn't forgive myself if you died because of me." He frowned and refused to meet Nephi's gaze.

Nephi wrapped his arms around his friend. "I owe you my life. Thank you."

He stepped away, and Enoch almost smiled his old, easy smile. "Yeah, I guess we're even then." He scowled down at the gun in his hand.

"You shot Ammon?" Nephi asked quietly.

"If I hadn't, you'd be dead right now."

Nephi nodded. Then his eyes caught the other man lying dead in a pool of blood.

"Brother Ryan." Nephi dropped to his knees. "He was always so kind to me. He gave up everything for the work." Now he'd given up his life, too. "God rest your soul in His kingdom forever," he whispered. "I promise to take good care of your family for you."

"You know this won't do you any good," President Black said. Nephi stood to face him. Hyrum still had Black on his knees, the gun quivering beside his head. "You can't hold me hostage forever. Help for me is on the way even as we speak. And if you kill me, the good people on this ship will rise up and destroy you for certain."

"Call them off, or you'll be dead before rescue arrives," Enoch said. "Maybe you aren't as beloved as you think. Ammon didn't seem to care if we killed you."

"Ammon wanted to inherit the Presidency early, I fear. A terrible waste." Black's eyes met Nephi's. "Holding me here is futile. Do you think you can just take over the ship, and everyone will listen and obey? You're no leader."

But he was wrong about that. Nephi stepped forward and put his hand on Enoch's shoulder. "It's time for us to go. Today. Right now."

"We're not ready," Sherem said from where he stood guarding the elders. "We're not in position."

"Black is right." Nephi said. "We go now or all of this was in vain."

For the first time, confusion passed over Black's face. "Go? You really think you can leave the ship and live?"

"Yes. You have no power over us anymore. You have rejected the true gospel, and the Lord has rejected you as leader of His church."

Black's expression turned stony. "How dare you presume to speak for the Lord? I am the President here. You have no authority."

"That's where you're wrong," Nephi said. "President Black, if you want to live, call off your elders and allow us to leave in peace. There will still be plenty of supplies and landers when the ship reaches Canaan. And you'll be rid of me at last."

Black glowered. Hyrum pressed the gun closer to his head. "Turn on the camera," Black said through his teeth. The trembling elder turned the camera back on and held it up so Black was visible. "Brothers and sisters," President Black began, "I wish to put an end to the violence and death these heretics have caused among us."

Nephi frowned, but didn't speak.

"Call off the counter-attack. The Lord has made His will known to me. The heretics are to leave this ship. We will no longer be troubled with their rebellion. We will cast them on the mercy of the Lord. Do nothing to interfere with their departure." He lowered his head, and Nephi signaled for the cameraman to turn the camera off.

"Good choice, President. We'll need the proper launch codes."

Black met his gaze. "You shall have them."

"And our tabs returned. All of them."

Black nodded once, his jaw tight. "God will send his justice upon you in the vastness of space. Now release me. I am a man of my word."

"No." Enoch leveled his gun at the president. "Not until we're safely away."

Nephi put a hand on Enoch's shoulder. "Let him go. He'll do what he says."

Hyrum looked doubtful. "Are you sure about this?"

"I'm sure."

Both Enoch and Hyrum lowered their weapons, and Black came to his feet.

Nephi nodded to his friends still holding the elders and the High Council. "Them too. Just don't give them their guns back."

As Black and the others moved away from the scene, the president faced Nephi again. "You and your followers will die out there in the cold emptiness of space. You have no idea what you are doing, but your blood is not on my hands."

"If that is the will of God, then I'll humbly accept it. All I ever wanted was to worship Him," Nephi replied.

Black's eyes narrowed, but he didn't respond, only turned on his heel and motioned for the other men to follow him.

"Give me that camera," Nephi said. The cameraman handed the device to Nephi and hurried off behind Black. Nephi turned the camera back on and held it up to face him. "My friends, if you've been watching all this, then you know what I'm about to say. The time has come for us to leave. Get to the landers as quickly as you can. Bring only the most essential personal items. Brothers and sisters, the first families boarded this ship with a dream for their descendants. It is up to us to fulfill that dream, whether you leave with me or remain here. What will your legacy be?" He paused. "May the blessings of God always rest upon the righteous." Nephi turned the camera off and tossed it aside. "Hyrum, where are Sal and Prissa?"

"I hid them in one of those empty apartments."

"Good." Nephi slapped him on the back. "I'll go get them. And what about Phoebe?"

"I let her go," Hyrum said gruffly. "I think she went to the chapel with everyone else."

"Thank you, Hyrum, for everything you've done."

Hyrum scowled. "Maybe not quite everything."

Nephi held out his hand. "Friends? No hard feelings?"

"No hard feelings." Hyrum shook his hand.

"All right, you guys." Nephi looked over the friends who had risked their lives to save him, and gratitude spilled over him. "This is it. Let's go."

It was hard with the press of people in the halls to get to a core access panel so he could go find the girls. It shocked and pleased him at the same time, and he hoped they had planned and prepared well enough to carry more than they expected.

"Nephi!"

Someone was waving at him, pushing against the crowd to get to him. His breath caught. Elizabeth. Her eyes were all puffy from crying.

"Elizabeth, you're alive!"

She drew in a sharp breath. "Forgive me. I couldn't face going back to Ammon. I couldn't bear it anymore. I figured if faking death would work for you it would work for me too."

"Ammon is dead."

"I know." She bowed her head. "I probably shouldn't be so happy about that."

Nephi put his hand on her shoulder and she met his gaze. "Nephi, I—I want to come with you. Please."

"I doubt your grandfather would be happy about that."

"I don't care," Elizabeth said. "He doesn't have to know. He thinks I'm dead anyway. I doubt he shed many tears. I told you I wanted to do what was best for my son. Now I know; this is it. Please. Let me come."

"I won't deny anyone who wants to come," Nephi said, "so long as you understand the risks. This isn't going to be an easy journey nor an easy life. You'll be hungry and cold, and I can't guarantee any of us will be safe."

Elizabeth drew herself up. "I've been hungry and cold for months. I can handle it."

She was brave. He'd give her that. "Then get to the landers. Just don't let anyone report it to your grandfather."

"I won't. Thank you." She threw her arms around him for half a breathless second, and she was gone.

Prissa looked up when Nephi opened the door of the apartment Hyrum had sent him to. She sat on the floor in the front room with Sal asleep on her lap. Her eyes were more swollen than Elizabeth's had been. "Nephi?" she whispered, barely audible. She started to cry again. "It worked, huh?"

"It worked." He lowered himself to the floor beside her and put his arm around her. She leaned her head on his shoulder. "Enoch saved my life," Nephi said. "Can you forgive him now?"

She laughed and hiccupped through her tears. "Maybe."

Nephi squeezed her shoulders. "Get down to the landers and find him. We're leaving now."

"Now?"

"Yes. We'll be free, Prissa. Look, when you get down there, will you find Elizabeth and make sure she's taken care of?"

"Elizabeth Black?" She raised her eyebrows.

"Yep. Can you do that?"

"I—sure."

"Good. I'll be there with Sal in a few minutes." He eased Sal off Prissa's lap and into his own. Prissa kissed him on the cheek and left.

Sal hadn't stirred. Phoebe must have given her something pretty potent.

"Sal." He ran his hand over her hair. "Salome, wake up."

She shuddered and blinked groggily. "Nephi? Am I dreaming?"

"Nope. I'm here." He lifted her up to lean against him. "Enoch's plan worked. Black is letting us leave. Do you need anything? You have your journal? We're not going anywhere without that."

"You're really here." She laid her head against his neck, and he felt her tears drip onto his collarbone.

"I'm really here." He kissed her forehead. "I know you're hurting. So am I. But we really have to go. I'll help you, okay? We can rest once we're in the lander."

Sal shook her head. "I can't. You should leave me here and go."

"Never." He pulled her closer. "I would sooner go cast myself out the airlock than leave you here. I'll carry you if I have to."

"Didn't Phoebe tell you what they did to me?"

"She did." Nephi kissed her head again. The ache returned to his chest.

310

Sal leaned back to look at him. "Then you should leave me here. You need a wife who isn't—broken." Her face crumpled.

"Salome, you are not a teacup and you are not broken. I never want to hear you say anything like that again. You are my wife now and forever, no matter what, understand? And the baby they took from us will be ours for eternity. You will hold it in your arms and raise it yourself. I promise."

Sal's lips quivered. "Are you sure?"

"Never been more sure of anything." He wished he had the words to make her understand what he saw when he looked at her. Her beauty and her majesty and the stunning destiny that awaited her. "Now tell me, do you have that precious journal of yours?"

She almost smiled. "I have it. And your Book of Mormon too."

"Good. And I have you, so we're ready."

He helped her up. "Don't worry, love. We'll take it slow. We'll get there together."

Many hours passed before everything was ready and everyone was onboard the landers. The number of people coming astonished him. The landers would be packed. It wasn't just leftovers, either. A large group of terrestrials had joined them—including Amaleki Cooper—and even a few, uncomfortable looking celestials.

True to his word, President Black sent Nephi the launch codes and returned all the tabs. The vast doors of the launching bay yawned open to reveal the stars in all their glory. Not the cold emptiness of outer darkness, but the awe-inspiring heavens and all God's numberless creations. They stretched on into eternity, wondrous and great. Welcoming.

Nephi bowed his head and commended them to God. They were in His hands now. Then one by one he watched the other seven landers full of believers launch into the brilliant expanse. And when he was certain they were safe, that Black really wasn't going to stop them, he ordered the launch of his own final lander, and he and his flock left the *Kingdom of Heaven* behind forever.

Epilogue

Nephi stepped down from the lander on shaking legs, weakened from hunger after so many months. Brisk air snapped into his lungs, startling and fresh. New. Filled with smells he couldn't quite describe, with a wild quality he'd never experienced on the *Kingdom of Heaven*. It invigorated him. He turned to help Sal down from the lander. Her eyes were brim with tears, mostly joyful, but some from her ever present sorrow. He wrapped his arms around her and held her gently. "We'll find a way, Sal," he whispered. "We'll have children. I promise." He'd told her before and he'd tell her again and keep telling her as long as he had to. "After all we made it here, didn't we?"

She nodded into his shoulder.

"I love you, Salome."

Hand in hand, they walked away from the lander. Nephi squinted in the bright sunlight and lifted his free hand to shade his eyes.

Sal at last uttered a cry of joy.

"What is that smell?" Prissa asked stepping up beside him, waddling a little with the heaviness of the child inside her, almost ready to be born. "I can *taste* the air." She wrinkled her nose. "That's so weird."

Enoch put his arm around her, laughing. "It's like if the filter room actually smelled good."

Nephi laughed aloud. That was as good a description of the air as any. He looked back to see Elizabeth coming down the ramp, her infant son wrapped in a sling across her chest. Phoebe was right behind her, and the rest of their lander company crowded in the door waiting their turn to come out. The other landers would be nearby, though he couldn't see them.

"Is this it?" Sal asked. "The place you saw?"

"It is." Nephi faced the scene again. He'd stood in this very spot a hundred times before. The golden field swaying in the wind, the sun so bright in the sky. He knew exactly where the settlement should go, where they'd build their temple. All of it.

Off to his right, he spotted something new. A pond as clear and blue as any on celestial deck. A wave of gratitude broke over him. In that moment all the hardships of the journey, the sorrow, the hunger, and the fear were swallowed up in the joy of reaching their promised land. He dropped to his knees and Sal beside him, then Prissa and Enoch, Elizabeth, Phoebe, and all the rest, still trickling out of the lander. They formed a circle in the golden grass. Nephi took Sal's hand on one side and Prissa's on the other. He drew in another deep lungful of the strange and wonderful air, and in a whisper that reverberated around the circle, he gave his thanks to God.

Acknowledgements

Bringing a novel into the world requires the help of many, many people. I wish to express my thanks to Tracy Lofthouse, Dave Butler, Heather Hansbrow, Danyelle Leafty, Summer Saxton, RaeLee Steinacker, Eileen Wyckhuyse, and Tina Yeagley. Special thanks to Suzette Saxton for her amazing editing skills and Paul Browning for the breathtaking cover design.

A huge thanks goes to my husband Tracy and our children for their unconditional love and support, and of course, I give my endless gratitude to my Father in Heaven, who provided the way.

About the Author

A ngie Lofthouse went to college with every intention of becoming a particle physicist, but through a series of misadventures, found herself studying Shakespeare instead. After college she combined her love of science and her love of words into a science fiction writing career.

She has published numerous short stories in online and print magazines and anthologies, as well as two sci-fi adventure novels, Defenders of the Covenant and The Ransomed Returning, in addition to The Glory of the Stars.

She lives in a little canyon in the foothills of the Wasatch Mountains with her family of writers, artists, singers, composers, illustrators and musicians.